THE

OFFER

K.SINKO

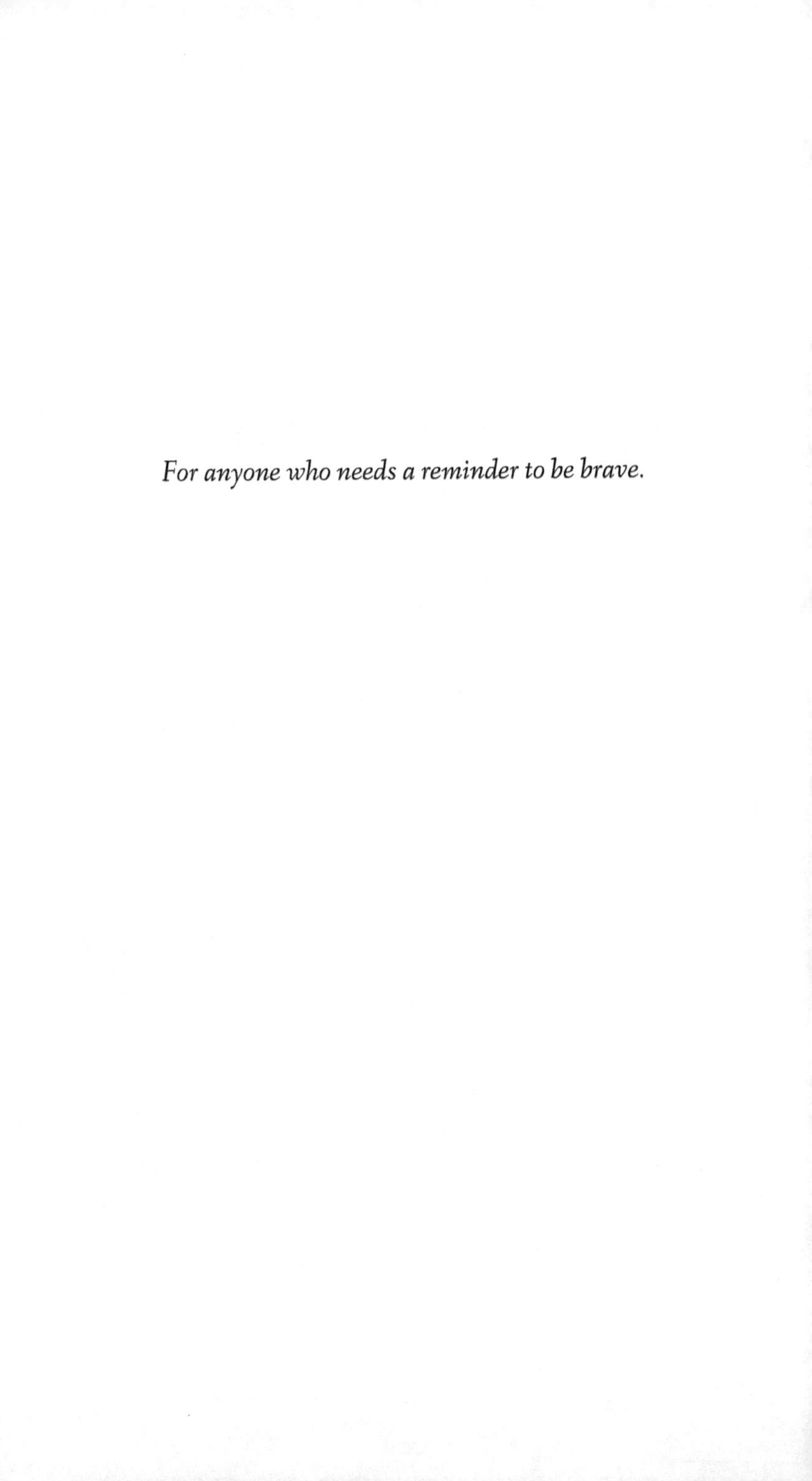

For anyone who needs a reminder to be brave.

Prologue

Five summers ago

Jess watched Charlie fiddle with the keys in his hands as he stepped up to the apartment door. "It's not the biggest place in the world," he admitted.

Jess wrapped her arms around his waist. His fidgeting slowed as he turned to face her. "It doesn't matter, as long as I'm with you."

He grinned and reached for one of her hands, then kissed her knuckles.

She stared up into his bright blue eyes, at his tousled black hair, and felt like she could melt right then and there. They were really doing it, moving in together. After everything they'd been through—the lying, the sneaking out late at night, the covered-up texts on her phone—they were finally going to be together. No more having to wake up earlier to go to school so she could kiss him. No more fighting with her parents or pretending like everything with Charlie was over.

She was free to be with the one she loved…even if it cost her everything.

Charlie slipped his hand into hers as he unlocked the door, tugging Jess through the entryway and into the apartment.

He was right—it was small. The door led into a main room that served as the living and dining room, attached to a tiny galley kitchen. To their left was a narrow staircase that she knew from pictures opened up to a loft bedroom. Even from here, she could see sunlight pooling in from the windows, casting a clean, bright ambiance.

"Like I said, it's—"

"It's perfect," Jess interrupted him, her eyes roaming over the space.

He smiled, tucking her under his arm and squeezing tight, kissing her on the forehead. "How are you doing?"

She shrugged. "The best I can…"

He kissed her again. "They'll come around," he mumbled, his lips brushing against hers as he spoke.

She nodded, holding back the tears that welled in her eyes. *I will not cry again today*, she thought. She'd done enough of that, and she was through with holding the pain in her heart.

She pushed away from him and scanned the apartment, brushing the water in her eyes with the back of her hand. "So how exactly is this going to work? What did your father say?"

Charlie nodded. "He told me that rent is due by the fifth of every month, and utilities are included…whatever that means."

Jess sniggered. *He's so naive. It's cute.* "Gas, water, heat? Those kinds of utilities. Didn't you ever play Monopoly?"

"Ohhhh," Charlie said, his eyes wide. "That makes way more sense now."

They remained silent, eyeing the empty apartment. Charlie eventually gazed in her direction but didn't look directly at her, his eyes somewhere at the top of her left ear. He reached for her, tucking a lock of her blonde hair behind it. "You going to be okay here alone?"

She nodded. "Yes, I think so. I have Scoops, and Ron said he's going to train me to make the cakes. That'll get me a lot more hours."

"I can't believe I have to leave you..."

"It's okay. I made my choice, Charlie. And you said you would help me pay for this place. *Our* place, as you like to call it."

"About that," he said, twirling a strand of her hair with his finger. A nervous tic she picked up on over the years. "You know, with me going to college and everything, I'm not sure how helpful I can be..."

She bristled. "What do you mean?"

"Paying for stuff. Rent and whatnot."

She nodded as her head spun, avoiding the queasy feeling in her stomach. This is what moving in with someone was about, right? Sacrificing for one another, taking care of one another? Charlie had been taking care of her since graduation, since the day she walked out of her childhood home and never looked back. He was the one who advocated for the apartment, one of the many properties his father managed in Haverport. He made all of the arrangements necessary for them to move in—even though he'd technically be away until he graduated college. Maybe it was her turn to sacrifice. He would help her out soon. Eventually.

Jess wrapped her arms around Charlie's neck. "Don't worry about it, I got it."

He grinned, pulling her close. "We did it, Jessie. No more hiding."

She pressed her lips to his. Even if the queasiness in her stomach had yet to subside, she knew it would. The nerves would go away, and eventually, everything would be as it should be.

And maybe Charlie would be right. Maybe they'd all come around.

Chapter One

Present day

JESS SAT at the small kitchen table, the surface covered in papers. She ignored her half-eaten grilled cheese sandwich, the plate perched atop her stack of bills. The laptop beside her was moving too slow to get anything done. Even if it was ten years old, she had to make it work; there was never enough money left over for a new one.

She tossed a stack of receipts to the table and placed her face in her hands. The headache she woke up with lingered, but if she didn't get ready in the next five minutes, she was going to be late for work.

The springs of the mattress upstairs squeaked as Charlie got out of bed. She listened to his movements as he splashed water on his face and brushed his teeth, then made his way down the narrow staircase.

He paused at the table, taking in the mess. "Grilled cheese? For breakfast?"

"We don't have anything else," she snipped. "No cereal, and we ran out of eggs and milk yesterday."

"Aren't you at the grocery store every day? Can't you pick some up?"

She tossed her pen to the table, looking up at him. "With what money, Charlie? I have to pay rent in two days and it's going to suck everything out of my account."

Charlie brushed a hand on Jess's back. She flinched. It was the first time he'd touched her in a week, and it felt strange. He traced small circles below her neck.

"I can pay it this month," he said. "Rent, I got it."

She looked up at him and frowned. "All of it?"

"Yes, all of it," he answered, brushing his thumb across the crease in her forehead. "No need to stress, Jessie."

"I'm always stressed, Charlie."

"Why? Because of money?"

"*Yes*, because of money," she replied, crossing her arms. "Something I never seem to have enough of."

"You don't need money to be happy," he grumbled.

"But you need it to *survive*, Charlie." She lifted her plate. "Grilled cheese. For *breakfast*."

"Okay, okay, I get it." He backed away from her into the kitchen. "Grab some groceries today, all right?"

She scowled. "You promise?"

"Promise what?"

Jess pinched the bridge of her nose, slamming her eyes shut. "Rent, Charlie."

"Oh, right," he said, opening up the practically empty fridge, like food might miraculously appear. "Yes, I promise."

Her phone buzzed in her pocket.

Shit. She ran up the stairs as she answered the phone, wedging it between her shoulder and ear, reaching for her uniform that was hanging dry. "Yes?"

"Jess, hey," Calvin said on the other line. "I'm going to need a favor. Are you free tonight?"

"Depends on what the favor is."

"Night shift," he answered. "No cake orders today, but—"

"I'm in," she said. "Six?"

"Yep. Thanks, Jess. See you then."

She tossed her phone on the unmade bed and slipped on her Post Road Market uniform, tucking the black polo inside the matching black pants. She twisted her hair into a claw clip and grabbed her glasses on the nightstand, then descended the stairs. She slowed as the twinkling sound of a video game booted up downstairs.

She eyed Charlie as she grabbed her purse and coat by the door. He plopped down on the couch, holding a controller she'd never seen before.

"What is that?"

"It's the new Switch. It finally came yesterday."

She froze, staring at the expensive-looking video game contraption on their cheap entertainment center, the wood sagging further down the middle compared to when she first bought it at a consignment shop four years earlier. "You...bought it?"

"Yeah, like, two weeks ago," he answered.

Her shoulders tensed as she stared at a completely oblivious Charlie, his eyes bouncing across the screen as he played.

"You bought an expensive video game console two weeks ago?" Her mind raced. *How?*

"Technically it's not *that* expensive, not as much as a PlayStation 5."

"Charlie...how are we able to afford that?"

He paused the game, finally looking up at her. "Huh?"

She was fuming. Grilled cheese for breakfast. No coffee. A table covered in bills and receipts because her finances were an absolute wreck.

She dropped her purse, holding up her arms. "How the *fuck* are we going to afford that, Charlie?" she screamed, her voice cracking "We barely have the money to pay rent!"

Charlie dropped the controller on the couch and stood up, his eyebrows raised. "Jess, for shit's sake, it's *fine*. I put it on my credit card."

She sucked in a breath. She might be broke but there was always one thing she *never* messed with—her credit. Even if she didn't use her card much, she made sure to always pay it off. She couldn't afford to have a bad credit score. Bad credit meant never getting out of this tiny apartment and finding something bigger. Bad credit meant not replacing her ancient car, whenever that day would come. Even if she shared everything else with Charlie—*everything* —she had yet to share a credit card with him. And right now, staring at a brand-new Nintendo Switch that could've likely paid for three months' worth of groceries, she was thankful for the little voice in her head that'd told her not to.

Except, of course, she knew Charlie. Knew that he never would've used his own credit card on something like this. He hoarded money and only paid the bare minimum she needed from him, month after month. Which meant only one thing.

"Jesus fucking Christ," she roared. "Which card did you put it on?"

His shoulders dropped, his gaze softening. "Jess..."
"WHICH CARD?!"

He didn't have to answer her, because it was clear. Charlie used the credit card connected to his father's bank account, the one he'd kept in his wallet since he was sixteen.

"Jess, someone is standing outside." The relief in his voice was palpable.

Jess whipped around, noticing a figure standing in the outside entryway. She stormed over and flung the door open, finding her coworker Rory standing there, wide seafoam-green eyes staring back at her with a mix of shock and pity.

Jess glared at her. "What are you doing here?"

"I-I just—"

She couldn't take any of this girl's bullshit high school drama right now. Not when she had her own problems to worry about. "Leave *now*."

"Jess, is everything—?"

"*Now*, Rory!"

She nodded and shuffled backward, but Jess didn't bother waiting for her to leave. She slammed the door and turned back to Charlie. "I thought you said you got rid of it."

"I said I wouldn't *use* it," Charlie corrected.

"And what do you call this?" She gestured to the TV.

"I haven't used it for like, four months now. I told him I would pay him back."

"With the money you have saved for rent?"

"I'll pay him back when I get my next paycheck," he answered tersely. "I'll be able to afford rent *and* a new video game."

"But god forbid you do a grocery run," she grumbled. She needed to get out of there before she did something she'd regret. She grabbed her purse. "I'm going to be late tonight, Calvin asked me to cover the night shift."

"Jessie, wait—" he started, reaching out for her.

She jumped from his reach and went for the door, not looking back. She wouldn't fall for it again, the soft touches and the *I'm sorrys* and the *It won't happen agains*. It was the same thing over and over with him, and she fell for it. Every time.

She needed to think. She slammed the door in his face and rushed to her car, praying that her boss didn't fire her for arriving late. Again.

CORY WAS PISSED, but not enough to give Jess another warning. "Three strikes and you're out," is what Cory always told his Post Road employees, and she already had one on her record after arriving thirty minutes late for a shift one blustery cold day this past October. She had no other choice, though; the electricity had been out and Charlie was already at work, so it was Jess who waited for the electrician to show up. Thankfully, Jess was currently on Cory's good side after willingly working during the holidays a few months back—a job no other employee wanted. But what else was she going to do, stay at home alone while her boyfriend was off enjoying the family Thanksgiving dinner she was never invited to?

At this point, Jess was convinced every single Sullivan was a secretly blood-thirsty vampire. Not the kind that sparkled in the sun and had feelings like in paranormal romance books—no. Charlie's family were of the completely soulless variety, caring about nothing but their next kill. Especially Charlie's father.

She finished up frosting a half-sheet pan cake for a birthday party, her palms cramping from squeezing piping bags. She dropped the bag and sighed, pressing her hands into her back as she stood up straight, the relief feeling extra delicious after three hours of crouching.

"Looking good, Jess," called Cory as he stepped behind the glass case and into the grocery store's bakery. "You always make it look so easy."

She shrugged. "Years of decorating ice cream cakes will do that. These are more forgiving since they don't melt so easily. Or at all, really."

"Yeah, I can imagine," he said. "Hey, got a minute?"

Jess frowned, wondering if she should brace for that second strike. She couldn't afford to lose the job, even though she detested it. Post Road was her off-season gig, a place to work and bring in money when Scoops was closed. But as they approached summer, she wondered if it would be foolish to give up her shifts. The double paycheck every week was going to be hard to say no to.

"Here's the deal," he said, hopping up on to the counter. Jess flinched, calculating the number of health codes he was violating by sitting on her work station, but she nodded and bit her tongue.

"As we both know, things aren't doing so well in here," he started.

Jess clenched her fists, then immediately stuck them into the pockets of her denim apron so he wouldn't notice. This conversation always occurred in different ways, at least once a month. Cory came to her with his "I'm the store manager" bullshit and explained why utilizing her only in the bakery was bad for business, and that he'd need her stocking shelves or behind the register. She would counter with the numbers, explaining how the bakery *was* in fact bringing in a significant amount, and how it could be a driver for the market if they doubled their output.

But for some reason, Cory was dead set against Jess being back here, and by the looks of it, he was going to force her over to the chip aisle.

"I've been doing some thinking, and you know, between trying to compete with Grampy's and now with Scoops being open...I'm thinking the bakery should take a pause," he said, crossing his arms. "And I really could use your help elsewhere."

She nodded, turning away so he wouldn't see her let out a shaky breath. She wanted to scream and tell him how ridiculous he was being. This man knew so little about running a business it astounded her. Sure, she still had a lot to learn herself. But becoming friends with Calvin and learning the ropes at Scoops taught her what was important to focus on and what wasn't. She knew pausing bakery production outright would seriously hurt this place.

"You're going to lose business," she said sternly. "It's going to cost you."

"I think it will cost me keeping it *open*. Seems a bit ridiculous, really," he answered, hopping down. "Listen, Jess, I was planning on closing up this part of the market when I took over last year anyway. You're a great baker and your cakes are impressive," he said, gesturing to the colorful assortment of ready-to-purchase cakes in the glass display. "But being a manager means making hard decisions, and right now, this is what's best for our team."

He walked away without giving her a chance to respond. Fuming, she checked the clock behind her, relieved her shift was officially over. She slid the cake she finished inside the display case, then untied her apron and stuffed it in her tote. She shrugged on her coat as she stepped out the sliding glass doors, the cheap material of her jacket doing little to block out the chilly March wind whipping through the parking lot. Inside her car was also freezing, but at least it protected her from the wind as she slammed the squeaky door closed.

She turned on the ignition, music immediately blasting through her speakers. She leaned her head back and let the sounds of the screeching guitar and the rhythmic base soothe the pounding headache that had returned with a vengeance. Unclenching her fists, she pressed her hands into her lap and took three long breaths. It was something she'd picked up from a YouTube video she watched weeks ago after her desperate online search of "how to decrease stress." The meditation guru said this very small moment of "grounding" was supposed to somehow calm you. She gave it a try, and to her surprise, it worked. *Slightly*. Enough to pull her out of her funk.

Jess pulled out of the parking lot, turning a corner before stopping abruptly at a red light. Someone walked across the crosswalk, a pair of wired headphones plugged in as he bobbed his head. At first she didn't recognize him, but as he got closer, she realized she knew the golden-haired boy who was walking across the front of her car, his face practically in the clouds as he made it to the other side of the street.

It was the haircut that caught her off guard.

She rolled down the window and honked.

Kevin whipped around, and when he saw who it was, he burst into a grin. "My dear Jessica!"

She rolled her eyes. "I see you chopped off the mop," she said.

"Yes, so glad you noticed," he replied, flicking his hair slightly, his mouth still pressed into that casual grin.

Kevin always kept his hair long, his honey-brown locks hanging just below his shoulders. He'd had it that way since moving to Haverport from Vermont their sophomore year. But now his hair was shorter, his waves hanging to his chin, the pieces at the front layered to round out his face. His tattoo was much more noticeable now without his hair in the way, the black ink snaking up the side of his left shoulder and around the back of his neck.

A car horn flared behind her. She jumped, quickly pulling off the road. Kevin kept grinning as he leaned down onto her open window, transferring his groceries into one hand.

She furrowed her brow. Kevin was far off from the bike shop down on Main Street, and it wasn't like the market was walkable. She glanced around, realizing they were at the bus station.

"Are you waiting for the *bus?*" Jess asked.

"Hey, I'm sensing some judgment with that tone," he said, wagging a finger at her. "Not all of us have the means to drive ourselves to the grocery store."

She frowned. "I thought you had a car."

"*Had,*" he emphasized. "Past tense. The beauty is no longer."

"That piece of crap finally met its end?"

"Nope, I sold it," he answered. "Gave me enough to afford the next few months."

She frowned again, glancing away from him and out over her steering wheel. She knew things at Port Wheels were bad; that winter, Calvin had mentioned that if Kevin didn't start bringing in more business, doors would be closed by the end of the summer. But she had no idea it was sell-your-car bad.

She sighed, turning toward him. "Need a ride back to town?"

"Oh my god, ride in the Jess-mobile?" he said. He opened the back door and tossed his bags on the seat without hesitating. "Sign me up."

Jess shook her head as Kevin climbed into the front, sitting at an angle so he could close the passenger door.

"You can move the seat back, you know," she said.

"Oh, okay, wasn't sure if you wanted me to sit here in this little clown seat," he quipped, sliding the chair back with a thud to make room for his long legs.

She rolled her eyes and turned on the ignition. Music blasted through the speakers again. Her face flushed as she quickly turned off the stereo.

Kevin laughed. "Jessica, what was that?"

"Nothing," she grumbled, pulling back onto the road.

"Obviously not nothing," Kevin said, reaching for her stereo. "That was some serious—"

She swatted his hand away. "Don't."

"Oh come on," he pleaded. "What was that band? You're gatekeeping."

Jess scowled at him. "I am not *gatekeeping*. You've just never heard of them."

"That's literally what a gatekeeper would say." He chuckled. "Come *on*, tell me." He reached out and poked her shoulder and she couldn't help it, she swatted his hand away again.

"It's—Ugh. It's a band, out of Chicago," she answered slowly. "They're small, indie."

"An indie pop punk band out of Chicago?" he replied as they stopped at a red light. Jess glanced over at him, noticing the way he was still grinning to himself, his eyes peering out the passenger window. "I always thought you were a Taylor Swift girl."

Jess unlocked the doors. "Get out."

Kevin burst out laughing. "You're right, how rude of me," he said. "Now put the music back on before I start singing to you to pass the time."

"It's literally a five-minute drive. Can you really not sit in silence for five minutes?"

He scoffed. "My dear Jessica, do you even know me?"

"Stop calling me that."

"And not get to see that little crease in your forehead? Nah, never," he quipped, his leg now bouncing slightly, looking amused.

She grumbled a few expletives to herself as the light turned green. Pressing on the gas, she wondered if she made a mistake offering him a ride. Being with him wasn't doing anything for her headache.

"It's actually so funny," Kevin said, shaking his head.

"What?" she huffed.

"You see, *my* favorite band is this indie pop punk group from Chicago," he said. "And I've been dying to listen to them all day."

Before she could stop him, Kevin swiftly flicked on the stereo, sending the music blasting over the speakers. Instead of turning it off, she waited, gripping the steering wheel tightly as the lead singer's voice rolled into the chorus.

She couldn't help it, the words she loved so much pulsing through her veins. She nodded her head, and she sang the words.

Jess looked over at Kevin. Surprisingly, he wasn't paying attention to her, giving her the space to be free with the lyrics and the beating drums. He was simply looking out the window and bopping his head, a smile still fixed on that perfectly tanned face of his. Like the sunshine from last summer never really left.

They remained like that for the rest of the ride, moving from one song into the next, until she pulled up outside Port Wheels. She parked, reaching to turn the car off.

Kevin brushed his hand against hers, motioning for her to stop. "Don't. Let the song finish."

The tips of his fingers were rough. She hesitated, mesmerized at the way her skin tingled from the contact.

As if they both understood what was going on, they wrenched their hands away at the same time. Jess white-knuckled the steering wheel again as Kevin shoved his hand in his pocket.

The song ended. She turned off the ignition.

Kevin coughed. "Heading back home?"

She shook her head. "Nope. Working the night shift over at Scoops."

Kevin frowned, something she rarely saw. "Are you planning on working both jobs this summer?"

Jess leaned back in her chair, thinking through her conversation with Cory. The bakery was the only thing drawing her to Post Road. At Scoops she didn't have much creativity—it was just simple ice cream cakes and colored frosting, nothing truly *special*. At the market she had room to experiment, offering different types of cakes and even some pastries like chocolate croissants and cranberry orange scones and kanelbullar sweet cinnamon buns. But if Cory was planning to pull her from the bakery...

"I-I don't know," she confessed. "I need the money."

"Has Charlie been helping out at all?"

She swiveled her head and glared at him. "That's none of your business."

Kevin held up his hands. "You're right, it's not. But he's living with you full time and can't use the excuse of college or the pandemic to not pay rent anymore. That was lunacy."

"Again, this was never any of your business," she said. "And now, I would like you to get out of my car."

Kevin sighed, reaching for the door handle. "Jess, you know if you ever need anything—"

"I don't. Get out, Kevin."

He nodded, sliding out of the car and grabbing his groceries. Jess watched as he turned the corner, making his way to his apartment above the bike shop.

She let her shoulders drop on a sigh, wondering if it was worth the detour home to eat something quick. She swore softly, realizing she forgot to stock up on groceries when she stormed out after finding out Cory's "brilliant" business strategy.

Ice cream for dinner it was.

Her phone dinged as she turned the car back on. She checked it, finding a picture from Kevin. He sent an image of a small bakery box open on his table, filled to the brim.

KEVIN

The kanelbullar are my favorite.

She smirked, shifting gears. They were hers, too.

Chapter Two

Jess never expected to work at Scoops By The Sea for this long.

When she first got the job there, she figured it would be a summer gig. Freshly sixteen, working at Scoops was going to be her way of making a little extra cash. Never did she think she'd still be working here seven years later, or that it would've graduated from being "a little extra cash" to one of her main sources of income.

All of the people she worked with that first and second summer were gone. Some graduated college, some had bought houses, some had already birthed humans and now walked around town with strollers and diaper bags. But she was still here, scooping ice cream and making cakes and pulling apart horny teenagers who loved to make out in the bathroom or closet.

At least Calvin wasn't planning on leaving. He was in line to be the new manager; Ron announced at their employee meeting last week that Calvin Ball would officially be taking over next summer. He'd always been close with Ron, the only father figure in his life.

Thinking about her own father made Jess sick to her stomach, so she pushed the feeling down like she always did and focused all of her attention on the pile of dishes in front of her, scrubbing the metal cups and utensils aggressively until they gleamed.

Calvin walked through the open doorway that led to The War Room, the tiny room in the back where the real action happened. The front of the shop was for scooping ice cream and serving customers, but The War Room was *her* domain. The place where she pressed ice cream and chocolate crispies and cold fudge into steel molds, piped colorful frosting, swirled curly letters. Despite spending hours leaning over cake after cake, the work grueling as the busy summer months flew by, she loved it. Whenever she took her deep breaths and counted down from three, her mind drifted to the methodical action of dolloping frosting on cake edges, the soothing motion making her feel a little more at peace.

She dried off the dishes with a rag, placing them on the counter as Calvin unlocked a desk drawer and pulled out a safety box. Jess feigned disinterest as Calvin counted the bills before tying them off and stacking them in neat piles on the desk. He marked something on a notepad from the safety box then nodded, stepping away from the desk and walking toward the front.

Jess froze, staring at the piles as she listened to the sounds of Calvin opening up the registers, emptying out the bills. She should keep working, keep going through the motions of closing up the shop so they could get out of there. But she couldn't tear her gaze away from the piles of money.

He wouldn't notice if one went missing, she thought to herself. *He's young, he could have miscounted.*

And she needed the money—desperately. Charlie may have offered to pay rent this month, but what about next month? Would she have enough to afford her portion of rent *and* pay for groceries and gas and all the other tedious expenses that came with being an adult? It would be nice to have a little extra, just once. It would be nice to replace some of the clothes she had in her closet, the same ones she's worn since high school, now a little tight and uncomfortable. She made it work, but *god*, it would be nice to buy a few new pairs of jeans that fit her curves rather than her boyish figure from high school. Or even a jacket that actually kept her warm.

"Everything okay?"

Jess looked up, noticing Calvin had stepped back into The War Room. He was standing there stiff as a board, his hands clutching the money from the registers. The way he was looking at her felt like half warning, half worry. That maybe Jess *was* capable of swiping a few stacks of bills and bolting.

Embarrassment built up in her throat. She shook her head and waved him off. "Yep, all good."

She could tell Calvin was still watching her warily as she returned to putting the dishes away. She did a final check that everything was locked and sealed, making sure all ice cream freezers were properly closed so there weren't any literal meltdowns in the morning.

Jess stepped up to the desk as Calvin locked the safety box back in the desk drawer. He handed over her tip money for the night and she mumbled a thank-you, stuffing it in the back pocket of her khaki pants as she turned to leave.

"Jess, wait."

She turned, looking over at Calvin who was still sitting at the desk, his elbows propped up casually as opposed to his usual posture of arms crossed tightly around his chest. The way he was looking at her also wasn't his usual tight-ass, militant personality, but one of sorrow. She wanted to throttle him for it.

"Calvin, I've had a long day."

"I heard, working here and Post Road this morning."

She rolled her eyes. Besides Charlie—who never had any need to talk to Calvin—there was only one other person who knew about her pulling a double today. "Let me guess, a certain hippie bike boy texted you."

"He's worried about you."

Jess felt like steam was coming out of her ears. She squeezed her eyes shut and took a deep, centering breath before continuing. It was the only way she was able to control her anger from spewing everywhere these days. "I don't need his worry, or your worry," she replied, eyes still tightly shut. She didn't want to look at his pitying face. "Everything is fine."

"Jess, I've known you a long time. I know everything isn't fine. You look like shit."

She huffed, daring to open her eyes so she could glare at him. "That's what every girl wants to hear."

"How bad is it?"

She shook her head, looking down at her sneakers. They were the same ones she'd worn on her first day at Scoops, and she realized the frayed canvas near her right big toe had finally ripped into a small, mortifying hole.

The sight of it drained all of her anger, all of her energy, all of her will to try to fight her way out of this conversation. Like soapy water disappearing down the sink. "It's not great," she grumbled. "We're scraping by each month. I'm going to have to work both jobs this summer, and Cory just said he's closing the bakery."

Calvin's eyebrows bent. "Why would he do that? He makes a killing from it, that's the dumbest move."

"I don't think it has to do with money. From the sounds of it, he doesn't want to be competing with Grampy's or even Scoops this summer."

He huffed. "What an idiot."

"But now with Charlie living at home full time, things keep getting more expensive. More food, more gas money, more *everything*. I feel like...I feel like—"

She looked away, feeling her throat close up. Calvin may be the only true friend she had in this town, but that didn't give him the right to see her break down. She spent so long pushing away the tears and the emotions that she grew accustomed to that numb, hollowed-out feeling in her heart. She almost forgot what the sensation of crying felt like; that stinging feeling in your cheeks and your nose and eyes as tears began to form.

She took another deep breath before continuing, not looking him in the eyes as she finished. "I feel like I'm stuck. Like this is my life forever. That it will never get better."

"Have you told him this?"

"Charlie? God no. He's always so chill about money. He grew up spending it freely, and it never seems to be a problem with him."

"And that bothers you," he said. Not a question.

Irritation pricked her chest as she slammed her hand on the counter. "*Of course* it bothers me, Calvin. I'm the one constantly trying to budget and keep things afloat, eating fucking *grilled cheese* for breakfast because there's nothing else in the fridge, and he's off still using daddy's money buying video games and not even offering to pay for stuff unless I beg for it."

"Grilled cheese for breakfast actually sounds kind of good," he mumbled.

She glared at him.

"Is he still working for his father?" he asked.

She nodded, circling her wrist, realizing how hard she slammed it on the counter. She forced herself to relax a little. "Yes, but he's taken on a bigger role since graduating. He's basically his second-in-command now."

"Sounds like he should be making more..." Calvin started, then hesitated. Almost like he was waiting for her to explain the rest of it. To make sense of it.

But there wasn't more to it, and none of it made sense. Charlie *was* making more money at the boatyard these days, managing their books and their important client relationships. But he was stingy with how much of it he actually spent. His new paycheck was enough for him to split the cost of rent, which did put Jess somewhat at ease after five years of paying it all herself. But then her car broke down in January and needed serious repairs, draining all of her savings from working extra shifts at Post Road, and set her back to living month-to-month. Without any kind of cushion to fall back on this summer, she'd be spending a lot more time in the chip aisle.

She tried relaxing her shoulders as she looked at Calvin. "We'll figure it out, because that's what you do for the person you love. You figure it out."

"And you do? Love him, I mean?"

Jess barked out a laugh. *Unbelievable.*

"Do you really still want to be with him?" Calvin pressed. "Because by the sounds of it..."

"What, so you fell in love last summer and think you're now the expert here?" Jess snipped at him. She was happy for Calvin, for meeting Melanie and letting his hard edges soften around her, for allowing her to see the dark parts of him that not many people did. Melanie was one of the good ones; one of the only ones Jess felt she could trust with assisting her on ice cream cakes, which wasn't an easy job for her to share. But he was still so young—*they* were still so young. He had no idea what being in a long-term relationship really looked like.

"I've been with Charlie for almost nine years," she continued. "And in that time, I've learned a lot about what it means to sacrifice and care for someone else. Because that's what you do when you're in a relationship—you sacrifice."

"You don't have to lecture me about sacrifice and caring," he rumbled. "You know better than anyone the shit I've been through. The shit Mel has been through."

Jess rubbed her neck, looking past the windows at the front of the shop, the parking lot outside blanketed in darkness. She knew she was being unfair. Calvin and Melanie both dealt with family members that suffered from addiction. The disease had taken Melanie's brother last summer, and Calvin lost his mother years ago in mind and spirit—lost to the power of pills and her need to constantly have more. He was right—she shouldn't be lecturing him about sacrifice.

"You said you've been in a relationship for nine years," he said, skipping over the fact that Jess was being a complete dick to him. "But you still haven't answered my question."

Her body trembled in panic. Saying "I love you" to Charlie was the equivalent of saying "pass the remote" or "what's the weather." It didn't mean anything, at least not as much as it used to. Their love transformed from a thing of passion and urgency to a thing of sobering calm. No heat.

No fireworks. She "loved" Charlie for so long, she forgot what it really meant to be *in love* anymore. What it felt like.

She figured that was how it went in a relationship—that the intensity softened over the years, that the relationship simply moved into a new phase. You changed. You grew.

Jess brushed him off, trying to make it look casual. "Of course I am, that's a stupid question."

Calvin shook his head slightly, looking defeated. He reached for his phone on the desk. She watched as he read the text that was lighting his screen, a smile curling on his lips. "Kevin says hi."

She wanted to throttle him again. "Tell him to lay off and mind his own business."

Calvin chuckled. "You know that will only entice him."

Jess rolled her eyes. She watched as Calvin began typing.

"Calvin...how bad is it?"

He looked up from his screen, confused.

"The bike shop, his finances," she clarified. "He said he sold his car. It...it can't be good."

Calvin sighed, placing his phone back down on the desk as he leaned back in the chair. "He's doing his best to keep his expenses low, but he's still not bringing in enough business. The car was able to buy him another month or so. But the boost he gets from summer people might not be enough this year."

Summers in Haverport were known as the busy season —the town population tripled with tourists (or "summer people" as they called them) between May and September. Small businesses in town made enough during that short summer season to last them through the dead of winter. But not all of them could survive it, including a charming little bike shop.

"Does he have a plan?" she pried. "Is he going to try to switch things up?"

"That's what we're trying to figure out."

Her brow furrowed. There had to be another way. There *had* to be. "What would happen if the shop closed? Do you think he'll stay in town?"

Calvin shrugged. "It depends on how broke he is. If things don't turn around, he might move back in with his parents in Vermont."

Jess felt that panic rising again in her chest. Kevin was annoying as hell, but having him around was a constant. Kevin was one of the few people from their graduating class who had done what she did. Knowing he'd chosen to stay and work rather than head off to college had made her feel a little less lonely in this tiny, suffocating town. Even if he drove her nuts.

Calvin stood up, sliding his phone in his pocket. "One more thing before you go."

She looked up at him, his face stern.

"If you ever need money, talk to me," he said.

Jess glared. "I would never ask—"

"I would know if you swiped it from the box," he said matter-of-factly. "So do yourself a favor and avoid that mess. I'm your friend, Jess, come talk to me first."

She huffed.

"Promise me?"

She gave him the finger, heading for the metal back door to exit the shop. "I can handle myself, Ball. Stay out of it."

CHARLIE WAS ALREADY ASLEEP when Jess got home, so she didn't bother making the trip upstairs. She kicked off her sneakers and tiptoed toward the bathroom, flicking on lights as she went. She glanced over at the table on her way, noticing a pizza box from Penny's sitting on top of her tax papers and receipts from earlier. Her stomach growled as she stopped and flipped the box open, only to find a few crumbs left. She swore softly and discarded it in the recycling bin, trying to not get too angry at the small grease stain that'd leaked onto their bills.

She tugged off her Scoops uniform and tossed it in the laundry basket, then slipped on the sweats she'd left in the corner of the bathroom that morning. As she brushed her teeth, she stared at her reflection in their tiny mirror.

Calvin was right—she did look like shit. The bags under her eyes were more pronounced than they'd ever been. Her lips were cracked, and her face was ghostly pale, like she hadn't seen sunshine in ages. She sighed and spit out the toothpaste, rinsing off her toothbrush. She should probably add ChapStick to her list of groceries to pick up tomorrow, maybe a small bottle of concealer to mask the dark circles around her eyes. Buying makeup wasn't a priority in the budget anymore—it felt a little frivolous. She shook her head and scrapped the idea.

Jess removed her glasses and popped them into her case, then climbed into bed next to Charlie, not feeling the least bit tired despite how long she'd spent on her feet that day. Instinctively, Charlie rolled over, swinging an arm around Jess and curling her close, nuzzling his face into her neck.

During their first few months of sleeping in the same apartment, in the same bed, this small moment each night made Jess's skin prickle with excitement. The way he cuddled her and wanted her close after months of sneaking around. At the time, his neediness was sweet, because she was head over heels. But now? His hot breath smelled like pizza and it kind of made her want to punch him in the face, and she wished for space more than anything.

What changed so much for her to feel this way?

Deep down, she knew. She thought back to the moment when Charlie Sullivan IV went from being a family friend to something far greater, from a boy she used to play with to one she couldn't help but fall for.

It was the summer before their freshman year of high school. Jess and her sister, Dakota, were helping their father at his boatyard after lunch, checking to make sure everyone had their permits, while also checking the docks to make sure the areas were safe and clean. The summer season was about to begin, and the boatyard was now a central hangout spot in Haverport thanks to Mr. Sullivan, Charlie's father.

Before Jess's dad brought him on as a business partner, Cap's Boatyard was rather simple. A place to dock the boat and grab a burger and a cold bottle of beer, maybe some french fries if you got in before they ran out. That was until Mr. Sullivan came along. Cap's exterior went from chipped charcoal paint to a crisp white. The aging rugs were ripped out and replaced by polished wood floors. The plastic table and chairs were swapped with hand-crafted wood fixtures, tablecloths, and plush armchairs. And the menu upgraded significantly—from burgers and beers to oysters and Chardonnay, and a chef who served a breakfast and lunch menu with prices that Jess's father felt the citizens of Haverport would never be able to afford. But the patrons who blew in for the summer—with their motorboats and small yachts—didn't even flinch at the menu. Soon, Cap's became a destination spot for the entire state of Connecticut.

Jess remembered her father's private complaints over

how much changed, but he never voiced it to Charlie's father. Business was much better now that he was on board, and their family actually had money to spend. Jess would pretend to side with her father when he grumbled, but she would never tell him how much she loved sneaking into the kitchen, watching as the new chef piped little cakes and topped perfectly sliced fruit on tarts for the guests. She was mesmerized by it, wishing she could learn how to do the same.

That's where she was when Charlie found her that afternoon. Jess kissed her father on the cheek, wishing him luck on the kickoff day of the summer season, and left to go use the bathroom. Dakota had rolled her eyes at her, knowing fully well that Jess intended to slip into the kitchen.

She crouched down and watched from an open archway as Chef Barrios worked meticulously on the dessert for the day—mini strawberry shortcakes with billowing homemade whipped cream.

"Should we steal one?" whispered a warm, familiar voice next to her.

She whipped her head around and covered Charlie's mouth with her hand. "Be quiet or he'll find us."

To her surprise, Charlie kissed the center of her palm. She felt her cheeks flush as she pulled away. "Gross, Charlie."

"Is it that gross?"

Her heart fluttered in her chest. She'd always thought Charlie was cute, but this felt different. Like standing on the edge of a cliff, feeling her body start to tip over. "That's —that's just—"

"Come on, Jessie, you've never thought about kissing me?"

She didn't allow others to call her Jessie—only her family. But Charlie adopted the name quickly after her father had the Sullivans over for dinner two years ago, and the nickname stuck despite her protests. Yet now, with the way his sparkling blue eyes danced in her direction, the nickname on his lips didn't seem so bad. Maybe the taste of his lips wouldn't be so bad, either.

Charlie smirked at Jess's silence, reaching for her hand and squeezing. "Kiss me, Jessie."

She pulled her hand away. "You're crazy."

"You know you want to."

She felt the tips of her ears turn pink and looked back into the kitchen. Chef Barrios was lifting a pan of strawberry shortcakes, heading in their direction.

She reached back for Charlie's hand and dragged him into a tiny alcove, out of sight. Chef had a habit of reprimanding anyone who entered the kitchen without his permission.

Her heart was hammering in her chest as she listened to the metal doors leading to the dining room swing open, the small crowd applauding his entrance.

She didn't take notice at all of the ways their bodies were pressed together, not until Charlie traced his fingers up her side then curled a hand around her back. Goosebumps flecked her arms as she looked up at him, his face dangerously close.

"Don't you want to know?"

"Want to know what it's like to be kissed?"

"Not just kissed," he murmured, cupping her head with his other hand. "What it's like to be kissed by *me*."

The thudding of her heart grew louder in her ears as Charlie brushed her cheek with his thumb, waiting.

"Yeah," she whispered. "I want to know."

He smiled, pressed his lips to hers, and completely changed her world.

From that very first kiss, Jessica Valerie had been in love with Charlie Sullivan IV.

Yet now, as she relived the memory in her head, she couldn't summon those tingling feelings it usually pushed to the surface. The way he so boldly grabbed for her and took the plunge, tipping over that cliff from friendship and diving into something more.

Instead, she felt hollow, and she wondered if she would ever feel that way again.

Chapter Three

Jess was in her happy place—hovering over an ice cream cake with a bag of yellow frosting in her hands. She was testing out a new design for the trim; tiny flowers made with yellow petals and edible pearls at the center. She knew it was probably excessive, but the lines at Scoops were slow and she had a few hours to kill before her shift was over and she was due at Post Road for the evening.

She sensed Melanie approaching her station, peering down at the cake but keeping enough of a distance so she wouldn't be in the way. Melanie remained silent as she watched Jess create the last little flower at the bottom right corner of the cake.

"This one is stunning, Jess," Melanie said breathlessly.

She huffed, pushing her glasses up the bridge of her nose with her index finger. "Probably won't have time for something like this during the season."

"Will you make one for my birthday?"

Jess straightened, looking into Melanie's blue doe-eyes. The girl's cheeks were wet, and she watched silently as a few tears trickled down to her chin.

Jess smiled softly, and to her surprise, reached out and grabbed Melanie's shoulder, giving it a gentle squeeze. This was going to be Melanie's first birthday without her twin brother by her side, yet the girl was insistent about having all of them over for a party next week. She kept saying she wanted to fill the day with joy, in honor of Duncan.

"Of course," Jess whispered. "Anything in particular you want?"

Melanie smiled and brushed a tear away with the back of her hand. "You're the artist, I'll let you decide."

Jess nodded, her gaze lingering out beyond The War Room and into the front of the shop, already calculating the different combinations and possibilities.

"But add something purple in there," Melanie continued. "It was…our color, on our birthday."

"Sure, I can do that."

"Jess?" Calvin asked as he trudged down the narrow staircase from the storage room upstairs.

Jess dropped her hand, frowning. "Ball?"

"Got a minute?"

She nodded, securing a plastic lid on top of the cake in front of her and carefully sliding it in the freezer. She glanced back over at Melanie and noticed Calvin had his arms wrapped tightly around her, whispering something softly in her ear. She nodded and kissed him on the cheek, then headed back to the front.

Jess crossed her arms. "What's up?"

Calvin pointed to the stairs. "Upstairs."

She rolled her eyes. "If you're about to give me another lecture about money—"

"I'm not," Calvin said. "Not a lecture. Something better, I hope."

Curious, Jess followed him up the narrow stairs and into

the storage room littered with boxes of extra napkins, spoons, cups, cones, and toppings. But to her surprise, they weren't the only two up there.

Perched on top of a box was Kevin, digging into a big bowl of Black Cherry Chunk.

She scowled. "What are you doing here?"

Kevin grinned. "You know, I can't wait for the day I see you and it's a smile and a *hello* instead of immediate hatred."

Jess shuffled from side to side. "I don't hate you," she mumbled.

"It'd be okay if you did," he retorted. He winked at her, then looked back down at his bowl. "I like a challenge."

She shook her head and looked back at Calvin. "Care to explain what's going on?"

Calvin crossed his arms, clearly in business mode. "Jess, you know from our conversations the state of Kevin's shop and his financial predicament."

Jess swiftly glanced in Kevin's direction. He wasn't looking at her, but his cheeks were flushed with embarrassment. For a brief moment, she felt the need to protect him from this.

She crossed her arms and glared up at Calvin. "Get to the point."

He nodded. "You said yourself that Kevin would benefit from a new way to bring in more business, and so we thought of a solution."

Jess gestured with her hands to move this tedious conversation along.

"There's a commercial kitchen in the back of the shop," Kevin chimed in. "The space used to be a café, but they closed down and then Kimmy flipped it into a bike shop. She never demoed the kitchen, though. It's still there."

Jess could feel the cadence of her heartbeat speed up as he continued.

"When I took over, I thought about taking the kitchen out to make more space for inventory, but I don't know, part of me had this crazy idea..."

Jess looked over at Calvin, who was already staring back at her, head tilted and a knowing smirk on his lips. "Crazy idea?"

Kevin's eyes remained on the empty cup of ice cream that now sat next to him. "I was in Chicago once, and I came across this bike shop that was also a coffee shop. It was absolutely slammed, so many people there, so many *dogs* there."

"And?" Calvin added, guiding Kevin back to his point.

"And so many delicious pastries," Kevin said, his hazel eyes now meeting hers.

She blinked once. Twice. "What are you saying?"

"That the bike shop was booming," he replied. "Mind you, it's Chicago—not Haverport. But what if my bike shop borrowed from the same model? What if it was a bike shop...and a bakery?"

Jess sucked in a breath, finally understanding what Kevin was getting at. "You want to use that kitchen to open up a bakery."

"And he wants you to run it," Calvin said.

She looked from Kevin to Calvin, then back to Kevin. "You're demented."

Kevin grinned. "Or *brilliant*."

Jess rubbed her face and shook her head. "Your solution to saving your business is opening up *another business?*"

"We wouldn't need to open up another business, it would all be a part of the shop," Calvin said. "We would just need to get the right licenses and permits to have a working kitchen, and an inspection, of course."

Jess crossed her arms, her mind reeling. "How are you going to afford supplies? Renovations? And I'm assuming you want coffee at this bakery as well, right? Espresso machines are not cheap."

"We have an investor who's willing to front the money to get this project going," Calvin explained.

"Who in their right mind would do that?"

The two guys looked at each other. Kevin shook his head just slightly, winning whatever silent exchange passed between the two of them.

"Fine," Jess said, deciding not to press any further. "It doesn't matter, it's your dumpster fire of an idea."

"Sixty thousand."

She looked up at Calvin, her mouth agape. "Excuse me?"

"That's what Kevin can pay you as a starting salary. It's full time, so you would have to drop Post Road. I'll allow you to work some night shifts here if you like, but no more pulling double duty every day."

Jess felt bewildered, shaking her head. "That is...absolutely insane, guys."

"We'll also have the means to hire someone part time to help you at the counter. Minimum wage is the best we can do for them, unfortunately. But hopefully tips will make up for it."

"And you'll get free rein of the menu," Kevin added, his soft eyes landing on Jess.

She stared back at him, realizing what he was offering her. The chance to have her own bakery, to be as creative as she wanted. To finally leave Post Road and Cory and his terrible business decisions for good.

But deep in her gut, she had a feeling there was more. It sounded too good to be true. "What's the catch?"

Kevin and Calvin glanced at each other again, which made her bristle with irritation.

"You have five seconds to tell me or I'm heading back downstairs."

"You have to leave him," Kevin answered softly.

Jess froze, staring up at her friend. Or a guy she *thought* was her friend. Because what he was asking of her was absolutely, one-hundred percent, diabolical. "*Excuse me?*"

"The salary, the bakery, the freedom, it's all yours," Kevin said. "But only if you leave Charlie and move out."

It was more than her usual anger bubbling in her chest now. This was *fury*, the need to tear things apart and scream at the top of her lungs. How *dare* they dangle this in front of her just to pry their way into her relationship? What right did they have to make such a bold claim on her life?

"You'll move in with me and Gram," Calvin added, in a frustratingly calm manner. She despised him for it. "There's an extra room in the house that's all yours. Originally, I was thinking until the end of the summer, but Gram said it's yours for as long as you want. You can stay until you're comfortable finding something on your own."

"Who the fuck do you think you are demanding—"

"Jess, he's sucking you dry," Calvin said. "You're constantly paying for him for everything."

"Not *everything*," she sputtered, her voice rising. "He offered to pay the rent this month."

"For what? The first time in four years?" Calvin snipped, his quiet resolve cracking slightly.

"And you're not happy," Kevin added faintly.

The fire in her belly fizzled, her anger smothering out.

She clenched her fists and closed her eyes, then began her three deep breaths. *Deep one in, one. Deep one out.*

"Jess—" Calvin started.

"Shut up, Cal, let her finish."

Deep one in, two. Deep one out.

Deep one in, three.

She opened her eyes, feeling calmer. More like herself. With a quiet resolve, she glanced back and forth between the both of them. "You are out of your fucking mind, and you crossed a line," she said coolly. "Feel free to find another baker."

Jess turned slowly, heading for the stairs.

"I don't want anyone else, Jessica."

She turned her head, looking over at Kevin. He was now standing, like he was about to come after her. She watched him hesitate before shoving his hands in the pockets of his hoodie. "The offer stands. If you don't want it, then I won't go through with it."

"So essentially, the success of your business falls on my shoulders," she replied. "No pressure or anything."

"I can't guarantee that the bakery would save the business," Kevin added. "But you're the smartest woman I know when it comes to this stuff, and I can't imagine doing this with anyone else."

She rolled her eyes. "You've got your buddy Calvin over here. You'll be fine."

"He's got his own business to run, and he only agreed to help manage this transition so I don't have to..." He hesitated, looking down at his shoes.

"So you don't have to move back home," Jess finished for him.

He nodded, a small section of his honey-brown hair

flopping in front of his eyes that were now back on her. "Please," he said softly. "Please think about it."

She gripped the railing and glanced down the stairs. "It is a good offer, but what you're asking of me is too much. I decline."

She bounded down the stairs, not daring to look back up at the face that was no longer full of sunshine. All because of her.

Jess sat on the couch, a sliver of light from their tiny back patio streaming in through the blinds, and nursed a glass of red wine. She shouldn't have bought the bottle, but after a grueling shift on the register and stocking shelves, she found herself walking out of Post Road with a bag of groceries in one hand and the cheapest bottle of wine in the other. She was halfway through the bottle now, still in her uniform, letting the sharp tannins coat her tongue as she replayed the offer over and over again in her head.

A bakery, all to herself. Even if Kevin's offer was outright absurd, she flirted with the idea of *what if*. What if she had her own spot, a chance to create what she wanted and actually have a say in how things were run? What if she could ditch Post Road and late-night summer shifts at Scoops for a more balanced schedule? Could she do it? Could she work side by side with Kevin every day with his constant smile and all of his frustratingly positive energy? Could she really leave Charlie behind?

Leaving felt prosperous. She was nine years in with Charlie. *Nine years*. She'd given up so much of herself to be with him, to live this life she wanted. Sure, things were hard right now, but relationships were never supposed to be easy. Things would get better, right?

Right?

She shook her head and took another gulp from her glass, wincing slightly at the sharp, potent taste. It wasn't anywhere near the best wine in the world, but it was doing the job. Her hands were no longer shaking in frustration. Her mind wasn't racing as quickly as it had when she looked into Kevin's eyes, watching them droop with disappointment when she refused his offer.

The front door clicked as Charlie stepped into the apartment. He was still in his work clothes, slightly rumpled from the day. He locked the door behind him and shrugged off his coat, glancing over at the couch and startling slightly.

"Is that *wine?*" he gawked, walking over to sit next to her. He slipped an arm around her waist and kissed her cheek. "Got any more?"

Jess shook her head. She technically did, but she'd hidden it away. Despite the cheapness of the bottle, this was her small luxury. She wasn't in the mood to share.

"Damn," he sighed. "Could use some right now. It's been a long day."

Jess didn't respond at first, just looked up at Charlie's raven-black hair. She used to love running her hands through it, the motion always soothing whatever worries were going on in that head of his. But the desire to do so wasn't there anymore, so she swirled her wine, keeping her eyes on the glass. "He's got you working late?"

"Yeah, there was this event tonight for all the boatyard vendors. He said he needed me there to *charm* them."

"And I'm sure that worked," Jess said, her tone coming off flat and a little bitter.

Charlie didn't seem to notice. "It did. They were eating out of the palm of my hand."

Jess made a face, thankful that his gaze was angled toward the porch blinds.

"Jessie," he whispered. "I have to tell you something."

Her stomach turned. He still wasn't looking directly at her, but she could see the anguish on his face. Her chest tightened. "What did you do?" she snipped.

Charlie's attention snapped to her, his eyes wide. "Me? I didn't do anything, I swear."

She exhaled. "Okay, then what's going on?"

"It's about the Cape."

Feeling her hands starting to shake again, she placed her glass down on the scuffed-up coffee table in front of them. "The Cape" referred to Cape Cod, the place where they took a vacation every year. Jess...hated it. Hated that the only place she could get away to each year was another beach—a little different to Haverport, but a beach none-theless. But Charlie's parents had a house out in Brewster, so getting to stay there, just the two of them, meant *free*. It wasn't her ideal vacation, but it was what they could afford. And more importantly, it was an entire week off.

But with the way Charlie was looking at her, she had a feeling her blissful week of nothing was about to get ripped out from under her feet.

"My father decided to put the house up for short-term vacation rentals this year," he started. "He says he has a lot going on here this summer and won't have the opportunity to use it. So our family is getting one week at the end of April before rentals start."

She began wringing her hands. "So...you're saying that our week will now involve the family? And it's happening next month?" *It will be colder this time of year,* she thought. *But still lovely. And still an entire week off.*

"Actually...the week *will* be for family, but only for immediate family members and spouses," he rushed out, looking sheepish. "And since we're not married..."

"That means I'm not invited."

Charlie simply nodded, his eyes searching Jess's face for something that she knew wasn't there. Grace. Forgiveness. Kindness. Love. She wasn't giving him any of it. Instead, she bolted up from the couch and rubbed her neck. She felt like she was on fire. She reached for her glass and downed the dregs of her wine, gripping the stem hard.

"Jessie—"

"Shut up," she demanded, not looking in his direction. "I knew they hated me, Charlie, I've known for a while now...but this? This is cruel."

"They don't hate you," he whispered, his voice hesitant. Like even he was grasping at a truth that wasn't there.

"Oh really? Tell me, how many times have I been invited to a family holiday since moving in with you? When's the last time I was over at the house, or even talked to your parents?"

He frowned. "Jessie, you know the rules—"

"Married couples only, got it," she spat. Her throat felt singed, raw, like any second she was going to open up her mouth and scorch the entire apartment. Reduce her entire life to ash. "So does this mean we'll have to go somewhere else for vacation? With our own money?"

Charlie stood up, reaching for her, but she was too quick. She snatched her hand away and stumbled a step back.

"I-I don't think I'll be able to get away this summer," he

uttered. "There's a lot going on at the boatyard this year, and you know how the season can be."

"So no vacation," she said. "No week off. No nothing."

"Maybe—maybe this fall? We could get away? The house...it won't have any rentals anymore. We'll escape, just you and me."

Jess slammed her eyes shut. She knew she was probably being unreasonable. It wasn't like this was Charlie's fault. He was following what his parents wanted, and he didn't have any say on the house. The fact that they were even allowed to stay for a whole week was already generous enough.

Yet part of her wished that Charlie tried, just this once. To fight for her. To prove how much he wanted her there, a part of his family. Or at least tried to make some kind of vacation plan that was different, a new adventure that wasn't the same old routine they lived out year after year. Something that would reignite the passion in their relationship that was sputtering out day after day. She couldn't be the only one who felt it.

"Do you even want me there?" she whispered, feeling helpless. Vulnerable.

Charlie hesitated at first, his eyes wide. "Of—of *course* I want you there, Jessie."

"Did you tell them that?" she asked. Her voice sounded steady and lethally calm, the complete opposite of the emotions raging inside her heart.

"I—" He broke off, his sentence dying in his throat.

Jess waited for him to respond, but nothing came. His face colored in shame as he looked down at his loafers. She simply nodded, placing the empty wineglass back down on the coffee table and stepping around him. "Do yourself a favor and sleep on the couch tonight," she demanded coolly.

"I have an early morning shift at Post Road so I'll be out before six."

Charlie nodded, not bothering to fight with her as Jess quietly took the stairs up to the loft, waiting for the tears to come. But after slipping on her sweats and sliding into the cool bed, her face remained dry. She let her mind drift to the methodical motion of kneading dough, the pressing and folding and pulling drifting her into a restless night of sleep.

Chapter Four

JESS WAS BACK in her least favorite place in the world—the chip aisle.

She was trying her best to be gentle with the bags she placed on the shelves, but when her mind drifted to her conversation with Charlie the night before and the fact that she wouldn't even get a scrap of a vacation this year, some of those bags took the brunt of her anger. She sighed, and rearranged them so they weren't the first ones customers grabbed, then closed her eyes. *Deep breath in, deep breath out.*

Charlie had still been tucked up on the couch when she left that morning, hugging a throw pillow to his chest, a blanket tossed to the floor. She'd had her moments when she wanted to throw Charlie to the couch for the night, but he always said something to her that made her soften and forgive him.

Not last night though. He hadn't even tried to fight her, and she didn't care.

Maybe because deep down, in her heart, she was giving

up. And maybe there was a part of him that felt the same way, too.

"Jessie?"

Her eyes flew open at the sound of that soft, familiar female voice. The voice that reminded her of whipped cream or meringue—light and soft and pillowy. Like it came from the clouds.

Jess turned to find her sister standing there. She was wrapped up in a pink checkered coat, wearing black leggings tucked into white workout socks and comfortable-looking sneakers, her soft blonde hair pulled back in a low ponytail.

But it wasn't her outfit that made Jess stare with eyes wide at the sister she hadn't seen in years. It was her round belly.

Jess sucked in a breath. "You're pregnant."

Dakota gave her an impish smile. "Four months."

"Wow," she breathed. "That's just—wow. Congrats, sissy."

Jess watched her sister wince at their familiar nickname for each other. The word rolled so easily off her tongue, yet it tasted stale in her mouth.

"Jasper?" Jess asked in a whisper.

"Is the dad, yes," Dakota said. "We're also, um—"

She didn't finish her sentence, but instead, held out her left hand. Jess stared down at the glistening princess-cut amethyst stone on her ring finger.

Jess stared wide-eyed, and her sister's eyes flooded with tears. One sprung free and trickled down her cheek.

"When we found out, Jasper proposed immediately," Dakota explained, pressing the tear into her cheek with the palm of her hand. "We had been talking about getting married for a while anyway. This little one clearly wanted us to move things along."

"And you're happy about it, yes?" Jess asked, feeling her defenses flare up for her older sister.

Dakota's mouth split into a grin. "Over the moon."

Jess exhaled and nodded, not sure what else to say, her insides tossing and turning over the revelations. How much she'd missed because she was no longer part of their lives.

"We're going to wait until next year for the wedding, get settled first," Dakota explained, instinctively rubbing her belly.

"Are you guys in town now?" she asked, curiosity getting the best of her.

"Not...yet," Dakota answered, the tone of her voice apprehensive. Jess knew there was more she wasn't saying. "We sold the condo in Stamford."

Jess's mouth flew open. "You *owned* a condo?"

Dakota shifted on her feet. "Yeah, I guess you wouldn't have known that either."

Her heart twisted in her chest. There was so much she didn't know. But then the thought of that night after graduation came flooding back to her, and she clenched her fists. She knew this wasn't all on her. So why did it always feel like that way?

"They miss you, by the way," Dakota said softly, like she could read her mind. "You should...you know..."

Jess glared at her. "No."

"Sissy." The word causing her sister's face to twitch when she said it. "Just, please—"

"It's been almost five years," Jess said sternly. "And not once have they reached out."

It was her deepest, darkest wound that continued to fester and suck the life out of her. During that first year in the apartment, when Charlie came home on his college breaks and they'd spend a blissful week or two together, he'd say the same thing over and over. *They'll come around, Jessie. Give them time.*

But slowly, as time ticked by and the seasons blended into each other, he stopped saying it, like he'd finally come to the same conclusion she'd already made in her heart. They would never come around. They would never try to win her back.

She hated that what happened between her and her parents also meant blocking out her sister. It made sense at the time; she'd taken their side. But now, with Dakota in front of her with that beautiful round belly and the ring that sparkled like hope under the fluorescent lights of Post Road's godforsaken chip aisle, Jess felt tired of pushing her away. She missed her sister—and she needed her.

"Can I see you again?" Dakota asked softly. "Coffee, maybe?"

Jess opened her mouth to try to fight her on it, that old feeling of frustration withering in her gut whenever Dakota tapped into their bond—that old ability her big sister had of reading her. But they were adults now, and her sister was extending an olive branch to her.

She let out a soft breath. "Okay."

"Text me," her sister replied. "It's, um, the same number. Nothing new there."

Jess nodded.

Dakota shuffled around her and her cart, heading for the checkout line. "You look—"

Jess frowned, staring down at her hands. *Like shit? I know,* she thought. She examined her uneven fingernails, pale and devoid of any color, hiding her disappointed expression so her sister couldn't read that, too.

"It's good to see you, sissy," Dakota said instead. She turned quickly and walked down the aisle, leaving a trail of peppermint and vanilla behind her. Jess closed her eyes and felt a pang at the memories it evoked.

She turned back to her cart, carefully lifting a bag of chips and placing it on the shelf, letting tears run freely down her cheek for the first time in a very, very long time.

PREGNANT. *Marriage.*

The two words swirled around in her head, the image of her sister wrapped in that pink coat always at the forefront of her mind. More importantly, the idea that she *got pregnant*, and then Jasper proposed, and Dakota was thrilled about it.

What if I woke up one morning and found out I was pregnant, she asked herself. Intimacy between her and Charlie had ground to a near halt, but it only took one slip-up for the little stick to show two pink lines instead of one, and the idea made her stomach roil. Would Charlie propose like Jasper did? There was a period of time when all she could think about was Charlie getting down on one knee, but somewhere along the way that daydream had transformed into a pipe dream—one she'd eventually given up on. Now the idea made her bitter and mad...especially if the only reason he did it was because she got knocked up.

She knew it wasn't like that with Dakota and Jasper. They met in their freshman year at Boston University, the same year Jess started high school, and Dakota had fallen head-over-heels. Jess thought back to that first holiday break, how Jasper drove three hours from his hometown to see her and have dinner with them. Jess sat there and watched the way Jasper's eyes sparkled every time they drifted to Dakota, wondering if Charlie also looked at her that way.

Jess had been with Charlie just as long as Dakota had been with Jasper, and yet everything felt starkly different. Dakota was still clearly in love and happy. Why didn't she feel the same way?

She couldn't seem to get her mind off the image of Dakota's smiling face and rounded belly, even as she sang "Happy Birthday" to Melanie and sliced the cake for everyone—a double layer with Strawberry and Birthday Cake ice cream for Melanie and Duncan's favorite flavors, trimmed with purple frosting. She knew she had to really be out of it when Kevin's goading over her uneven slices didn't rile her.

Now the whole group sat on the porch, lazy and content after demolishing the cake, watching as the sun slowly dipped below the bay. A black convertible pulled up in front of Melanie's cottage in Sandy Cove, and Jess peered over to see Zach smoothly stepping out of his car and locking it.

Blake yelped at the sight of his boyfriend and bolted, hopping down the stairs and snaking his arms around Zach's shoulders so he could reach up to him for a kiss. The sight of them made her heart twist, made her think of Dakota and Jasper, of Calvin and Melanie wrapped up tight on the porch swing next to them.

"Must be nice," she hummed to herself, not realizing how loud she said the words. She ignored the way Kevin awkwardly shifted next to her.

"You could just break up with him," Calvin responded.

And take us up on your offer, Jess finished for him in her head. She curled her hands into fists, wondering if the reason she was questioning her relationship so much was because of *them*.

Her phone rang in her pocket. She grumbled when she noticed it was Charlie, but was happy to have an excuse to step away from her loved-up friends. "Speak of the devil."

Jess entered the cottage, pressing the phone to her ear. "What?" she answered.

"Jessie, hi!" Charlie said cheerfully. They still hadn't talked about their fight a few weeks ago, and now Charlie was off on his family vacation in the Cape. Without her. And sounding like he was having fun, no less.

She took a deep breath, forcing herself to be civil. "How's the Cape?"

"Cold right now, but beautiful," he said. "Not the same without you here though."

"Yeah, I'm sure," she gritted out.

Jess heard the porch door swing open and turned abruptly. She saw Kevin step inside, Calvin at his heels. She frowned, rolling her eyes as she turned away from them.

"Hey, so I was talking to my dad," Charlie said. "He was wondering when you were going to send rent for April? He said you're usually good about it so he was surprised it didn't roll through."

Jess froze. "What do you mean send rent in? I thought you said you had it handled."

"Wait, what?"

She removed her glasses and rubbed her face with the back of her hand. Thank god she couldn't afford makeup anymore, because she would just be smearing it down her cheeks for the number of times she did this in a day. "You told me you would handle all of April's rent, remember?

After you watched me eat grilled cheese for breakfast over a pile of unpaid bills?"

Jess slid her glasses back on and noticed the way Kevin cocked an eyebrow at her. She heard him mutter something under his breath that sounded like, *For breakfast?*

"Oh, I, well—" Charlie spluttered, hesitating.

Jess waited for one beat, then two, hoping he would remember. Praying that he would offer to do so anyway.

But after an uncomfortably long silence, she shook her head. "Charlie, I have to pay my portion for May in a couple of days. I can't pay double the amount, I don't have the cash."

Jess watched as Kevin and Calvin looked at each other —damn them and their silent exchanges. She shook her head and stepped away, walking toward the kitchen sink.

Laughter sounded on the other end of the phone at something someone said. Her stomach churned as she wondered what was so funny. Wondering if *she* was the cause of that laughter.

"Look, Jessie, I gotta go. I already gave him my half, and he says you can send the rest with your May payment."

She blanched, unable to form sentences, unable to defend herself. Paying rent for April *and* May was going to clear out everything she had in her checking account, and Post Road wasn't paying her again until next Thursday.

"Love you!" he chirped, then dropped the line.

Jess just stood there in a daze, looking at the lock screen of her phone, her wallpaper a picture of kanelbullar she made two months ago that she was particularly proud of.

She felt a soft hand on her shoulder. "Hey, you okay?"

Her gaze drifted to Kevin's wavy locks and the hazel eyes that looked intently at her. Her gut reaction was to brush him off. But his hand on her shoulder felt like an anchor as she battled the anxiety building up in her chest. As if he knew, he gave her a gentle squeeze, waiting patiently for her breathing to slow. She simply shook her head in response, and he squeezed her shoulder once more.

Jess looked past Kevin and realized Calvin was already back on the porch, leaving the two of them alone in the cottage.

"What can I do to help?" Kevin asked her softly.

"Do you have eighteen hundred dollars?"

Kevin let out a low whistle. "Jesus, I wish."

Jess grimaced, feeling embarrassed over hearing how desperate her voice sounded. But he didn't seem to care, his thumb brushing up her shoulder, down to her collarbone, and back.

She was afraid to look into his eyes, afraid of what she would find there. "I know what you're thinking."

"You do, do you?"

"You want me to take you up on the offer."

"And why won't you?"

She finally looked at him, that lock of hair now tucked behind his ear. "Because I can't leave him, Kevin. I can't."

"Jessica—"

"Nine years."

He let out a shaky breath. "I know."

"I can't give up after *nine years*."

"It's a long time."

"I don't know anything else," she admitted.

The vulnerability that rolled off her lips surprised her, but Kevin didn't skip a beat. He simply nodded, that thumb still tracing the front of her shoulder, his touch making her skin hum.

Kevin shifted so he was facing her and cupped her other shoulder. "Does that mean the rest of your years have to look the same? You still have a whole lot of life waiting for you, Jess."

"But this is what I thought I wanted for my life. How could I want it so bad then, but want nothing to do with it now?"

Kevin froze then, his thumb no longer tracing her collarbone. "What are you saying?"

She grumbled and shook out of his grasp, stepping away from him. "Nothing. I'm saying nothing."

"That didn't sound like nothing," he said, trailing after her. He reached for her shoulder again, turning her away from the cottage door and guiding her back toward him. "It sounds like you don't want it anymore."

She shrugged him off again. "It doesn't matter," she said pointedly.

"Why not?" he pushed. "Why does it not matter?"

"Kevin, seriously, I get what you're doing," she said, her voice rising. "You want me as your baker for your bike shop so you don't have to move back home. But I need you to back the fuck *off*."

Kevin's face fell. Silence lingered between them until the faint sound of the porch door opening roused him back to life. "The bakery isn't to just save my business, Jess."

"It's not? Don't tell me you're doing it for *me*."

"So what if I'm—"

Calvin stepped in, placing a hand on Kevin's chest. "Hey, leave her be."

Kevin huffed and shook his head. But instead of storming off, he looked back at her. "Forget me and the bike shop, Jess. What I really want is for you to be happy, and I care about you enough to make sure you get that happiness. Does being with him truly, honestly make you happy?"

Jess scowled, but she didn't have the words to respond.

She worried if she tried fighting him, tried pretending that she was happy, the truth would come tumbling out instead.

"I have to go," she grumbled, grabbing her jacket and purse as she headed out the back door, making sure none of the Scoopers on the front porch saw her teary departure. She'd never cried in front of any of them before, and she intended to keep it that way.

Chapter Five

JESS WAS able to pay her portion of the rent, but it meant loading her schedule the following weeks with extra shifts. She kept her head down and focused, avoiding Kevin at all costs. She saw him walk into the store one morning as she worked the register, watching the way his shoulders sagged when he looked at the deserted bakery. She'd snuck away conveniently for her break. She didn't want to hear about the bike shop or his inevitable move home—it wasn't fair of him to dump that on her in the first place.

Toward the end of the month, Jess had enough in her account to pay next month's rent plus some, which released some of the long-held tension in her shoulders. She hated living month-to-month like this, but maybe if she started saving small pockets at a time, she wouldn't feel so strained when a new month rolled along. She decided she would transfer some of that money into savings as she drove home after working a double at Post Road.

She stepped into the apartment, fully expecting a dark room and for Charlie to be in bed, but when she stepped in, she was greeted by the sight of candles, takeout boxes, a bottle of wine, and a smiling Charlie on the couch. He was already in his sweats, his hair a little disheveled, but his expression was bright.

Jess dropped her purse to the floor with a defeated thud. "What's this?"

Charlie flipped open the boxes of food. "Dinner for my Jessie."

She smirked. "You bought me Chinese?"

"*And* wine," Charlie said, already pouring her a glass as she took a seat next to him. "And don't worry, I paid for it."

She rolled her eyes, but any fighting words left her body at the smell of vegetable lo mein and kung pao chicken. She moaned. "Thank you."

He smirked, reaching in to kiss the corner of her mouth. "That was a fun sound."

She swatted him away. "Food first."

Charlie chuckled. "How was work?"

"Brutal," she grumbled as she took a bite of noodles. "Cory kept me at the register the whole time."

He frowned. "What happened to the bakery?"

Jess paused. "Did I not tell you he closed it down?"

"No, you did not," he replied. He shifted closer to her and reached an arm around her shoulder, kissing her cheek. "I'm sorry, babe, you must be upset."

Babe? Jess took a gulp of her wine, trying to think back to the last time he called her that. Weeks? *Months?* "Yeah," she responded with a huff. "It's fine, whatever."

He kissed her again slowly, then started dropping a trail of kisses down her neck. He curled a finger at the collar of her polo, pulling it down as he continued his path.

She took another sip of wine. "My, are we desperate."

"Come on, Jessie," he said into her neck, his breath warm. "It's been so long."

"I know," she sighed, placing her glass down.

She gave in, peeling his T-shirt off his body and running a hand along the side of his abs like she always did, because she knew it made him shiver. She knew exactly what Charlie liked; at this point, it was well practiced. And it was the same for him—he was an expert at extracting her soft moans and frantic touches, shifting her into the positions that were familiar and easy.

Charlie lifted her and carried her up the stairs, stripping off her uniform and laying her down on the bed. It was always good with Charlie, but for the first time, she wondered if there was *more.* If there was something else they could do to spice things up.

She let him cuddle her after, holding her close underneath their duvet as he planted a lazy kiss at the back of her neck. She let her body go slack, releasing the stiffness that came with standing at the same register and craning her neck back and forth as she mindlessly scanned items on the belt. Charlie traced circles on her stomach with his thumb as she drifted off to sleep.

The sound of pots and pans and a few curse words in the kitchen woke her up the following morning. She bolted upright and checked the clock, realizing that Charlie was already out of bed and doing something in the kitchen before seven in the morning.

She tied her robe tightly around her waist and padded downstairs. She peered into the kitchen and caught Charlie trying to flip a pancake, cursing when it hit the side and folded over.

"Are you...*making breakfast?*" she asked, flabbergasted.

"Trying to," he grumbled, pointing to the plate next to him. "But they're coming out a little burnt."

She stepped up next to him, letting him curl an arm around her waist. "It's okay, I like them crispy."

"Liar," he mumbled, sliding another pancake on the plate.

"Is there a special occasion I'm missing or something?" she asked, picking up the plate.

"No, just—" Charlie started. "Sit, I'll be there in a minute."

She frowned but followed his orders, slathering her stack with maple syrup before taking a bite. The pancakes were flat and flavorless, but she didn't comment. He'd been uncharacteristically sweet the past twelve hours, and she didn't want to ruin it. She couldn't help but feel hopeful as he kissed her cheek before sitting down next to her. What if things were finally going to turn around? What if this rough patch they'd been in was finally over?

"What do you think?" he asked, taking a bite.

"They're great, thank you," she said. "Definitely better than my usual piece of toast."

He smirked. "You're welcome."

They ate in silence. Jess chewed methodically as she watched Charlie, his eyes on his plate.

She put her fork down, deciding to break the silence. "Charlie, what's going on?"

He tipped back in his chair, and the mixture of guilt and worry on his face made her chest fall. It was one she was far too familiar with at this point.

She crossed her arms. "Spit it out."

He winced, then ran a palm over his face. "Dad offered me a promotion. A big one."

"Okay..." Jess said, dragging out the word. "And that's a problem because?"

"Because the job is in Garrison."

Her brows shot up. "So you won't be working at Cap's?"

"No," he said, finally looking at her. "He wants me to manage his real estate listings at his firm...at the office in Garrison."

Jess gripped the table in front of her, keeping her eyes on the half-eaten pancakes on her plate, now soggy from the syrup. "What does that mean?"

"That—that I would likely have to move," he said softly. "To Garrison. By the end of the summer."

"That's a forty-five-minute drive from Haverport," Jess said. "That's a really long commute for me."

Charlie's silence had her looking up at him. His cheeks were flushed and he was bouncing his knee under the table. "Or...or you stay here."

Her eyes went wide. "Are you breaking up with me?"

"No—no. Jessie..." He reached for her hands but she pulled them away and tucked them underneath her arms. "We could do long distance or something, maybe just for a little while."

Jess stood up, her arms still crossed. "What does 'a little while' mean? A few months? A year? Do you not want me to move there with you?"

"*I* do," he admitted. "*He* doesn't."

His father. She shook her head, at a loss for words.

"He told me that it might be good for me to be on my own for a little while," Charlie explained in a rush. "He said I could have the job and stay in a brand-new apartment if I did."

"He wants you to leave me," Jess said, rolling her eyes. "Un-fucking-believable."

"No, he never said leave you," Charlie said. "Just...to spend time. On my own."

"In hopes that we'll fizzle out," Jess said. "Because god forbid I be his daughter-in-law."

"That's not fair."

"It isn't?" she squeaked. "Please explain to me how *I'm* being unfair, Charlie. Please tell me how, after watching my family blow up, he could be so apathetic and cold toward me even though *I took his side.* And now he wants me to be okay with him trying to drag us apart?"

"He's done a lot for you," Charlie said, holding up his arms and gesturing toward their apartment. "*I've* done a lot for you."

She coughed out a laugh. "Are you kidding? You couldn't even pay last month's rent!"

"For an apartment that he let you have without any credit score or anything else to your name," Charlie spat. "All I've ever done is take care of you, and he thinks it's unfair that I haven't had the chance to go live my life yet because of it."

Jess took a step back, like she'd been punched in the gut. "You—you think I'm holding you back from living your life?"

Charlie's eyes went wide. "No, he said that, not me—"

"But do you agree with him?" she interrupted. "Do you feel like you haven't been able to live your life?"

He hesitated slightly, then an explanation poured out of his lips. But the hesitation was all she needed. She ignored his words.

"I'm done," she whispered.

"You don't mean that," he argued.

"No, I'm done, it's over," she said. "We're done, Charlie."

Tears trickled down his cheeks, but after weeks of breaking down in front of gas station pumps or hidden away in stock rooms, her thoughts on Dakota and how much they had grown apart, her eyes remained dry. The admission from his father, the truth of what Charlie felt deep down in his heart from that hesitation—even if he was afraid to admit it...Jess knew.

She looked around their apartment, feeling embarrassed by all of it. How long had he felt this way? Had he always felt the need to take care of her, to give up his life for her? Did any of this life she clawed at desperately mean anything to him?

He kept reaching for her but she slapped at his arms, warning him not to come any closer as she stormed up the stairs. She pulled her suitcases out from underneath their bed, covered in a layer of dust, and tuned out the sound of Charlie's pleading. She ripped open the closet and started pulling her clothes off hangers, throwing them into the bag.

"Jessie, stop. *Stop!*" he yelled.

She paused her haphazard packing for a moment, then shook her head, not allowing herself to do anything for him anymore. "No. I made up my mind. Move to Garrison. You're free of me."

"You know it's not like that," Charlie said. "Please, Jessie, don't go."

"Go live your life, Charlie." She moved on to the dresser and emptied out handfuls of clothes and keepsakes into an old duffel bag. "I'll go live mine."

He crawled onto the bed, trying to reach for her, but she swatted him away, the aggressive motion making the nightstand beside her shake. Her glasses fell and cracked on the hardwood floor.

Her small slap seemed to be his last straw, his begging switching to anger. "This is all pretend anyway," he sneered. "It's not like you have anywhere to go."

She threw on an old stained tee and shimmied into a pair of jeans, then tossed her broken glasses into the bag in front of her and zipped it up. "Yes, I do. I've had a plan in the works for a while."

It wasn't like she'd been the one to make the plan, but her words did what she intended them to. She hated the way she reveled in the wounded look on Charlie's face. She picked up her bags and carried them downstairs.

"But what about the rest of your stuff?" he asked, right on her heels as she entered the bathroom. "You're going to leave it here?"

Jess popped in her contacts, then shoveled the rest of her toiletries into her purse. She snatched her uniform that was tossed on the floor from the previous night, then scanned the apartment. She shook her head, stuffing it in her duffel. "Nope, toss it for all I care. It's all cheap crap anyway."

Charlie gawked at her as Jess threw open the door and popped the trunk of her car, tossing the first few bags in.

"How could you do this to me?" Charlie asked, his words gravely with emotion as Jess grabbed the rest of her stuff from inside. "After all this time?"

She slammed the trunk shut and looked at him, *really* looked at him. In that gaze she saw the boy she fell in love with, with his sparkling blue eyes and the midnight-black hair she loved to run her hands through. But he wasn't a boy anymore. He was a man, someone completely different from who he was nine years ago, and she was finally ready to admit to herself all of the ways they'd changed over the years. She couldn't live in the past for the rest of her life, wearing the same clothes and doing all of the same things. It was time to grow up and be the woman she was meant to be.

"Do you really think it was going to work, Charlie?" she

asked, her voice softer and gentler than before. "Truthfully, where did you think this was going? Did you see us ever leaving this apartment? Getting married, having kids?"

The last bit made her heart twist, thinking of Dakota. She pushed the thought of her family away. One disappointment at a time.

Charlie looked down at his bare feet on the sidewalk.

She wasn't sure what made her do it, but she leaned into the small stroke of gentleness she felt in her heart and reached out to him, cupping his face for a moment. "Me too. We tried hard to hold on to something that was never really meant to be."

She dropped her hand and got into her car, then pulled away from the apartment and the life she always thought she wanted, and toward something that felt a lot scarier: a life she never expected.

Jess stood on Calvin's porch, listening to laughter inside, remembering it was Memorial Day. *Of course this was the moment Calvin decided to break out of his shell*, she thought. He was scheduled to work the night shift at Scoops that evening, and by the sounds of it, all the other Scoopers not working this afternoon were here as well.

She felt the urge to turn around and bolt, but she had nowhere else to go. She clenched her jaw and closed her eyes and took her three deep breaths, focusing on the sounds of the distant waves at Scallop Shell Beach and the smell of Gram's freshly baked oatmeal chocolate chip cookies.

After her third exhale she held up a fist and knocked.

Everyone inside went silent. A few words were exchanged as she heard a pair of flip-flops clapping toward the door. It swung open, but it wasn't Calvin on the other side of the porch door. It was Kevin.

The room remained silent as her eyes flicked over to Calvin making his way to the door. She looked back at Kevin, his eyes wide as he scanned the bags that surrounded her feet. The left corner of his lips twitched upward.

When he finally gazed back into her eyes, she nodded her head and asked, "Is it too late to take you up on the offer?"

Kevin's mouth split into a giddy grin. "Of course not, my dear Jessica. It would never be too late."

Jess rolled her eyes. "And if your business already went under and you were halfway to Vermont, that still wouldn't have been too late?"

"You're ruining the moment. Stop being so practical."

"If you don't want practical, then don't take me on as a business partner," she deadpanned.

She didn't think it was possible for his smile to get any bigger, but Kevin's smile grew wide, like a cartoon character. Goofy, perhaps. Jess shook her head, pretending to ignore the way Calvin was rubbing his face trying to contain his own smile before gesturing to Tyler on the couch to help him with the bags. She grumbled about how she could have handled them herself, but Tyler brushed her off, picking up two duffel bags and a suitcase as if they weighed nothing and carrying them down the narrow hallway.

Calvin grabbed the rest of her stuff as Kevin led her inside, the porch door slapping shut behind them. She felt her cheeks flush as she looked down at Melanie and Rory, surrounded by scraps of paper with what seemed to be sticker designs for Scoops, the two of them sitting there with mouths agape.

Rory scrambled up from where she was sitting. "Jess, did you—"

"Yes," she said, not waiting for Rory to finish her sentence. "I left."

She heard Melanie cough out an exasperated laugh, then slapped a hand in front of her face.

Kevin stepped away from Jess and ran a hand through his wavy hair, then let out a shaky breath.

Jess felt her cheeks flush again, her hands sweating. She hated having all of this attention on her.

Somehow, like the former high schooler *knew* that this entire interaction was bothering her, Rory reached out an arm and wrapped it around Jess's shoulders. Never would she have allowed this in the past. But never in her life had she thought she would leave Charlie. It seemed today was a day full of firsts.

"We were about to pick up pizza from Penny's," Rory said, shifting subjects. "You hungry?"

Jess nodded. "Yeah, pizza sounds good."

Chapter Six

Jess wasn't sure when she'd last stepped into Port Wheels, but when she arrived the following morning, she was certain there was barely a third of the bikes usually cramming the tiny shop. They were still parked neatly next to each other along the walls, but none were dangling from the ceiling like in summers past.

Kevin was leaning over a bike at his workshop in the back, his hands black from bike grease as he twisted a brake tighter with a wrench. He blew on the strand of wavy hair that flopped in front of his eyes, only for it to fall back down in front of his face.

"I think someone stole all of your bikes," Jess quipped.

Kevin grinned as he kept twisting. "Good morning, Jessica. Boy, is it going to be fun getting your sunshine personality every morning."

She snorted, looking around her. "Seriously, Kevin, where did they all go?"

Kevin tossed the wrench onto his small desk, wiping his hands with a dark rag. "I'm not selling as many, so I opted for less inventory this summer. There are a few older models in the back I need to bring up here, though."

He started making his way to the back of the shop. She followed. "Won't it be hard to try making more money if you have less bikes to sell?"

"Most of the shop's money comes from repairs," Kevin explained. "Usually people will bring their bikes in for a repair then head to Seabreeze Café for a coffee and wait. But now with the bakery—"

"People might just stick around here and buy from us," Jess finished. "Very smart."

Kevin turned toward her and beamed. "Did you just call me *smart*?"

"Don't let it get to your head," she grumbled, shaking her head at the way Kevin laughed as he pushed a set of double doors that led to the back of the shop.

But it wasn't a storage room he was taking her to. It was the kitchen.

Jess stood there for a beat, awestruck. A commercial oven, counter space, and an industrial-sized mixer were along one wall. A deep chest freezer sat parallel to her left. She stepped around the extra bikes toward the back and eyed a decent-sized walk-in. Nothing was humming, which meant everything was currently unplugged.

"What do you think?" Kevin asked softly.

Jess turned to him, noticing he was smiling at her. It made her squirm a little. "It's fine, it will do."

"Jessica, you're such a liar. You should see your face right now. You're *glowing*."

"I am not glowing," she snipped.

"You are too," Kevin jested. "You're probably already imagining that menu of yours."

She scowled and turned away from him, not wanting to tell him that she spent the previous night hunched over a notepad, dreaming up exactly that. *Her own bakery.*

"As long as you promise me there will be kanelbullar, you can do whatever you want," Kevin continued.

Her heart fluttered thinking about how she'd soon be able to make her favorite pastry again—and any other pastry she wanted.

She pulled her mouth into a scowl, trying her best to contain her excitement. She didn't want to give Kevin that satisfaction quite yet. "I can't exactly make *anything* with all of these bikes in here."

"Oh, you don't want to bake around the bikes? I thought it would give this place a little charm," he teased.

She rolled her eyes, grabbing the handlebars of a shiny purple one. "Very funny."

The two of them pushed bikes out of the kitchen and into the main shop.

"You're not wearing your glasses," Kevin observed.

She nodded, flicking a kickstand out for a bike and parking it. "They broke in my frenzied move out of the apartment."

He nodded, his face flushed. "I'm sorry, Jess," he whispered.

She frowned. "Why? You're getting what you want."

"I already told you, all I want is for you to be happy," he responded softly. "Even if my methods were..."

"Asinine?"

He huffed a laugh. "Something like that."

She observed the golden boy, the way his shoulders slumped, his hazel eyes dim as he stared back at her, looking like he really, truly screwed up.

"This whole thing has made me realize something," she said.

He cocked a brow. "Yeah? What's that?"

"That I actually hate wearing glasses."

His laughter was bright, ringing through the tiny bike shop like shining silver bells, the sound making her smile.

"Why are these back here anyway?" Jess asked, turning her face from his as she made her way back into the kitchen.

"I've had these models for ages, they just don't sell," Kevin said as he followed. "But it would be dumb to get rid of them, so they sit back here."

"Could you rent them out?"

Kevin's brow furrowed. "Rent them?"

Jess shrugged. "Yeah. Shops along the Cape do it all the time. Vacationers will rent bikes for a day or even a week so they don't have to travel with their own," she said. "It was also a big date-night thing for, well—"

She looked down at the handlebars, squeezing and releasing one of the brakes.

Kevin tapped a finger to his lips. "Maybe we could make it some kind of package deal. Date night at Port Wheels. Rent two bikes for a couple of hours, get two free treats of your choice."

Jess smiled, nodding her head. "Now we're talking."

When they finished pushing all of the bikes to the front, Jess pressed her hands into her back, scanning the room. "So how exactly is this going to work? The shop is tiny as is, but we'll need some kind of storefront for the bakery."

Kevin nodded. "Most of these bikes will go outside during store hours, which will give us some room. I was thinking," he started, turning toward the right wall next to the shop windows, "the bakery will go here."

Jess watched as he held out his hands. "Counter and register," he explained, then shuffled closer to her. "Glass display case next to it," he said, shuffling again. His arm brushed up against hers as he held out his arms. "We'll leave this space open for you to easily get in and out."

Jess took a step back, aware of the heat from his body.

"Sorry," he mumbled, then walked past her and continued on with his vision. "Back counter here with the espresso machine and other coffee accoutrements, and a little work space for you when you're taking orders or working on admin."

Jess let out a shaky breath. "This feels like a lot of work."

"It's a good thing I have contractors coming tomorrow," Kevin said. "If all goes to plan, everything should be done by this time next week."

She gaped at him. "You already have contractors? There's no way they agreed this last-minute."

Kevin simply winked at her, a twinkle in his eye. "Maybe it wasn't last-minute."

She stuttered, feeling stunned. "But...but how did you..."

"I had faith in the kanelbullar. I knew you wouldn't be able to go that long without baking your next batch."

Her mouth fell open as Kevin propped the front door and started pushing bikes outside of the shop, getting things ready for opening. Even before she left Charlie, before she decided to take him up on the offer, Kevin had things set in motion believing that she *would*. Contractors hired, plans in place. She wondered if there was something else going on behind the scenes she wasn't aware of, or maybe someone else who was pulling the strings. Kevin did mention a mysterious investor for the whole project, and there was only one person Jess could think of who'd want to drive Charlie out of her life.

She inhaled sharply as he walked back in to grab another bike. "Kevin?"

He looked up at her. "Mmm?"

"Who's the investor behind this project?"

Kevin opened his mouth and closed it a few times, like a fish. "They, um, asked to remain anonymous."

"But shouldn't I—" She caught herself, thinking through what to say next. She technically was only an employee of Port Wheels, not an outright owner like Kevin was, so she wasn't really in a place to make demands. But she needed to be sure.

She scrunched her hands into fists and slammed her eyes shut. "Can you promise me that it isn't Charlie's father?"

There was a beat of silence between them as Jess held her breath. She heard shuffling, then a pair of warm, calloused hands on her bare shoulders. "Jess," Kevin breathed.

She peeked her eyes open. His own gaze was soft, his expression careful.

"I would *never* do that to you. Charlie Sullivan the Third will never be in business with us or in charge of this property. He would have to rip it from my cold, dead hands."

She coughed out a laugh at his morbidity, which made him smile.

"Okay," she exhaled. "That's all I needed to hear."

"Good." Kevin nodded, dropping his hands. She watched him grimace after he did, looking at her shoulders.

She frowned. "What?"

"I might have, um, left some grease stains on your tank top."

Jess looked down at her shirt, at the remnants of bike grease from his touch. She shrugged. "I've had this thing for almost a decade, I literally don't care."

"You sure?"

"I don't care about any of my clothes," she said matter-of-factly. "They're all old from high school. I had to stop caring about clothes long ago."

"Jess that's...so sad."

She glared at him. "We're not here to be sad, we're here to work." She pulled her hair into a ponytail. "I'm going to grab supplies to clean that kitchen."

Kevin's face brightened, as if he couldn't believe this was really happening. "Want me to help?"

"Kevin, no, you have to *work*," Jess said, pointing to his half-finished job of opening up the shop. "We still need to make as much money as possible to keep this place afloat, and if we're doing renovations soon, you need to—"

"Okay, *okay*, boss lady," Kevin said in an amused tone. "I get it! Go clean, I'll be up here."

Jess nodded and turned back toward the double doors, flinging them open. She glanced around her kitchen—*her kitchen*—and cataloged what needed to be done. She smiled to herself, letting the excitement in her chest bubble to the surface as a few tears of pure happiness rolled down her cheeks. She wiped them away, her hands trembling slightly at the mere thought that this time next week, she would be baking all the kanelbullar her heart desired.

Jess sat on her new bed, in her new room. It felt jarring sleeping by herself after sharing one with Charlie for so long. She didn't realize how horribly she'd been sleeping until her first morning at the Balls' cottage when she woke up feeling well-rested for the first time in years. Or maybe it was the fact that the stress etched in her chest from constantly worrying about rent and bills dulled slightly in her new environment. Either way, she vowed to never share a bed with someone again.

She scanned the notebook on her lap, making edits to her recipes. They were the same ones she used at the bakery at Post Road but with major improvements now that she could do her own thing. She flicked through the pages, wondering if it would be crazy to sell a few loaves of sourdough bread and French baguettes each day. She scribbled it down, noting for later.

A soft knock came from her closed bedroom door. "You can't hide in there forever, my dear."

She sighed and tossed her notebook aside, then headed for the door, creaking it open slowly. Gram stood on the other side in her pajamas, wrapped up in her soft robe.

"I don't want to be a bother," Jess admitted. "As soon as I can afford my own place again, I'll be—"

"You be quiet with that nonsense," Gram interrupted. She held up her hand and patted Jess's cheek. "Calvin is your family, so you are my family. Now get in the kitchen and eat some dinner."

Jess gave her a bashful smile. "Yes, ma'am."

She followed Gram into the kitchen, sitting down at the table covered in an intricate lace tablecloth, a peony-scented candle burning at the center. Gram pulled out a wrapped-up pie container from the fridge.

Her eyebrows raised. "Dessert for dinner?"

"My house, my rules," Gram replied, placing a slice of cherry pie in the toaster oven, then took a seat next to Jess. "So. How are you?"

"Good." Jess nodded. She shifted in her seat, feeling uncomfortable. She'd only really spoken to Calvin's grandmother in passing. How much had Calvin told her? How much did she know?

"You break up with someone after nine years and you're just...good? I don't buy it, dearie."

Okay, so she knows a lot, Jess thought to herself. "I'm still, um, in shock, I think."

"I would be too, that's a long time to be with a person," Gram replied. "Calvin's grandfather has been gone for eleven years, and I still think I'm in shock."

"How long were you married?"

"Forty-one blissful years."

Jess smirked. "Were they *all* blissful?"

Gram nodded, no hesitation in the slightest. "Yes. Even when we fought. Even when things felt hard. Every second with him was worth it."

Jess wrung her hands underneath the table, her mind drifting to her years with Charlie. *Blissful* wasn't exactly the word she'd use to describe their relationship. Sure, parts of being with him in the beginning felt magical, the first kisses and the stolen moments when she'd sneak out of her parents' house. But in the end, on the brink of finally being on her own after almost a decade, she was surprised at how little she mourned what they'd become. Or maybe it was her excellent night's sleep that was making her feel a little jaded.

The timer from the toaster oven dinged.

Gram slid the slice of pie from a spatula onto a plate,

handing it to Jess. She took a tentative bite, expecting the filling to be overly sweet and the crust to be crumbly and dry.

Oh, how wrong she was.

The cherry filling was perfectly bright and tart, the liquid syrupy and thick enough for the pie to hold its shape. The crust was buttery and flaky and easy to fork into. She took another big bite of the pie, closing her eyes, feeling embarrassed by the moan that escaped her throat without her consent.

Gram chuckled. "That good, huh?"

She speared another chunk, shoveling it in her mouth, not caring that she was talking with her mouth full. "Can I have this recipe for the bakery?"

"Of course, why else do you think I made it?" Gram's eyes twinkled.

She picked up the end with the crust, biting into it. "And your oatmeal chocolate chip cookies?"

"Now that one is top secret. Grampy has been after it for years."

Jess frowned. "What would it take for you to hand it over to me instead?"

"Seeing he's got two decades of free blueberry coffee cake in his favor, you'll have your work cut out for you."

She groaned, looking down at her empty plate, wondering if it would be extremely rude to lick it clean. Grampy's blueberry coffee cake was a staple in town—the townies went absolutely nuts for it. She'd wanted to get her hands on that recipe for years, but it was sealed tight in his vault of buttery, sugary secrets. And apparently Gram's oatmeal chocolate chip cookies were of the same caliber. There's no way she would choose Jess to give that recipe to.

Jess leaned back in her chair, running a hand through

the long, wispy blonde strands cupping her face—the result of trying to grow out the bangs she'd given herself last summer. Another mistake to add to her list of horrible life choices. "Do you think Grampy is going to flip about us opening up a bakery?"

Gram tutted. "His deli brings in as much business in the afternoon as his baked goods do in the morning. Sometimes more."

"Yeah but...still," Jess huffed. "Haverport is always up in arms anytime a new business pops up."

It was why chains of any kind couldn't survive on Main Street; they were protested heavily by townies who didn't want big corporations to take over their beloved mom-and-pops downtown. The nearest chain was a Starbucks, which was a twenty-minute drive out of town, right off the entrance to the interstate.

Opening up her own spot wasn't as bad as a chain, but trying to compete with one of the oldest and most successful businesses in town? She could already picture the headlines. *Self-Taught Baker Thinks She's Better Than Grampy. Don't Go, She Sucks.*

Gram reached over and patted Jess's hand on the table. "I can see that mind of yours spiraling. Don't fret. It will all work out for the best."

She exhaled. "Will it? Will it really all work out for the best?"

"Yes," Gram replied, again without hesitation, like she was a fortune teller revealing the future. "You have a great partner in this. I know you will be just fine."

Jess frowned. "You mean Kevin?"

"He's a good boy. A little...aloof, sometimes. But kind-hearted and passionate. And very excited about working with you."

Her chest tightened. "He told you that?"

Gram smiled, that little twinkle still in her eye. "He didn't have to, dearie. It's written all over his face when he looks at you."

Chapter Seven

Jess was skeptical that the space would be up and running in a week. And yet, somehow, it came together without any issues. As if some kind of magical fairy was behind it all, spinning spells to make sure renovations went smoothly and appliances were delivered on time and installed with ease. In six days, Port Wheels was transformed as Kevin's vision for the bakery came to life.

She dipped a roller in a tray with beige paint, carefully lifting it before turning back to the wall. Even though Jess was meticulous about keeping her dripping to a minimum, she'd shielded the entire storefront and the bikes in plastic just in case. Which proved to be the correct choice when Kevin kicked the front door open, causing Jess to flinch and splatter paint on her shirt and the plastic covering the shiny new espresso machine next to her.

Jess set the roller down carefully and scowled at Kevin as he came marching in, one hand holding a couple of canvas totes filled to the brim, the other balancing a pizza box.

She frowned. "Weren't you supposed to be at Lowes?"

"I was at Lowes," he replied brightly, plopping the bags down before setting the pizza on the plastic-wrapped counter between them. "But they didn't have everything you requested so I also had to stop at True Value and Target, and Penny's was on the way home."

"Can you even afford pizza?" Jess chuffed.

"I told Penny her next repair is on me," Kevin said, lifting a hand and pointing at her face. "Also, stop being such a Debbie Downer. It's depressing."

"I'm not being a Debbie Downer, I'm being honest. We shouldn't be frivolously spending on anything. We should be focusing on getting in the green as quickly as possible."

Kevin groaned, tilting his head back. "Jess, working together is supposed to be *fun*."

"If you wanted fun, you should have asked someone else to work with you," she replied. "Now hand me those bags."

He raised an eyebrow at her. "Now hand me those bags....?"

Jess frowned. "Kevin..."

"Manners are such an important life skill, Jessica."

She growled at him, which only made his smirk stretch wider. He lifted the bags in front of her to make a point, swaying them back and forth. "Say the magic word, and they are yours."

"You're insufferable," she grumbled. She rolled her shoulders, making sure to glare at him the entire time, she conceded. "Now hand me those bags, *please*."

"So polite," Kevin said, taking a step back from her, bags still in hand. "But no. You can have them after you take a break and eat a slice."

"*KEVIN!*"

He pointed to himself. "Boss, remember? Now eat."

She swore to herself, watching as he placed the bags on his desk at the opposite end of the shop.

"Fine," she snipped, flipping open the box. When she noticed the toppings on the pizza, she paused.

"Veggie is your favorite, right?"

She glanced up, realizing Kevin was standing back at the counter, holding a paper plate in midair.

"Ye—yes," she breathed, taking the plate from him. "How did you know that?"

"How could I not? I was at Scoops visiting Calvin one time and he had ordered pizza for lunch since you were both working a double. You stepped into The War Room to give him shit that he got you a slice of pepperoni and not veggie."

"And you...remembered that," Jess said. It wasn't a question, more of a statement. That somehow Kevin remembered such a small detail about her from *years* ago.

He shrugged. "It's not a big deal."

"You're willing to...eat a vegetable pizza with me? Literally no one lets me get it because there's broccoli on it."

"I don't mind broccoli," he continued, lifting a stringy slice and setting it down on her plate. "Believe it or not, I actually order the veggie sometimes myself."

"Yeah right," she replied. She pulled a slice of mushroom from her pie and popped it in her mouth. "You're probably saying that to be nice. Just like you were about my favorite band."

"Definitely Maybe? Oh but I wasn't lying, they *are* my favorite band," he said, placing his half-eaten slice down on the counter before pulling out his phone from his back pocket. "'You and Me' is an absolute bop. Should we listen to it now?"

Her mouth fell open. "You looked them up?"

"You + Me" blasted through the speakers at Port Wheels at an ear-piercing volume. Kevin grinned, his eyes not leaving hers.

She shook her head at him and bit into her slice, watching as he bobbed his head. He danced with his slice of pizza dangled between his fingers, lifting his hand to pull the cheese with each bite.

At some point, Jess found herself on the other side of the counter joining him, another slice in her hand as they danced along to each song in the plastic-covered bike shop, not minding that she was sweating through her ratty Haverport High varsity field hockey shirt.

When the last song of the album came to end, Jess found herself laughing as Kevin dipped low into a curtsy like a ballerina at curtain call.

He popped back up and grinned at her laughter. "That has to be the most beautiful sound," he said.

She reached over and slapped his arm. "Stop that. You're being weird."

"No, I'm serious." He followed Jess as she tossed her paper plate in the garbage and went back to her painting behind the counter. "Jessica, when's the last time you actually *laughed* like that?"

A long ass time, she thought to herself. She racked her brain trying to recall her last truly joyous moment, but nothing came to mind. It was always work and stress and paying bills and occasional sex with Charlie when she had the energy for it. Nothing had felt amusing to her for a while.

Her silence was telling enough, so she let it linger as she lifted the paint roller and dragged it up and down the primed wall.

"Come on, I'm serious," he said, reaching around her to

grab the other paint roller. "You told me what you thought you wanted for your life isn't exactly what you want anymore, right?"

She bristled at his abruptness as he recited her words from weeks ago, but decided not to lash out at him quite yet. He *did* have a point. So she nodded.

"Okay, then what do you want now?" he asked.

She rolled a few strokes of pale beige on the primed white walls. "I'm not sure. Everything feels so...new and strange right now."

He nodded, reaching to fill in the white spots near the ceiling that were too high for Jess to reach. "That makes perfect sense, you lived that way for so long."

"Right. So how in the world can I know what I want when it hasn't even been a week?"

Kevin froze mid-stroke, his abrupt pause causing Jess to slow herself.

"I have an idea," he said, dropping the roller back into the tray and charging for his desk. Jess watched as he ripped a piece of blank paper out of a legal pad and grabbed a pen, heading back toward her. He leaned against the counter over that piece of paper and wrote the number one at the top.

"You're right. Trying to figure out what you want for your new life probably feels like a lot."

"No shit," Jess grumbled.

"Manners, Jessica. That mouth of yours won't get you anywhere."

She rolled her eyes and flipped him off.

He laughed in response. "Let's focus on the *now*. What are the things you want to do right now?"

"What do you mean?"

"Like..." He tapped the pen in his hand as he thought

through his response. "You've spent your whole life working to make money and live in this reality that you thought you wanted. But in that time, there were probably things you never got to do. So...what do you want to do?"

"As in...activities?"

He grinned. "Exactly! Think of it as a bucket list of all the things you want to do that you haven't had the chance to since graduating high school."

"A bucket list," Jess repeated.

"We could even kick it up a notch," he added, tapping the pen incessantly. "Let's pick ten things we should do by the end of this summer."

"*We?*" she balked.

"Oh yes, this is a *we* activity. Consider it team bonding. An extended clause on the offer."

"Or what? You'll fire me?"

"Yes," he deadpanned. "I'm the boss. You must do as I say."

"I feel like you probably shouldn't be using that excuse all the time..."

"Or what? You'll call HR?" he teased. "Because I *am* HR."

She groaned. "You really are insufferable."

"I take that as a compliment," he said, clicking the pen. "Now, let's start. Number one."

Jess set down the paint roller, realizing there really was no way out of this. Plus, would it really be so bad if she spent her summer doing the things she'd always wanted to do? It seemed a little silly but...it also sounded nice.

She crossed her arms. "Open up my own bakery."

He pointed the pen at her face. "That's a cop-out."

"My summer bucket list," she quipped. Before Kevin could quip back, she cut him off. "You seriously telling me that all the work we're doing to start this bakery can't count?"

He huffed. "*Fine*, but no more work stuff on this list. Number two."

She tapped her finger to her lips, glancing at the glass display case and thinking of all the treats that would soon fill those pristine-looking shelves. "Take a professional baking class."

"I said no work stuff!"

"That's not work stuff, that's fun stuff," she answered, pointing to the paper. "Write it down, boss."

He smiled, his teeth gleaming as he shook his head, scribbling it down. "Yes, ma'am."

Jess felt an unfamiliar tightening in her chest at his *yes, ma'am*. She watched the way his mouth twitched as he wrote. She tore her lingering gaze away before he could notice, then paced back and forth about what else she really wanted to do.

Her mind went to the vacation she'd miss out on this summer, how she would never go to the Cape with Charlie again. But that also meant she would...*never have to go to the Cape ever again.* She was free to go wherever she wanted. Charlie's idea of a vacation was visiting a carbon copy of their hometown. Now? She was free to vacation however she pleased.

And buy whatever she pleased. And spend her time how she pleased.

Her mind began racing with the possibilities.

"I want to go camping," she said. "Not backpacking, just camping. Somewhere far from here, out in the woods. Maybe Maine or New Hampshire."

"Or Vermont," Kevin said, winking at her before he looked back down at his paper. "Love it. Writing it down."

"I want to go to a grungy underground rock concert," she added, the ideas now spilling out of her. "And the location has to be extra sketchy. I want my shoes to stick to the floors from spilled beer and god knows what else, and for there to always be the possibility of someone getting punched in the face."

"How...oddly specific. I dig it."

"I want to watch all of *The Lord of the Rings* movies in a single sitting—the extended versions. Charlie *hated* those movies and I haven't had the chance to rewatch them since high school. I want to drink gross energy drinks to stay awake and eat lots of popcorn and end the marathon with the sun rising and feeling utterly sick to my stomach from junk food."

"An absolute rager with Frodo and Samwise. I'm in."

Jess whipped around from where she was pacing to face him. "You'd really watch all three of them with me? That's a twelve-hour commitment."

"Jessica, if you're doing it, I'm doing it."

Her chest tightened again. She rubbed at it as she turned away, hoping it would ease the feeling as she brainstormed the rest of her list. "I need new jeans. I'd like to find the perfect pair."

"Oh now see, I draw the line at shopping." He said it with such a straight face.

Her shoulders sagged. "Really?"

For a beat, he was silent. But then he smirked, and she realized he was toying with her. She reached over and shoved his shoulder as he laughed.

"Jessica, we will find you *the* pair of jeans," he said, writing it down. "Where you go, I go."

She crossed her arms, deciding it was time to start

playing with *him*. "If that's the case, then I also want to go skinny dipping."

She relished the way his cheeks turned pink, his eyes widening.

"Where you go, I go, right? Looks like you'll have to hop into the Long Island Sound butt naked."

"But that would also mean *you* would have to get butt naked," he said, that infuriating smirk curling up the side of his face again.

She wanted to wipe it right off, and thought of just the way to do so. "I want to hook up with a stranger."

His face paled. *Success.*

"I-I, well—"

"I mean, it's been so many years with Charlie...I never really got to try the whole one-night stand thing," she said. "You could be my wingman."

He ran a hand through his hair, brushing it out of his face. "I don't think—"

"That it's a good idea? This is my list, but hey, if you'd rather we not do this, we could scrap the whole thing..."

"No," he said rather abruptly. "We're doing this. You deserve this."

Her chest did that weird thing again as they stared at one another. Kevin coughed to break the silence, looking back down at the sheet of paper. "You, um, have two more."

Jess paced, thinking through what her life would be like without Charlie. It hit her then—for the first time in almost a decade, she was *single*. Alone. Well...not completely alone; she had Calvin and his Gram and the staff at Scoops and her infuriating friend turned bossy boss. But as she wondered whether she'd feel that familiar loneliness this summer, something she'd never had the capacity to do with Charlie hit her square in the face.

"I want to get a dog," she whispered

Kevin's face brightened, as if he himself were a dog and Jess had offered him a treat. "A dog?!" he squeaked.

"Calm down, tiger," she said, shuffling through the logistics of what *having* a dog would entail. "Out of all of these, that feels the most unrealistic. They're so expensive, and with the bakery opening I'm not even sure if…"

"Stop, stop, stop," Kevin said. He moved around the display case to her side of the counter, then placed his hands on his shoulders. His favorite position with her, apparently. "We can easily find solutions. And you're about to have *money*, Jess. You won't have to pay rent for a little while."

"I can't mooch off the Balls forever, Kevin."

"Yes, but they're in no rush to have you leave. You can take your time."

She huffed. "I should probably ask them if it would be all right before we get our hopes up."

He squeezed her shoulders with a little too much enthusiasm. "Did you say *we?*"

Jess felt her face flush. "I-I, shit, I didn't mean—"

"Aww, you want to be co-parents as *well* as co-workers, how cute," he teased, booping her nose with his finger. "I would love to be the father, you didn't even have to ask."

She scowled at him. "I *didn't* ask."

"Minor detail," he said, shooing her comment away. "I've kept a note of different dog names I like in my phone for years now. I'll send it to you for your consideration."

"How kind of you," she grumbled.

"Thank you. Now, I believe you have one left," Kevin said, snatching the list and writing *DOGGIE!!!!* in bold for number nine.

Jess reached for the roller in the tray and began aggressively painting the walls again. She knew what her last one *should* be, but sharing it with Kevin felt way too intimate.

"Hey, hey, don't shut down on me," Kevin said softly, reaching for her again. She twisted out of his reach.

He got the message straight away and took a few steps back. "Okay, how about this."

She paused, peering over her shoulder at him.

"How about we each pick something for number ten, something that we do at the time of our choosing."

Jess frowned. "But then that would make it eleven things."

"We won't have to finish them this summer, they can exist outside the list."

She considered it for a moment, then nodded. He handed her the paper and pen, encouraging her to write it down. Jess leaned over, then with a shaky breath, wrote down number ten.

10. See them again.

She exhaled, then thrust the list back into his hands. Kevin glanced down, nodding at what he saw, then added the last item to the list. He folded it up and slipped it into the pocket of his board shorts.

Jess frowned. "I don't get to see what you wrote?"

"Don't worry, you will soon."

She scowled. "But this is *my* list. Shouldn't I be the one to hold it?"

"Yes, but I am the *keeper* of the list. I make sure that you're not cheating and you actually do all ten things here."

"Has anyone ever told you how frustrating it is to be your friend?"

"Aww, Jessica, we're friends? I'm touched."

"I hate you."

"There she goes *lying again*," he said. He pulled a bandana out of his pocket and tied it around his neck, then grabbed the corner and pulled it back, tucking his hair neatly behind. "All right, put me to work, boss."

"I thought *you* were the boss."

"Oh yeah, that's right," he said, taking a step back. "Should I leave then?"

Jess reached a hand out and grabbed his arm, his skin warm against her palm. "No, stay. Help me paint."

She felt his bicep flex at her touch and wrenched her hand away quickly.

He laughed, grabbing a roller. "Then paint I will."

Chapter Eight

"You worked at a coffee shop for two years, but it recently closed?" Jess scrolled through the open résumé on the tablet perched on her lap.

Zach nodded. "Yes, the building sold so the shop closed. My manager decided not to reopen."

"That sucks, I'm sorry," she said.

He nodded once. "It was a long drive from here, so it'll be nice to work in town."

"Completely understand that," Jess replied. Thoughts of Charlie in his new apartment in Garrison crossed her mind, how far he must now be from home. She coughed, pushing past the thoughts, moving along with the interview. "You're familiar with basic espresso drinks. Americanos? Lattes? Cappuccinos?"

"Basic drinks, and a little extra. We could get creative with some of our flavors and what we offer, if you're willing."

"Amazing, you're hired," Kevin butted in.

Jess leaned over and elbowed his side. "Just because we *know* him doesn't mean he's the right fit."

"Oh come on, Jessica, Zach is perfect."

"I know I only got this interview because of Blake," Zach said. He lifted a leg up and crossed his ankle over his knee. "But I don't want you to hire me for that reason alone."

"We do love Blake, yes," Jess said. "And you're right, being his boyfriend can't be the only qualifier. We do have to consider all of our options."

Kevin rolled his eyes. "What options? Zach is willing to take a *pay cut* for us."

"Kevin, you want to hire him so you can work with your friends."

He beamed. "Is that such a bad thing?"

Jess shook her head, eyes back on Zach's résumé. It *was* impressive—he'd finished his second year at the local community college, had experience in coffee shops and restaurant settings, and was willing to take a pay cut *and* work the crazy early hours required for a bakery. But asking someone to work for *her* felt like a whole different kind of commitment, especially the significant other of a friend she respected. It felt like a really, *really* big ask.

Soft fingers covered in silver rings brushed her hand, matching bracelets dangling from his wrist. Jess looked up at Zach, understanding etched on his face as he gave her a reassuring squeeze.

"If working for you is going to cause strain on your relationship with Blake, then let's not do this," Zach said. "I love him and I love this little family you all have. I don't want to ruin anything. Scoops means so much to him."

Her throat tightened. Even though the Scoopers were quite a bit younger than her, that place and those people meant everything to her, too. Scoops had been her little sanctuary away from her hell for so long. But she would never admit that to them. Jay certainly would never let her live it down. And Rory probably wouldn't stop hugging her.

But Zach *was* perfect for the job, she couldn't deny that.

She cleared her throat. "How about this. We'll try this out for the summer and see how we're feeling by Labor Day. We keep an open line of communication, and if absolutely *anything* comes up, talk to me. I've never managed someone before, and like you said, we don't want to ruin any relationships. So let's be honest with each other."

Zach squeezed her hand again then sat back, a dimple appearing on his devastatingly handsome face. "Sounds perfectly reasonable."

The tension in her chest eased. "How often are you willing to work? We'll likely be open every day."

Kevin scoffed. "Every day? No, that's not happening."

Jess frowned. "We have a shop to save."

"But that doesn't mean we have to work ourselves to the bone to do it. No, I'm the boss, I set the boundaries. We're closed on Mondays."

"Do you really think that's wise with so much more on the line?" She waved an arm around the renovated shop and bakery.

"When else are we going to work through your list, Jessica?"

Zach raised a brow. "What list?"

"Nothing, ignore him."

Kevin grinned. "Jessica has a summer bucket list that she must finish in order to keep from getting fired."

"You won't actually fire me," she growled, tapping away on the new tablet courtesy of their silent investor. She hadn't thought too much of it when Kevin set it up for her, claiming it was essential for taking orders and running the business. It's not like he was wrong—her laptop wouldn't be speedy enough for what they needed.

"Is that like...an employee requirement or something?" Zach teased.

Kevin barked out a laugh. "Do you want it to be?"

"My only goal this summer is to make sure Blake isn't working at Scoops during Haverfest this year, buy him all the cotton candy he wants, and ride the Ferris wheel until he's sick of it."

"That is so cute I might scream," Kevin replied.

"Please don't," Jess quipped.

"Speaking of...I know this is absurd to ask right after getting hired, but can I have that day off?" Zach asked.

She nodded. "If that's really your only goal for the summer, then yes. Kevin and I can handle it that day."

"Hmm, maybe we should do a booth on the street like everyone else and close down the storefront," Kevin dreamed.

"That's actually not a bad idea," Jess mused.

"See, Jessica, this is why we make a good team," he said, reaching up to boop her nose again. She slapped his finger away, which only made him laugh.

Zach leaned forward. "Just to be clear, do you go by Jess or Jessica?"

"Jess," she answered at the same time Kevin said, "Jessica."

Zach looked back and forth between them, then made the correct decision. "Jess, what day would you like me to start?"

"The bakery's opening day will be this time next week. Can you be here at six thirty in the morning next Wednesday?"

"Absolutely. Mind if I poke around the shop and get my bearings?"

Jess lifted an arm in invitation. "Have at it."

Kevin leaned over to Jess when Zach was a safe enough distance from them. "Is it just me or is it absolutely crazy that Blake scored him?"

"Blake is unfailingly loyal and loving, doesn't surprise me at all," Jess responded, scrolling through her list of to-do's. Pick up the dishes and mugs she ordered from the restaurant warehouse. Stock the bins with flour and sugar. Write out the bakery menu on the chalkboard they hung up yesterday. Swing by the discount shoe store and see if she could find a new pair of clogs to work in.

"So Blake can get it." Kevin leaned back into his chair.

Jess whipped her head around and glared. "Do you take *any* of this seriously? We have so much to do and you can't seem to ever focus on the task at hand."

Kevin's eyes went wide at her abruptness. "Geez, Jess. Not everything is about work."

"You have a business that's failing. Right now, everything should be about work."

He looked like she punched him in the gut. "Twist the knife, why don't you?"

"I'm only being honest."

"Yeah, me too." He shifted in his seat so he was fully facing her, his knees knocking against hers. "Listen, I am pumped that we're working together and that you're getting things organized for us. But there is nothing stopping us from having fun while we do it. So I'm going to need you to lighten up a little bit."

"Lightening up won't get us anywhere."

"Neither will forcing yourself to be miserable your

whole life. It's like you're a glutton for punishment or something."

She sucked in a breath, ready to serve the snark right back, when the front door slapped open. Rory looked frazzled—her mahogany hair tied up in a bun, her rainbow painted nails chipped, her seafoam-green eyes blazing with anxious energy.

Jess stood up, instantly worried. "Everything all good?"

"Um, well, actually—" Rory started.

"Do I need to beat Tyler up?"

Rory's shoulders relaxed. "No, no, this has nothing to do with Ty."

She couldn't help being protective of this girl. When Rory came into Post Road that past fall, makeup running down her face from crying and a phone perched to her ear, something cracked in her chest. Despite her best efforts to stay out of all of the Scoopers bullshit drama, she found herself offering advice. Because god knew that's what she needed when she was seventeen—someone to speak truth into her life.

Even if she warned Rory off falling in love in high school, the girl seemed hell-bent on dating her best friend. But now when she saw her and Tyler together, constantly touching when they thought no one was looking, for some reason their relationship felt *different*. Like Calvin and Melanie's. It made her wonder where she'd gone wrong.

Jess ignored the regret that always seemed to simmer in her stomach when she thought of Charlie. "Then what's up?"

"Do you want the good news or bad news first?"

"Good news," Kevin blurted before Jess could reply. She decided not to fight him on it.

Rory reached into her canvas tote and pulled out her laptop. "The good news is, I finished the logo."

Kevin whooped as Rory opened up the screen. At the center of the logo was a simple drawing of a bike with a basket, and inside the basket was a loaf of bread. *Port Wheels* was written in a clean sans-serif font below the bike, with *Bikes + Bakery* in a smaller version of that same font below.

Kevin gasped, holding his hands to his chest. "Rory, it's perfect. You're perfect."

"Yeah?" Rory flushed, looking at Jess for confirmation.

She nodded. "Yes, this is awesome, thank you. What do we owe you?"

"Literally nothing, you're doing me a favor by helping me expand my portfolio. I'm already nervous enough about art school this fall with nothing really to show for it except my yearbook designs."

Jess rolled her eyes. "Fine. But only if you promise to never, ever work for free again. You are an artist now and you deserve to be paid what you are worth."

Rory's cheeks went pink. "Well, I don't know about *that*."

"Seriously, promise me."

Rory glanced up at her and after a beat, agreed. "Okay, Mom, I promise."

"I hate when you children call me that."

"But we're *your children*," Rory said, flinging her free arm around Jess's shoulders.

Jess grumbled a few curses as Rory squeezed tighter. "What's the bad news?"

Rory stiffened. She released her hold and looked at her screen. "Okay, don't freak out."

A few taps later, Rory hesitated, then turned her laptop

toward Jess and Kevin. It was a Haverport community group on Facebook, and at the top was a long post from an unrecognizable username followed by paragraphs that had Jess's head spinning. She sucked in a sharp inhale when she scanned the first line at the top.

Who does she think she is?

"What is this," Kevin mumbled, his breath ghosting her ear. She didn't realize how close he'd stepped.

Jess ignored him and read.

Here in Haverport we are proud of our small businesses. We thrive on taking care of one another, of making sure our local business owners succeed. So why would we allow for someone with such limited experience to open a business that would directly compete with Grampy's, our town's most precious jewel? At least Seabreeze partners with Grampy's to sell his baked goods in their café. But Port Wheels' newest bakery will be in direct competition. Is it her goal to drive him out of business?

Not only is she leaving Scoops high and dry, taking all of her cake customers with her, but her absence at Post Road Market is also telling. She's stealing business away from our beloved establishments without a care in the world.

Hopefully it won't last; her father's business dealings may be telling enough. If the lifeline that is Charlie Sullivan III hadn't appeared all those years ago, Cap's Boatyard would've ceased to exist. If the saying "like father, like daughter" is true, maybe this won't be something we'll have to worry about at all.

Needless to say, Haverport: spend your money wisely

on the people who are actually there for you. Not the
people with a greedy hand in your pocket.

Callused fingers brushed her shoulders from behind, squeezing them tight. "Jess."

"How could someone possibly post this?" Rory whispered. The girl had tears in her eyes.

"Because it's controversial and moronic," Jess said flatly. She pointed to the hundreds of likes and comments below the post. "This is the kind of shit that gets attention."

"But it's *awful*. Like, truly insane. Yours is a business in town, too. Why would they not support you?"

Jess swept an arm toward the front windows, toward Main Street. "Because we *are* directly competing, and if you haven't noticed, we don't have doubles of the same kind of businesses in town. Capitalism doesn't exist here."

"But Grampy's isn't just a bakery. He sells sandwiches and deli meats and—"

"Rory, I knew this was coming," Jess explained, her voice calm despite the crushing sensation in her chest. "There was a reason why my boss at Post Road didn't want to keep the bakery open. Competition in this town is like this evil sin. We knew we were going against the grain when we decided to open."

Rory let out a jagged exhale. "Okay. Anything you need me to do?"

"Just send us the files for the logo. You've already done so much."

"You sure?"

Kevin dropped his hands, and she found herself missing their grounding weight. "Rory," he started, "could I pay you to write Jess's menu on that chalkboard? Make it look nice and pretty, maybe draw the logo somewhere on it?"

Jess exhaled, thankful that he was taking some initiative.

"I have to be in Scoops in fifteen, but I could come tomorrow before my night shift?"

Kevin nodded. "Great, come any time after nine."

Rory gave Jess one last pointed glance, then slipped her laptop into her bag and bolted out the door.

As soon as they were alone, Jess felt every muscle in her body tense, that crushing sensation making her feel like she was going to cave in. She sucked in sharp inhales, struggling to get any oxygen in her lungs.

"Whoa, it's okay, it's okay." Kevin snatched her hands and squeezed tightly, anchoring her back into the moment. "Focus on something around you. Tell me what you see."

"Um, uh—"

"Pick something, anything."

"The...bags. At your desk. I still haven't opened them."

"Stop making a to-do list and tell me details. What do the bags look like?"

"Tan. With the old Port Wheels logo. We'll have to figure out how to get the new logo on our receipts. Maybe we could sell bags."

"Jessica, for the love of god, stop thinking about work. Tell me what's happening."

"Your hands. They are so calloused. Do you ever use lotion?"

Kevin sniggered. "Better. Tell me more about my hands."

"You're squeezing little pulses. Like a heartbeat."

"Better, Jess. Tell me more."

"They shouldn't be this dry, usually your hands are covered in grease."

"Can't ruin any more of your tank tops."

She huffed a laugh, realizing the sound had a smile

tugging at the corner of his lips. "They're also warm. And tan. I keep wondering if you go to a tanning bed to stay this golden all winter long."

"Nah, I'm just made of gold," he teased. "Feeling better?"

Her chest was still tight. Her eyes shuttered, and she shook her head.

"Let's try your breathing. Deep breath in for me, sweetheart."

She obeyed, concentrating on those callused hands instead of what he'd just called her. Then she took another. Then slowly, a third.

"There we go." His voice was soft. Gentle.

Before she could protest, Kevin was pulling her into a hug, sealing her up tightly to his chest. One arm wrapped around her shoulders, the other cradled the back of her head. Keeping her secure.

The tension in her chest melted away.

"Thank you," she whispered. "I need to work on that."

"You're going through a lot, Jessica. No one expects you to be okay with it all. Especially me."

She exhaled. "Why are you so nice to me? I'm *really* mean to you."

He was silent. Jess listened to the hammering in his chest, the beat speeding up with each quiet breath.

"Do you remember the day we met?" he asked.

She racked her brain. "Um...I think it was sophomore year? Biology lab?"

He nodded, his fingers massaging her scalp. "It was my second day in Haverport. I was wearing my favorite tie-dye T-shirt my mom made me, and my hair was tied up in a bun, like how my dad wears it. It made me feel confident, like it was my armor in this very new, very unfamiliar environment."

Images of a younger Kevin flashed through her head, his tie-dye shirt, his Chaco sandals, his khaki shorts, a hemp necklace at his throat that she later learned one of his sisters made for him. Jess remembered that confidence, the unashamed swagger as he stepped into the classroom.

She also remembered the snickering, the name calling, the way her peers pointed their fingers and laughed at his clothes. Her hands curled, grasping fistfuls of his soft cotton T-shirt.

"Do you remember now?" he mumbled, unbothered by the aggressive way she was clinging on to him.

"I remember their laughter," she admitted. "I remember getting angry."

"You stood up and screamed at them, actually," he recounted. "Told them to take their cookie-cutter clothes and their bland, vanilla personalities and shove it up their asses."

"So ladylike of me," she coughed.

"It was incredible," he continued. "Obviously, you know I sat down next to you and we ended up becoming lab partners and friends. But what you *don't* know is that after that moment, no one made fun of my clothes or my hair ever again. I've always admired you for that, Jess. Your ability to fiercely love the outsider, your desire to want to take care of others. Like you've done for Rory this year. Like what you did for me. Still do."

He combed his fingers through her hair, then rubbed her back. "I know your reasons for not going to college are a lot different than mine. I couldn't fathom having to do more school and tests and homework, and sitting in a classroom was never my thing. But...it's been nice knowing I'm not the only one. That you and I are kind of in this together, figuring out the world on our own terms, one day at a time."

She didn't know what to say, but it didn't matter because he continued. "You've always been a small comfort. Even if you kind of hate me sometimes."

"I don't hate you," she admitted, her lips brushing against the front of his shirt.

His arms tightened around her, like she was a little clam in its shell. The thought of clams made her heart ache, her mind drifting back to simpler times, to those early morning truck rides to the beach with her dad, and before she could stop herself, she was crying. Her tears dampened his shirt as she softly sobbed. Kevin held her tight, whispering into her ear things that she couldn't comprehend over the roaring in her heart. The sound of his voice was soothing. Maybe he had always been a small comfort for her, too.

Chapter Nine

EVERYTHING WAS READY. It was the night before opening, and Port Wheels was sparkling. Picnic tables were placed outside with yellow-and-white-checkered umbrellas tied up with matching bows. The glass display case glistened, empty platters ready for croissants, scones, muffins, slices of Gram's cherry pie, and kanelbullar. Baskets perched on shelves lined with white cotton cloths for freshly baked sourdough and mini baguettes. The chalkboard was bursting with color, with options for baked goods and specialty drinks and a little corner for the daily specials. Tomorrow was mini strawberry shortcakes, with homemade whipped cream and fresh strawberries Jess picked up from the farmers' market that day.

But she was behind—*so* behind. It was her first night as an official bakery owner, and already she was failing. Miserably.

She was slicing strawberries when the door creaked open. She flushed. Ever since their little moment in the shop last week, Jess had the hardest time being around Kevin. She hadn't allowed herself to cry that hard in *years*.

But in his arms, she let it all out in the open, and he'd held her the entire time. Soothing her with his words. *It will all be okay*, she caught him saying. *I'm right here. You're not alone.*

Right now, though, she *really* wanted to be alone. She didn't have time to fall apart again. So she kept her eyes locked on the strawberries as he lingered by the door and asked if she needed anything.

"Nothing, all good." She scooped the sliced strawberries and placed them in the stainless-steel bowl at her side.

"Really, I don't mind helping."

"Kevin, I have to get used to doing this every day, I can't rely on you all the time." She grabbed a fresh handful and kept slicing. "This is what you hired me to do, remember?"

"True, but tomorrow is the first day, I wouldn't expect you to be in your groove yet."

"Seriously, get out. I'm fine."

"Are you even going to look at me?"

Jess didn't respond and kept her eyes on the cutting board. Hull. Slice, slice, slice. Scoop. Drop in bowl.

"Are you feeling embarrassed?"

Sweat broke out across her brow. "By what?"

"By...the other day."

"No," she lied. "Trying to focus, that's all."

The door creaked again as he stepped fully into the kitchen and neared her workspace. He pressed a hand to her back. "All right, I'll see you bright and early then. Call if you need anything, I'm right upstairs."

Slice, slice, slice. "Pretty convenient living right above your work, huh?"

"Yeah. Especially when you don't have a car."

Jess smirked. "See you in the morning, Kev."

"Kev," he hummed. She felt him trace his thumb back and forth on her spine. "I like that. Call me that forever."

She bristled at his touch and shoved off his hand. "Okay bye, get out."

Without a word, he shuffled out of the kitchen, the door swinging gently from his exit. She kept slicing away, waiting to hear his footsteps in the apartment above them before she felt safe enough to drop her knife and place her face in her hands.

How in the world am I going to do this? What was I thinking?

Three hard knocks sounded from the kitchen's back door. Jess lifted her face from her palms, brow furrowed, wondering who in the world would be dropping in this late at night.

Before she could bolt or try alerting Kevin, a deep rumble came from the other side of the door.

"There's only one person in town who answers to three knocks," the gruff voice said.

Bewildered, Jess unlocked the back door and opened it. Still in his apron, clutching a knife bag under his arm, Grampy stood on the other side.

He stepped into the kitchen. "What do you need me to do?"

JESS GAWKED as Grampy washed his hands, too shocked to sputter out a sentence.

He waved a hand at her failed attempts to form a sentence. "Work now, explain later. Give me a task."

Words eluded her as she directed him to the recipes for

the sourdough loaves and the fed starter. He snatched the bowls above him and got to work, placing one on a kitchen scale and making the measurements.

Still speechless, she returned to the fixings for tomorrow's special, pulling the cakes out of the oven to cool. She then moved on to the scones and prepped the dough, then handed it off to Grampy to shape, cut, and place each pre-baked pastry on a sheet pan.

As she wrapped the baking sheets with plastic to go in the fridge, Grampy stretched and folded the loaves for the last time for their overnight rise. He slid each bowl to Jess so she could seal them tight.

They finished in less than an hour. She snuck glances at Grampy as he helped her spray the countertops and clean up the space and wondered if she was imagining things. If he hadn't showed up, all of that work would have taken her at least a couple more hours.

Jess opened her mouth to say something to him, but Grampy cut her off. "Let me see the place."

She snapped her mouth shut and nodded, holding the swinging door open as he stepped through. She flicked on a light as he strolled the bakery portion of Port Wheels, whistling low as he walked up to the espresso machine. She fiddled with the strings of her denim apron as the old man scanned the menu, his gray mustache twitching as he smirked at the different coffee options. Those matching gray eyes twinkled as he scanned the rest of her bakery—the baskets and the polished wood counters and the gleaming glass display case.

"Want to explain to me why you're here?" Jess whispered.

"Make extra baked goods and freeze them when you have any kind of lull," Grampy started. "This will help during the really busy summer days when you don't have a spare minute to make new batches. 'Sold out' doesn't mean you have to actually be sold out. You can save some stock for the following morning."

She snorted. "You say this like I'll actually have a steady stream of customers."

"You don't think you will?"

She crossed her arms. "Did you hear about that community group post? I really don't think we're going to last long if that's actually how Haverport feels about me."

To her shock, Grampy rolled his eyes. "Ignore it."

"But seriously, why are you here? According to this insane town, you should consider me public enemy number one."

"I remember how I felt the night before I opened my place. Way in over my head. I didn't want you to feel the same." He clasped his hands behind his back. "You will never be my enemy, Jess. And there's only one person in town who is power-hungry enough to plant that kind of story, and everyone who truly knows what's going on in the Port knows."

She sucked in a breath. "Mr. Sullivan."

Grampy nodded, waving his hand around the shop. "He's been after this building for years. Port Wheels closing would have been convenient for him to swoop in and make a sweet offer to Kimmy so she would sell."

"Does he want to own this whole town or something?" she asked through clenched teeth.

"Yes," Grampy answered, without an ounce of hesitation. "Ever since taking over Cap's he's been slowly procuring buildings down Main Street, hoping to flip them and turn them into businesses that bring in different kinds of clientele. Pricey shops, restaurants worthy of the Michelin guide...you get it."

"That's ridiculous," Jess spewed. "The summer people come to Haverport for our old-school, laid-back charm."

Grampy lifted a brow. "Do they? How's Cap's doing?"

Jess frowned, thinking about her father's old boatyard. It did draw a new kind of crowd, with fancier boats and people who liked to order overpriced oysters with lunch.

"I was surprised he would come after you like that, given that you're dating his son and all," Grampy continued.

"I'm not dating him anymore," Jess whispered. "I left Charlie."

That bushy mustache twitched again. "And the plot thickens. Where are you living now?"

"With the Balls. Just until I find a place on my own."

"Good. Do me a favor and find out that oatmeal chocolate chip cookie recipe for me."

"Who says I'm sharing?"

Grampy laughed. Jess shushed him and mumbled about Kevin sleeping upstairs. He probably wasn't though. She wouldn't be surprised if he had an ear perched to the floorboards right now, tuning in to every facet of their conversation. The side of her mouth ticked up at the thought.

He followed Jess back into the kitchen and they collected their things. Grampy placed a hand on her shoulder as she locked the back door for the night. "You're going to be fine, kid. If you need anything, you know where to find me."

"Three knocks on the back door." She smiled. "Thanks. But I should be okay."

"Asking for help is not a bad thing, Jess," he said. "I honestly wish I did it more when I was your age. Don't be like me."

As she watched Grampy leave, she realized that asking for help wasn't that easy. After relying on Charlie and his family for so long, she didn't know what it felt like to ask for help without any strings attached. Because for some reason, there always were strings. Even if she was often the last to see them.

THE AIR WAS sweet from sugar and yeast and pulled espresso and frothed milk. The shop was bursting with sounds of crusty bread and paper bags, bright music and echoing laughter. The line leading up to the bakery front trailed out the door and pooled onto the sidewalk.

Jess hastily rang up her current customer's order—two cranberry orange scones, one blueberry muffin, two Americanos, one cappuccino. Zach ripped off each printed ticket next to him, sticking them onto cups, placing them in a neat line next to him. He was quick and efficient, and had yet to get a single order wrong during their haywire first morning.

"Need me to slow down?" Jess called to Zach. "I can take a pause on these orders."

"Nope, I'm used to it," Zach replied. He sounded a lot more composed than she felt. "Keep going. Keep making that bread."

"How on brand." She turned back to the line that had yet to relent for the past three hours. "Next!"

As the following customers stepped up, the sound of billowing laughter pulled her attention to the other side of the shop. Kevin was grinning at a customer, coffee in hand as he pointed to a bike between them—a kid's magenta bike with training wheels and sparkly streamers on the handlebars. If she wasn't mistaken, she saw a couple of customers leave a half hour earlier with two shiny new bikes in tow as well.

"What are these heart-shaped things?" asked the woman on the other side of the counter, her pink sun-kissed nose pressing up against the glass. "They are adorable!"

Jess smiled. "Kanelbullar. They're like cinnamon buns."

The woman squealed. "I'll take four."

With gloved hands she placed the pastries in a large paper bag, still in disbelief at how the morning was turning out. Grampy was right; that community post he claimed came from Mr. Sullivan didn't reflect how the people of Haverport felt as many familiar faces came piling through the front door. Old high school peers, fellow business owners, regular cake customers from Scoops and Post Road who wanted a taste at her new pastry creations. The picnic tables outside were packed, people wearing sunglasses and ball caps, dogs happily lapping at the water bowls positioned along the sidewalk. She hoped Charlie's dad drove by this morning on his way to Cap's and saw the commotion. She wondered if Charlie would drive by, too.

She brushed off the thought of her ex—her *ex*. It had been over two weeks since she left, the longest she'd ever gone without talking to him. She felt a pang in her stomach as she bagged more pastries and rang up orders. She knew this kind of change was good—she was running her very own bakery this morning, for crying out loud. But she missed the comfort of having him in her life, that steadiness of knowing she always had one person she could turn to.

Her eyes drifted to Kevin again, watching as he exchanged bills with the customer holding the handlebars of the bold magenta bike. *You've always been a small comfort.* Maybe that was all she really needed; a small comfort.

Kevin examined the crowd after the customer left, then glanced at Jess. His mouth burst into a grin, his arms held out wide as he gestured toward the massive line crowding the shop.

I told you so, he mouthed.

She rolled her eyes but didn't bother containing the grin on her face. *Yeah, yeah, you were right.*

An hour later when the line finally dwindled, she scanned the inventory. One loaf of bread, a couple of strawberry shortcakes, a handful of scones and muffins, and no more kanelbullar in sight.

Zach placed down a latte—a beautiful leaf drawn at the top with frothed milk. The customer let out a blissful sigh, thanking them as she grabbed her paper bag with her muffin and exited.

Kevin sauntered over, placing his hands on the counter in front of Jess, a shit-eating grin on his face. "Great job, team. Zach, you are the coffee master."

Zach chuckled. "I think that should be my next tattoo."

"Oh, tattoos! Jess, why didn't you add that to your list?"

"Didn't think of it until now."

"Want to swap one out?" Kevin replied. He pulled the list out of his back pocket. "We could exchange it for number eight."

She eyed him, his look full of mischief.

She smirked. "Number eight remains."

He lifted both shoulders as if to say, *I tried.*

"Now I need to know what number eight is," Zach said.

Kevin ignored him, eyes on the pastries. "Wait, is there no more kanelbullar?!"

Jess reached for a paper bag she'd hidden underneath the counter. "Let's just say I've been in a relationship with one man for a *very* long time, and need to do some...experimenting," she explained to Zach.

Zach grinned. "Ah. I see."

Kevin continued ignoring them, pouting at the practically empty display case in front of him. Jess held up the paper bag to him.

His face split into another one of his shiny grins. "Oh my god, you didn't."

"You're welcome. *Boss.*"

He snatched the bag and opened it, taking a big whiff of cinnamon and sugar. His eyes brightened when he looked at the pastry. "It's in the shape of a heart!"

She shrugged. "Figured I'd try something a little different."

Kevin took a greedy bite, flaky pastry falling to the counter. "It's because you love me, isn't it?"

"No," she deadpanned. "Also, you're making a mess."

He pointed to Jess, looking at Zach. "She loves me."

Zach laughed, reaching for the rag in his back pocket and wiping away Kevin's crumbs.

"With that logic, I love every person who ate a kanelbullar today. Zach included."

"It was *so good.*"

"Jessica, you stop your flirting," Kevin teased. "Zach is spoken for."

"That's right, touch him and you DIE."

The three of them turned their heads to the possessive voice at the other end of the shop. Blake leered at them, his arms crossed tight against his chest, the rest of the Scoopers at his heels.

"Damn, Blake, that was hot," Rory said. She held tight to yellow balloons, tied with sparkly gold strings.

Jess frowned. "What are you guys doing here?"

"Hi, Mom!" Jay yelled. "Surprise!"

The group filed into the shop despite her protests. Blake snuck around the counter and gave Zach a long, lingering kiss. Rory handed Tyler some of the balloons, then pointed to different places for him to tie them up. Calvin clapped Kevin on the back, asking how things were going so far. Melanie skipped over to her and placed a large box down on the counter.

Jess peered up at Melanie. "Is that...?"

Melanie beamed. "We're so proud of you, Jess. Happy opening day."

She opened the box, and sure enough, it was a cake. A sloppy-looking cake, with yellow frosting and an amateur drawing of a bike on the front. In thin icing around the bike, each Scooper signed their name.

"I may or may not have made this from a box," Melanie started. "Don't hate me."

"The box stuff is honestly great. What flavor?"

"Uh...yellow?"

Jess chuckled. "Yellow is a great flavor."

"Jess, get over here so I can give you a hug that I know you don't actually want," Rory chirped.

She rolled her eyes and made her way from behind the counter, allowing Rory to throw her arms around her and squeeze tight.

Calvin wrapped her up in a hug next, giving her an extra squeeze. "Things look great, Jess. You should be proud."

She stiffened. "What if it's not enough, though?"

Calvin paused, an arm still around her shoulders, keeping his voice low so no one else would hear. "Let's regroup when you get home and we'll go through the numbers, all right? Bring Kevin."

She nodded. "Yeah, okay."

"Sissy?"

Jess felt like her heart jumped to her throat at the sound of that voice. She pulled away from Calvin.

Dakota stood by the door, one hand on her now very round belly, the other clutching a bouquet of wildflowers, her amethyst ring shining under the shop's downlights. Jasper was behind her with a hand on her shoulder. His hair was longer now, braided into thick cornrows that trailed down his neck.

"Dakota," she breathed, taking a step closer. "How...why..."

"I've been keeping up with the news on socials," she answered. "I wanted to see you in action. Sorry if we, um, disturbed something."

"You didn't. I'm with these losers all the time, it's fine."

"Mom, I don't like being called a *loser*," Jay quipped from behind her. "It's going to cause psychological damage, you know."

"Send me a bill," she jeered, not taking her eyes off Dakota.

Jasper chuckled, looking around the shop. He also wore an engagement ring on his left finger, a simple black titanium band. "This place looks awesome, Jessie. I actually can't remember the last time I was in here."

"Who are these people," Melanie whispered to Rory.

Jess turned toward the group. "Scoopers, meet my sister, Dakota, and her fiancé Jasper."

"You have a *sister*?" Jay balked. "How did I not know that!"

She looked back at Dakota. Hurt flashed across her sister's face, but she mastered it, tucking it away and giving Jay that sweet smile she knew so well. "Yes, she's my younger sister. And about to be an aunt," she replied, tapping her belly.

"Congrats, Dakota," Calvin said. He knew of her at least. As did Kevin, who was now standing close to Jess, his hands tucked into the back pockets of his jeans.

"Thanks, Cal. Congrats on Scoops, by the way. Ron told my dad you'll be taking over next year."

Jess blinked at her sister's casual mention of their father. Conversation continued around her but she couldn't seem to focus, the ringing sound in her ear distracting her until the feel of a warm, calloused hand at her back roused her to life. The ringing in her ears dimmed.

"Sissy, will you give us a tour?"

"Um, sure."

Jess went through the motions of showing her sister and Jasper the bakery, explaining the different baked goods on the menu and some of the plans for specials she wanted to serve later that summer. Dakota reached to grab her hand like she did when they were kids, then paused, letting her arm fall flat next to her protruding belly. "This is awesome. I can't wait to see this place flourish."

"You have way too much faith in me," she murmured, wiping at the clean counter with a rag. She wasn't sure what else to do with her hands.

Dakota exhaled. "They wanted to come, you know."

Jess ignored her as she kept wiping at the counter.

Getting the message that Jess clearly did *not* want to talk about this, Jasper chimed in. "How's Charlie?"

She cocked her head and paused her cleaning. "I don't know. I left him."

Neither of them said anything, so she peered up at them. Their expressions were clear enough; they knew.

"How?" Jess asked. "How do you know?"

"I assumed," Dakota answered, keeping her voice low enough so no one would hear. Not like it mattered, the Scoopers standing a couple of yards away were being rowdy enough for their conversation to be private. Kevin also kept his distance.

"There's no way you would have allowed yourself to do any of this if you were still with him," Dakota continued. "Opening a business is a big risk."

"What does that mean?"

Dakota bristled at her harsh tone. Jasper rubbed Dakota's back, taking the lead. "It means that you did everything you could to make that relationship work. To open a bakery would mean to choose yourself for once...which, let's be honest, Jess, was not something you were doing when you were with him."

She froze, staring at Jasper, too stunned to speak. In a couple of sentences, he was able to clearly articulate what took her years to understand, to pinpoint the long and short of their relationship's downfall. Jasper really was such a good partner for her sister, and was going to be a great father. She felt a desperate, belly-deep desire to be a part of their lives again. To be a part of her niece or nephew's life.

Jess glanced at her sister, who was now openly crying. She gave her a watery smile, taking the flowers from her hand. "Are you still up for having that coffee date soon? I want to hear everything about the baby."

Dakota beamed. "Yes. Next week, maybe?"

Jess nodded. "Mondays are my day off."

"You're busy on Mondays!"

Jess scowled at Kevin. "You can't claim the entire day. You have to give me some semblance of freedom."

"What's happening on Mondays?" Dakota asked around a short giggle.

"Kevin is making me, um, complete a summer bucket list," Jess admitted. "He says if I don't complete it I'll get fired."

The Scoopers yelled at Kevin for that, and he cracked up at their reactions. Dakota's sweet laugh joined their chorus, but Jess remained silent, her eyes on Jasper.

His gaze was full of unspoken warning. *Don't you break her heart again.*

Jess nodded, letting him know she understood what was on the line, even if it was a simple coffee date. Her sister's bright laughter brought a smile to his face, and he dipped his chin then traced his hand up to rub her neck.

Jasper's words bounced around her head the rest of the day. As she kneaded dough and shaped scones for the following morning, she concluded that he was right. By running this bakery, she was choosing herself for once. But that also meant protecting her heart, too. She knew deep down that everything between her and her sister—and her parents—wasn't her fault alone, and it would take a lot more than a simple coffee date to fix it.

Chapter Ten

Jess tapped her fingers on the coffee table as Calvin punched numbers into his phone, watching the crease in his forehead get bigger and bigger.

"You're killing me," she groaned. "Give me something. Anything."

"Don't worry, it's not bad."

"Your face says otherwise."

Calvin set down his phone, giving the tablet between them one more scan before looking up at her. "No really, it's not bad. Today went well."

"Of course it went well," Kevin chimed in. He was sprawled out on the couch, a plate of oatmeal chocolate chip cookies balancing on his chest. He reached for another and shoved it in his mouth. "I had all the faith in my dear Jessica."

"That makes one of us," she grumbled.

"Even after considering the percentage of your profits that will go toward inventory, taxes, salary, rent, you were in the green today," Calvin explained. "It was a successful opening."

Jess loosed a breath. "That's good to hear."

"But…"

The short-lived smile on her face fell. "But what?"

"You'll need to have days like this *every day* if we want to keep things afloat by the end of the summer."

"So a bustling crowd with a line out the door should be the norm?" Jess quipped. "Great. Awesome."

"You can do it," Kevin chimed in. "I believe in you."

"Believing in yourself doesn't bring in customers. Marketing does."

Kevin grunted, holding the plate of cookies steady as he sat up on the couch. "Call me Mr. Marketer then. What do you need me to do?"

"How do you feel about Speedos and spinning arrow signs that say *freshly baked*?"

Kevin cackled, the plate slipping out of his hands. Jess caught it before it fell to the floor, setting it down on the table.

"Are we really resorting to objectifying my body? We can't be *that* desperate already."

"Social media is a better place to start," Calvin replied. He winked at Kevin. "Although a shirtless picture of you on a bike eating a muffin wouldn't hurt."

"Is this what they teach you at business school? Should I be worried for you?"

"Calvin makes everyone at Scoops wear shirts a size too small to show off certain assets," Jess added in. "Biceps, pecs, boo—"

Kevin shoved him so hard he fell to the floor. "Calvin, we are going to have a serious talk…"

The sounds of her and Calvin's laughter interrupted him from finishing.

Kevin scowled and crossed his arms, his position similar to an angry-looking puppy. "This isn't funny, guys."

"I beg to differ, you should see your face right now," Jess said, catching her breath. His expression softened as he watched her wipe away tears. He tsked and snatched a tissue, handing it to her.

Calvin sat back up and crossed his legs. "Post photos of your specials, offer discounts, repost things customers tag you in, let people know about your Haverfest booth and other events. Adding location tags also helps with getting on certain explore pages for people in the area."

Her eyes widened. Managing social media on top of everything else—keeping up with inventory, baking at wee hours of the morning, saving enough money to find her own place, the list went on and on—it all had her head spinning.

"Jessica, c'mere."

She felt an invisible tug as she obeyed, standing from the floor and plopping down on the couch next to Kevin. He gently grazed his knuckles across her knee as he spoke, his featherlight touch leaving goose bumps across her skin.

"Today was amazing, *you* are amazing," he said. "We take this one day at a time, yeah?"

She took a deep breath. He smelled like cinnamon and honey from the cookies he just ate. It made her want to burrow under a blanket and fall asleep.

"I'm already so tired and it's only been a day," she confessed. "How am I going to do this?"

A section of his wavy hair flopped in front of his face. He removed his hand from her knee to push it back. "Do you still want this?"

She nodded, her words caught in her throat.

He grazed his knuckles against her skin ever so gently

yet again. His touch made her feel things she shouldn't be feeling.

"Then we do this," he said.

"We?"

"Yes, Jessica. *We.* You do not have to do this alone, because you're not alone anymore."

"We have your back," Calvin added. She felt embarrassed that Calvin was seeing her like this, but he gave her a reassuring smile that set her at ease. "And you really did have a successful day. Let yourself enjoy it."

Dakota was the only sibling she'd ever had, and Jess felt content with that. But somehow, these two men in front of her had become her brothers; two guys who cared about her enough to make an insane offer. One that would undoubtedly change the trajectory of her life—regardless of whether the business was successful.

Even if the way one of those "brothers" was touching her made her brain go fuzzy.

The three of them spent the rest of the night brainstorming specials and promos that could keep a steady flow of customers walking through the doors of Port Wheels for the rest of the summer. At some point Gram called Calvin into the kitchen, requesting his assistance with dinner.

Jess glanced down at Kevin's hand, at how close it was to her leg, his thumb sinking between the couch cushion and her outer thigh. She hitched a breath.

He followed her gaze and swiftly removed it. "I'm sorry," he rushed out. "I'm a physical touch kind of person. I have to remind myself that not everyone likes it. I don't mean to make you uncomfortable."

"It's okay," she whispered, surprising herself with how easy it was to admit that. Continuing to act on instinct, Jess reached for his hand and cupped it between her own. "Thank you."

She knew she could have been more specific with him, how thankful she was for his comforting presence, his friendship, his promise to never leave her alone. But when Kevin smiled in response and curled his fingers against her hand, his hazel eyes dancing as he looked down at her, she knew he was already well aware, and there was no need to say anything more.

"So, what's the first thing on your list?" Dakota asked.

"Technically I already achieved the first thing, which was to open a bakery."

The two of them sat outside Seabreeze Café, the sun warming her skin. She let Dakota sit on the other side under the patio umbrella with proper shade. She'd also bought her sister's coffee and pulled her chair out for her, helping her into her seat. Dakota insisted that she could have done all of those things herself, but Jess refused to listen. A few instances of over-the-top pampering was merely scratching the surface of all the lost years she needed to make up for.

Dakota took her last bite of the blueberry coffee cake in front of her, little brown sugar crumbles scattering across her dress. She wiped them off, then rubbed her belly, her engagement ring twinkling from a sliver of sunlight peeking through the umbrella. "What's number two, then?"

"I don't think the order of the list matters," Jess continued, taking a sip of her iced latte. "Kevin said we're scratching something off it today, but won't tell me what."

"Which one are you most excited to do?"

Jess tapped a finger to her cheek, then smirked. "Have a one-night stand."

Dakota choked out a laugh. "I did *not* expect that."

"Why? I was with Charlie for almost ten years."

"Exactly," her sister said, cocking a brow.

"Says the girl who's about to have a baby with her college sweetheart," Jess teased. "Tell me, haven't you ever thought of being with someone else?"

"Who says I haven't been?"

Jess gaped as her sister laughed.

"I was with a couple of other guys before Jasper, I will have you know. Until he blew my mind in the bedroom and I decided I was done-zo forever."

"I do not need to hear that."

"You just told me you plan on having a one-night stand, so we're even." Dakota sipped on her lemonade, tilting her head. "Although I don't think it will take you long to find someone."

Jess squinted her eyes. "What does that mean?"

"Oh, I don't know...there's this guy you know who has not only made it possible for you to open a bakery but has weaseled his way into spending every single day off with you this summer. Seems like a great contender."

Her mind drifted to the feel of his palm in hers. "We're just friends."

"You sure he knows that? Because the way he looks at you..."

"Dakota, come on. Let's not talk about boys. They ruin everything."

Her sister's shoulders fell. "Yeah. They kind of do."

The hidden meaning in her words hung heavy between them. Jess hunched back in her chair as she took another sip of her latte. Her skin felt too tight, the sun beating down on her making her break a sweat.

"I know...I know there's a lot to be said here, and I want to get us there, I do," Dakota started. "Just not today, maybe? We could just...enjoy this?"

The tension in her chest melted, the feel of the sun soft on her skin again. "Yeah, I'd like that."

Dakota lifted a hand in Jess's direction, reaching for her. But her belly bumped against the table, limiting her movement. She huffed and strained for a reach anyway, then gave up. Jess laughed at her sad little attempt to hold hands, and her sister kicked her under the table like old times.

"So, tell me everything about this little one. Was the first trimester really as awful as people say? Do you know the gender? What's been your weirdest pregnancy craving?"

"Yes. No. Chocolate-covered bacon."

"Chocolate-covered *bacon*?! You're a pescatarian!"

"This baby isn't," she grumbled. "I've eaten so much pork, I'm afraid I'm about to give birth to Piglet."

Jess grinned, scooting her chair forward so she could reach Dakota's hand, the gesture making her sister beam with happiness. "But it will be such a *cute* little Piglet."

Kevin wasn't kidding; physical touch was his thing. Telling him *it's okay* the other day was like opening up the floodgates, granting him access to touch her in ways that surprised her. When she was hunched over receipts calculating expenses, he came up behind her and ghosted a hand across her back. When she couldn't reach her recipe book on the top shelf, he grabbed it for her with one hand, the other brushing her shoulder. When she handed him his daily kanelbullar on a paisley-patterned plate, his thumb swiped across her pulse before slipping the plate from her fingers.

The old Jess would have screamed at him to back off, to keep his hands to himself. But this Jess...? She didn't hate it. His warm hands and the bump of his hip against hers felt like that small comfort during a chaotic first week. Even if the way he looked at her made her think comfort wasn't the only thing on his mind.

Dakota was right, he was *looking* at her. Tiny little lines crinkled at the corners of his hazel eyes every time he glanced at her from across the shop, the hint of a smile always on his lips.

But she was freshly single and he was *very* much off-limits. The last thing she wanted was to hop into another relationship and share a bed with someone again, let alone her boss (even though she used that term lightly). She slept so well now. She enjoyed star-fishing in the guest bed at the Balls' every night.

Kevin never pushed or asked anything of her, though. His touches were sweet and nothing more. They were safe. *He* was safe. So she let it happen, even let herself lean into it.

Kevin swung an arm around her shoulders as they walked down Main Street.

"You're not even going to give me a hint?" she grumbled.

"Think about it a little bit, Jessica, and I'll bet you can figure it out."

She scrolled through the list again in her head. "No one in town offers a professional baking class, so that's out."

"Very perceptive. You're so smart."

She pinched his side. He screeched and staggered back, feigning being hurt. But it only took him a few seconds to reach her again, fingers brushing back and forth on her tricep. "What else?"

"Haverport is too cute for a grungy underground concert, and we're not near a TV to watch Frodo for twelve hours, so those are out. I can't afford Lacey's, so I doubt we're going jeans shopping right now."

"You'll be able to afford Lacey's soon. We'll manifest that."

"Spoken like a true hippie."

"It is my roots."

"We don't have gear to camp and it's daytime, so no skinny dipping..."

Or hooking up with a stranger, she was going to add, but that look Kevin had given her on Calvin's couch the other night crossed her mind. She brushed past it.

"So that leaves..."

The sounds of yipping and heavy, open-mouth breathing and jingling tags interrupted her train of thought. They rounded the corner and halted at the entrance to the town square. The lawn was flooded with gleeful couples and families, their noses peering down at tiny fur balls with wagging tails safely tucked into small fenced-in zones across the green.

"Oh my god," Jess breathed. "Today?"

"Yes, my dear Jessica. We become dog parents. *Today*."

She whipped her head toward him. His hold on her shoulder remained firm, like he was preventing her from bolting. *Smart man.* "We can't afford a dog yet. We only just opened."

"Money is required for everything on our list," Kevin bantered.

"Then I want to rewrite the list. Only free things, from here on out."

"No, you're deflecting. We're doing this."

She growled. "How are we going to afford this, Kev?"

He shrugged, releasing his arm from her shoulders as he stepped into the square. "I'll put it on my credit card."

Jess froze. Kevin kept walking, oblivious to her still rooted on the spot as he drifted to a gaggle of Frenchies, his squeaky voice of delight ringing through the square.

Her hands curled into fists and she dug her fingernails into her palm. *He's not Charlie. He's not Charlie.* No amount of chanting could make her move from that spot, the words *credit card* pinging around in her head.

Kevin looked up from the dogs, mouth open to say something, and she watched his face fall. He made his way back to where she lingered by the entrance to the square.

"Jessica, what's wrong?" He brushed a hand up and down her arm.

"Do you do that a lot?" she asked abruptly. "Put things on your card?"

A whoosh rushed out of Kevin's mouth. He tightened his bandana at the nape of his neck. "Jess..."

"Do you have a lot of debt?"

His face flushed. "This seems a little pointed right now."

She turned on her heel and walked away from him.

"Jess, hold on...Jess, *stop.*"

He grabbed her wrist and pulled. She stumbled back, her body all but crashing into his. He caught her, and the two of them were left standing chest-to-chest.

"While it's not really any of your business—"

"It is my business," she said, cutting him off. "We're about to get a dog together."

"Fine, *fine*. I sold my car to pay off my debt. Are you happy?"

Her eyes widened. "I thought you sold it for the shop."

"I was too embarrassed to tell you the truth. You're careful with your money and I didn't want to seem like this big screw up. I want you to respect me as a friend. As a business partner."

"So you lied."

He stepped back, rubbing a hand down his face. "Yes. I've regretted it every day. I really, really want you to trust me."

"I do," she confessed, her words surprising her. "As long as you promise me two things."

He stepped into her, closing the distance between them. "Anything. Literally anything, Jessica."

"One, do not lie to me again."

"Done. From this point on, you know everything. I'll even text you when I poop."

"That's too much information, you sicko."

"Never too much information. We're about to become dog parents and deal with *a lot* of poop. What's the second thing?"

"Promise me that you will be responsible with your money. No more going into debt. If there's something on this list we can't afford, we can't afford it. Like getting a dog."

"That's the thing, I can afford to get a dog right now."

She cocked a brow. "You can?"

"After paying off my debt, I actually started putting money in my *savings*."

Jess smirked. "Look at you. An actual adult."

"I mean, I am about to blow it on a dog, but yeah. I've got the money."

She studied his face, thinking it through. She was about to adopt a dog with a man who had money habits that made her uncomfortable. But...she already made the choice to go into business with him. Would sharing a dog be any different?

Feeling reckless, she nodded. "Sure, yeah, okay. Let's get a dog."

He grabbed her hand and hauled her back to the town green. They shuffled through the different stations, booping wet noses and scratching little ears. Even if the puppies they passed were fuzzy and adorable and Kevin claimed he wanted to take them all home, she hadn't made a connection with one yet. She hoped to find a kindred spirit. She wondered if it was ridiculous to even hope for that.

They hit a collection of mutts toward the back, and Kevin about lost his mind. He hopped the fence and sat down in the middle, laughing as puppies climbed all over him and licked his face.

"Jessica, get in here. This is magic."

"I'm good out here, thanks."

Kevin held out a hand, curling his fingers and motioning for her to get in. She sighed and carefully climbed over the thin fence, then took a seat next to him. Puppies sniffed her shorts and her shoes and her hands. She smiled and scratched underneath little snouts, stroking the fur from their heads down to their wagging tails.

One brave golden pup climbed into her lap and took a seat on her thighs. The puppy stuck out its little tongue and panted, tail thumping back and forth.

"You're glowing."

"Stop, you're being weird."

"At this point you should know that's pretty much my motto," he said. "This little one likes you, I think."

Jess cupped the puppy's face and rubbed her thumbs against the fur on its nose. Its tail wiggled faster and faster.

"She's a mix, golden retriever and a lab," the rescue worker explained from beyond the fence.

Jess ruffled her floppy ears. "Does she have a name?"

"No name. I call her Honey but it doesn't matter. She can't really hear me."

Kevin frowned. "Is she deaf?"

"Partially. She was neglected, then got really sick. Her hearing hasn't fully recovered because she didn't get the right treatment."

"You poor baby angel," Jess said, petting her fur.

"I've had her for a little while now. Not many people want a dog that can't hear them. Makes training difficult."

Jess knew what that felt like, being abandoned. Her family let her walk out without a second thought, no matter how bruised or damaged she got during the process.

Kindred spirits.

"How much is she?"

The rescue worker's eyes widened. "You...want her?"

She smiled. "Yes. I want her."

Kevin shimmied his body closer to hers, reaching out to pet the pup in her lap.

"Honestly? Sign the papers and she's yours. She needs a good home, and I can't give that to her."

Jess grinned at the worker, then turned to Kevin. "Is that okay?"

A warm chuckle escaped his chest, that *look* on his face. "More than okay, Jessica. Let's take our girl home."

Chapter Eleven

Jess scrolled through the article on her tablet propped up on her knees. Rory was sprawled out on the floor, granting Honey access to hop up on her belly and lick her face. Melanie laughed, pulling out of Calvin's grip where she sat between his legs to give the dog a kiss on the forehead. Kevin sat on the other side of the couch scrolling on his phone as well, one foot next to Jess, the other on the coffee table.

"It says here that dogs who lose hearing from an infection usually get their hearing back, either partially or fully," Jess explained. "If it caused nerve damage, it might not."

Kevin frowned. "How do we know for sure?"

"We could test different sounds, see how she responds?"

"I can't believe you guys just like, got a dog," Rory interrupted.

"Me either," Calvin grumbled, glaring at Kevin.

"Dude, it's going to be *fine*. Jessica and I can handle it."

"Yeah, Calvin, it's fine, stop ruining it," Melanie added, leaning back onto his chest and kissing his chin.

"I want one now," Rory whined.

"You can play with her any time you want," Jess added with a flick of her wrist. "We'll probably need a dog sitter every now and then."

"Okay, so you really are like, *sharing* this dog," Rory said to her.

Kevin tapped her hip with his foot. "Jessica and I share a lot of things now. A business, a dog, maybe someday soon a bed—"

Rory and Melanie howled with laughter. The puppy cocked her little head at their reaction. Even Calvin covered his mouth with his hand to contain his grin.

She glared at him. "In your dreams. Plus, I refuse to share a bed with someone ever again."

Kevin sucked in an exasperated inhale, holding his chest like the drama queen he was. "*Never* again? Jessica, may I remind you that if you want to have a *one-night stand*—"

"WHAT?!" Rory screamed.

"—then you'll have to share a bed."

Jess smirked. "Technically, I don't need a bed for that, you know."

Kevin rolled his eyes and pushed his toes into her ribcage. She yelped, the tablet sliding between her and the couch as she snatched them and squeezed hard. He cowered in pain as he yanked his foot from her grasp.

"Besides, even if the act *occurs* in a bed, that doesn't mean I have to *sleep* in the same bed," she added.

"We are slipping *right* past Jess admitting she wants to have a *one-night stand*," Rory squeaked. "I want details."

"I don't," Calvin grunted.

"It's part of my summer bucket list," she explained, keeping her tone even. No part of her wanted to be talking to high schoolers about her sex life. Even if they did just graduate.

Melanie asked, "Why don't you want to share a bed with someone?" as she lazily traced her fingers along Calvin's arm.

Jess reached for the tablet, ignoring their gazes. "After sharing a bed with Charlie for so many years, I realized I hate it. If I decide to have a future partner, he'll have to be comfortable with separate beds or I'll walk."

"Noted." Kevin sat up and winked at her. "I'm okay with separate beds."

"You really are insufferable," Jess grumbled, and burrowed deeper into the couch. "It's like you expect me, after *nine years* of being a relationship, to settle down and call you *honey*—"

The puppy perked up, little floppy ears straightening as she turned toward Jess.

Jess sat up straight, brows raised, eyes on her dog. "Honey?"

The puppy stuck out her tongue and panted, recognizing the name.

"Oh my god, she heard that."

"Honey, Honey! Come here, Honey!" Kevin chanted, patting the couch aggressively.

Honey hopped off Rory's chest and ran for Kevin. She jumped for the couch but her paw slipped, causing her to stumble forward. Kevin scooped her up before her head could make contact and cradled her close to his chest. He nuzzled his nose into her neck as Honey yipped and nibbled his ear, tail wagging a mile a minute.

Jess scooted closer to them, reaching up to scratch the back of their puppy's head. "Would you like a treat, little girl?"

Honey didn't react to the word *treat* and kept nipping at Kevin's ear.

She pointed to the bag on the coffee table. "Calvin, shake that bag."

He lifted the treat bag and shook it hard a few times. Honey didn't budge at the sound, still content in Kevin's arms.

"Try the squeaky toy."

Rory did, squeaking it an obnoxious number of times. Nothing.

"Hmm." Jess tapped her chin.

"Honey," Melanie said.

The dog perked up again, turning toward Melanie, and let out a soft, hoarse yip. The puppy had yet to bark fully around them, and Jess wondered whether she was aware of how loud her voice could get.

"Maybe it's the cadence of it she can recognize, like the syllables and the tone," she pondered.

"My girls are so smart," Kevin mused.

Jess scrunched her nose and took the dog out of his hands. "I am not your girl."

"But she is, isn't that right, Honey?"

A little tail wiggled in response.

Kevin chuckled and leaned back, stretching an arm out on the couch behind her. "So what's the protocol here, dog spouse? What nights is she here, what nights is she with me?"

"Can she just...stay here, for a bit? I don't want her to get confused about having two homes until she's settled with us."

And I want her here with me. It was the whole reason she wanted a dog in the first place. A comfort and a companion. Kevin teased about being that for her, but the thought of hopping into another relationship felt like the ultimate threat to her freedom. The thought made her want to scream. Throw a mug across the room. Punch a hole in the wall. Rattle Calvin's massive bookshelf and watch all of his ratty paperbacks tumble to the floor.

Kevin's fingers brushed her neck and down her spine. She shivered at his touch and squirmed in her seat.

He dropped his hand. "She's yours, Jessica. She'll stay here," he whispered only to her.

She twisted back to look at his smiling face. "You've been so adamant about this being *our* dog."

"I know, and I am excited to be a part of this. But I'm not a dumb man. You need her right now as much as she needs you."

"Thank you," she whispered back, scratching beneath Honey's ears.

"Of course, sweetheart. I'm here whenever you need help, okay?"

Sweetheart. She scooted away from him to her side of the couch and resumed research on her tablet as Honey promptly fell asleep in her lap.

His touches, his casual use of *sweetheart*...it all felt like too much too soon, and the last thing she wanted was to give him false hope. So she stayed far out of his reach the rest of the night, keeping her distance, keeping her heart in the carefully caged box where it belonged.

Jess kneaded dough in the back. Massive headphones covered her ears, music blaring out the gutted silence of the shop. It was only their second week open and customers had already dwindled. The morning rush still felt steady enough, but by noon, the line died down. Zach kept himself busy with restocking paper goods and cleaning, always leaving Jess with a sparkling, spotless bakery by the end of his shift.

The door swung open and she jumped, not expecting Zach to step in the back and bother her during prep. She pushed the headphones down to her shoulders. "What's up? Need me out there?"

"Depends, do we take special requests?"

"You mean special orders? Like, for a cake?"

"Not sure exactly...want to come and find out?"

Jess removed her headphones and tossed them in her bag, then followed Zach through the door and into the front room.

Jan Fletcher stood at the counter, six jars of her signature jam in front of her. Jan owned a jam-making business in town with her husband, and if rumors were true, they made a killing at the local farmers' market every summer. Between the no-nonsense look on her face and the way she parked her hands at her hips, Jan certainly looked like she meant business.

Jess gave her best smile. "Jan, lovely to see you."

"You as well, my dear." She returned the smile and took a deep breath. "Jessica Valerie, I have come to make you an offer."

I think I might be tapped out on offers, she thought. "What do you have in mind?"

"Are you and Mr. Perkins doing a booth for Haverfest?"

"We were thinking about it," Jess answered honestly. "But at the rate we're going, I'm not feeling very hopeful that we'll afford one."

Jan grinned, pushing the jars of jam toward Jess. "Then this is your lucky day."

She frowned. "How?"

"Dan and I want to set up a booth this year, but we were thinking of offering something a little different than usual."

"Don't you guys make a boat load, though? Why mess with a good thing?"

Jan shrugged. "Keeps people on their toes. And right now, it's not about making money, it's about making *art*."

"Dearest lovely Jan, that is not the way to Jessica's heart," Kevin called out from the other side of the shop. "Money is all she cares about right now."

Jess flicked him off.

"That's right, dear, stick it to the man," Jan cheered, holding up a fist.

Jess bumped it with her own.

"Here's my proposition: What if Dan and I sponsored your tent? We'll sell our jars, per usual. But what if you made a special pastry or two using the jam to sell alongside us?"

"I love it, I'm in," Kevin said, now standing at the counter next to Jan with Honey cuddled up in his left arm.

"She wasn't asking you," Jess replied through gritted teeth.

"But I am the boss—"

"Are you?" Jan teased. "If I've been hearing Calvin correctly, it sounds like Jess has been running the show."

Kevin sputtered but couldn't seem to get out any real words.

Jess gave her a mischievous smirk. "I knew I liked you."

"We businesswomen have to stick together," Jan said with a wink. "So what do you say? We could also do some kind of deal with the bikes. Buy a bike, get a jar of Mel's Hot Raspberry Preserves for free."

"Throw in a pastry and that sounds like a sweet deal," Jess said.

"Literally," Zach teased, handing Jan her latte with a jam jar traced into the frothed milk at the top. Jan shrieked, throwing her head back in laughter at the latte. She leaned over the counter and planted a sloppy kiss on Zach's cheek.

"Don't tell Blake you just did that or he might murder you," Kevin joked.

"Oh, he's as harmless as this little puppy here," Jan said, ruffling Honey's ears.

Jess exchanged numbers with Jan and agreed to be in touch about what she was thinking for the jam-inspired pastries by the end of the week. Jan departed the shop with her half-finished latte in hand, leaving the jars of jam for her to experiment with.

She sighed at the lack of customers in the shop. "This is so depressing. We're never going to make it out of the red."

"Don't worry, it's the lunch lull," Zach explained as he wiped down the espresso machine. Jess noticed a massive lipstick stain on his cheek and tapped her own to warn him. He blushed and wiped it with the back of his sleeve. "Slower afternoons are normal for a coffee shop."

"Yeah but we're a *bakery*, we offer so much more than a regular coffee shop."

"Jessica, don't fret," Kevin chimed in. "I've sold more bikes this week than I did the entire month of May. Let's not worry too much about it yet, yeah?"

She frowned and crossed her arms. There *had* to be something more she could do to get customers through the door. There had to be.

Kevin stepped over and lifted one of Honey's paws. "*Don't be sad, Mommy. We'll be allllll right,*" he said in a high-pitched, childlike voice.

Jess rolled her eyes, and Kevin's attention shifted to something moving outside the shop window. He froze for a beat, then held Honey out to Jess. "Take her, will ya? Someone just rolled up with a bike."

She smiled, eyes on her puppy as Kevin headed outside. "Hi, my little Honey. Were you bored all day tied up near the big scary bike man?"

The dog licked her face, paws on her shoulders. She bounced, patting Honey's back like she was a baby.

Kevin stepped back into Port Wheels and came up to the counter. "Hey, customer wants a kanelbullar and a caramel macchiato to go."

She frowned. "They didn't want to come in and order themselves?"

"Nah, they have a nasty dog. Didn't want to scare Honey."

"But you said they had a bike?"

Kevin hesitated. "They have both?"

Jess placed Honey on her bed near Kevin's desk, then crossed the shop and washed her hands. She plucked the pastry from the display case and stuffed it in a paper bag with napkins.

"Want me to bring it out?"

"Nope, I got it," Kevin said. He snatched the bag and the coffee and darted for the door.

"Is it just me or was that weird?" Zach asked.

Jess huffed and reached for Honey again. "Zach, you should know by now that Kevin is *always* weird."

Zach chuckled. "Jess, I think *you* should know by now that Kevin brings out a special kind of weirdness when he's around you."

She ignored him and the tiny skip of her heart at Zach's words. She took note of what she needed to order for her next inventory fulfillment, not daring to look in Kevin's direction when he came back in.

Jess slipped a tray of lemon poppy seed muffins into the display case the following morning as Kevin dropped a six-pack of energy drinks on the counter with a dramatic *thunk*.

"Pop these in the fridge?"

She slid the glass door shut. "Care to explain why I'm storing your groceries?"

"*Our* groceries. Tonight is the night we travel to Mordor with Frodo and Samwise and watch Aragorn come in all sexy through the doors of Helm's Deep. We'll need our energy."

"But it's Sunday, I get the night to myself." She frowned. "We're supposed to do this stuff on Mondays."

"Think about it, Jessica. Do you want to do a movie marathon on Monday and then come in bleary-eyed on Tuesday just to botch the baked goods? You know the kanel-bullar deserves better than that."

She groaned. "Fine. That's fair."

He lifted the six-pack. "Fridge. And make a list of the snacks I need to get."

"Popcorn. M&M's. Pretzels and Nutella." She tapped her cheek. "We should probably eat real food, too. I'll make something."

His face brightened. "You're going to *cook for me*? What did I do to deserve such an honor?"

Everything, she thought to herself. But she knew she would never live it down if she admitted it. "If you're going to let me drool over Viggo Mortensen for twelve hours straight, you deserve a meal that's a little more substantial. Maybe even a bottle of wine."

"Oh, we're getting *crazy*," he teased. "Jessica, as long as you wear that cute little denim apron while you cook, I'm in."

She slit her eyes. "Why do you always make things so weird?"

Kevin reached over and booped her nose, the same motion she'd seen him do to Honey countless times in the past week since bringing her home. "For this exact reason. You get so ruffled. It's adorable."

He winked, then walked away, whistling. *Whistling*. She really was going to throttle him some day. Honey jumped up and down as Kevin approached, her long leash tied to his desk. Kevin flipped a bike upside down and clipped it onto the stand across from him, then sat on his tiny bench and tinkered away. Still whistling some tune she couldn't quite place.

THE GOLDEN AFTERNOON sun pierced through the back kitchen window as Jess drizzled sliced cherry tomatoes, minced garlic, and chopped basil in a bowl with olive oil, then added a couple cracks of fresh sea salt and black pepper. Tossing the bowl with one hand, she removed the plastic wrap from the sheet pan in front of her with the other.

"This is probably the hottest thing I've ever watched," Kevin drawled from the door.

She jumped, a few cherry tomatoes falling to the floor. "Dammit, Kevin. You can't do that when food is on the line."

He chuckled and bent down to pick up the rogue tomatoes, tossing them into the trash. "What are you making me over there?"

"You'll see."

She lightly drizzled more olive oil on her hands, then pressed dimples into the risen dough in the pan, gas bubbles popping up with each press. She dumped the cherry tomatoes on top and spread them out, then stuffed tiny mozzarella pearls in the empty holes.

A warm body pressed up beside her. She could feel his breath on her ear. "Step back, you're going to drool all over the focaccia."

He moaned. "Focaccia. My god. I do not deserve you."

"I know," she quipped. She washed her hands in the tiny sink by the door, then slid the focaccia in the oven.

Kevin cracked open two energy drinks he snatched from the fridge, handing her one. They clinked cans.

"To a night with Frodo," Kevin said before taking a long sip.

She scrunched her nose. "Frodo is the worst. Everyone knows Samwise is the real hero."

They debated this for a solid thirty minutes. She was surprised how much Kevin knew about *The Lord of the Rings*, even down to the particulars of the book versus the movie. Jess had attempted to read them, but never got past *The Hobbit*.

"I never had time to read the others," she explained.

"You should make the time," Kevin jested as he collected the empty can out of her hands. "You'll see the movies from a whole different perspective."

The timer buzzed on her phone, then a soft yipping noise came from the front room.

Jess straightened. "Where's Honey?"

"Don't worry, Jessica, she was sleeping in her dog bed. She must have woken up."

She relaxed and pulled the golden focaccia out of the oven, the smell of roasted tomatoes and basil wafting past her. "Wanna get her in the car? I'll wrap this up."

"We can't watch at full volume if we're in the same house as Gram and Calvin. No, sweetheart, we'll be heading upstairs."

"To your *apartment*? No way."

"Yes way. It's the *only* way."

"When's the last time you cleaned?"

"This morning."

"Liar."

"Jessica, I *swear*, on my beautiful little Honey's life, that I cleaned my apartment this morning. I also piled extra blankets and pillows next to the couch, and I even have a surprise for you in the freezer."

She scowled but grumbled, "What kind of surprise?"

He smiled, holding the door open for her. "The kind that involves a carton of ice cream from Scoops."

"Not much of a surprise anymore."

He placed a hand on his hip, not taking her shit. "I do have one warning, though."

She lifted a brow.

"I only have one bed, so if you decide you want to sleep, well..."

She kept a tight hold on the hot pan with an oven mitt as she shoved him with the other. He cackled, offering to take it for her, but she shook her head. "There's a bottle of red wine underneath the counter."

Kevin seized the bottle, then grinned. "When did you have time to get this?"

"Zach offered to grab it for us after his shift. He already deserves a raise."

Kevin scooped up Honey then flicked off the lights as she followed him out of the shop. "I know it's hard for you to comprehend, but people actually like to do nice things for their friends without expecting anything in return."

"That is hard for me to comprehend." The words whooshed right out of her. She couldn't control them. But they were the truth, and now they were out there.

His gaze softened. She instantly felt pathetic and shook her head. "Please don't," she pleaded.

So he didn't. The two of them remained silent as he locked the front door of Port Wheels. She followed him around the building and up the stairs to his apartment.

His place was small but cozy—a living room with a two-seater couch, a television, a coffee table, and a small book-shelf used as an end table. Along the back wall was an open kitchenette with a microwave, a toaster oven, and a two-burner stove. Honey jumped out of Kevin's arms and beelined for the bedroom that was just big enough to fit his bed. She placed the focaccia on the coffee table next to the bags of junk food she'd requested and followed her dog, peering into the tiny bathroom with a standing shower.

"Intimate," she chaffed as she meandered through his apartment. She made her way back to the living room, watching as Kevin pushed the coffee table to the side. He'd spread blankets out on the floor and tossed pillows to the center.

"Do you have a bread knife so I can cut this?" she asked.

"Top left drawer. I also have wineglasses in the cupboard above the microwave."

"Wineglasses, huh? I fully prepared for us to drink out of mugs."

"I will have you know that I have wineglasses *and* whiskey glasses. It's not very impressive to the ladies to drink out of mugs."

She placed the glasses down on the counter and turned toward him with a smirk. "Ladies, huh?"

"I'm not celibate, Jess. I can pull the ladies."

"With wineglasses."

"Now you're the one being insufferable," he rumbled, pouring her a glass.

She sliced the focaccia. "So how many, then? One, five, ten?"

"Are we really on the topic of how many partners I've had?"

She shrugged, licking the olive oil and tomato juices on her fingers. "I'm kind of curious."

He remained silent as he took a sip of his wine, then reached for two plates in the cupboard and handed her one. "Six," he finally answered.

Her gut clenched. "Wow, six. Did any of them ever—"

"Go anywhere? Nah. I also haven't been with someone in a year. You might be into having a one-night stand, but after having a few myself, I realized that I'm not a one-and-done kind of guy. I'm more of the commit-for-a-lifetime kind."

She hummed, following him with plates and glasses in hands to their sanctuary on the floor. "It's not all it's cracked up to be."

"Committing for a lifetime? How would you know?"

"Nine years feels like a lifetime."

He took a sip and shook his head, placing his glass down on the coffee table beside them. "It's not, though. Just because you dated the same guy since eighth grade doesn't mean you know what it feels like to commit for a lifetime."

Her face flushed. "Oh yeah, and how would you know? What do you know about commitment and long-term relationships? I've had my fill of sacrifice and compromise and sharing *everything* I own to realize that it's not something I enjoy."

Kevin tapped a finger on his propped-up knee, thinking it through for a beat. "You're right, I don't know. But I've always assumed that a person is willing to sacrifice and compromise and share if they love the other person. Those things are easier to deal with when you're with your person. Yet you make it sound like chains."

Her fingers trembled. She gripped her glass and took a long sip, the wine smooth on her tongue. It tasted ten times better than the three-dollar stuff she used to buy at Post Road.

Kevin didn't wait for her to give him some kind of retort. Instead, he tapped her knee, his hazel eyes bright despite the dim lighting of his apartment. "Have you heard from him?"

"No," she whispered. It should bother her that she hadn't heard from her ex of *nine years* that entire month. He was radio silent. He didn't even reach out to her about the opening of her bakery. Surprisingly, she didn't care.

"Jess, we're friends, so can I be honest with you about something?"

She sucked in a breath, then nodded.

He took the glass out of her grasp with gentle hands and placed it beside his, then brushed her trembling fingers with his own. "Being with him for that long doesn't mean you were treated well, sweetheart. You may have loved each other in the beginning, but watching from the sidelines...I could tell. You were unhappy. And he didn't do anything to make it better for you."

Tears leaked from her eyes and trailed down her cheeks. He cupped her face and brushed them away with his thumbs. "That relationship probably felt like chains. But I think maybe if you open yourself up to it someday, you'll find someone you're willing to sacrifice for and compromise with and all the rest without a second thought. Someone you can love, and who will wholly love you back."

She released a jagged breath, and emotion built up in her throat. She closed her eyes. "I'm so mean to you, yet you keep being nice to me. It doesn't seem fair."

When he didn't immediately respond she opened her eyes, noticing the *You've got to be joking* look he was giving her, his right brow cocked high. It made her smile.

"Let me remind you of the conversation we literally just had downstairs," he replied. He dropped his hands then lifted her plate and handed it to her. "And believe it or not, I enjoy spending time with you. You make me a better person."

She smiled at that and took a bite of her focaccia. She frowned. It wasn't nearly salty enough, and it was missing something. Oregano? Crushed red pepper flakes?

"For all that's good and holy," Kevin moaned. "This is freaking *fantastic*."

"It's not. I think it needs something—"

"Stop being so critical and enjoy the inappropriate sounds I'm making while eating this incredible thing you made me!"

She laughed and took another bite. "We don't have time for orgasmic noises. We have to gather the fellowship and go on a journey."

Kevin cheered and turned on the television. They ate in silence for the first thirty minutes of the movie, but it didn't take long for Kevin to start chiming in with his commentary.

They debated and laughed and finished off the focaccia and bottle of wine, Honey falling asleep soundly between them. As the credits rolled and Kevin switched on the second, Jess sprawled out on the blanketed floor, brushing a hand softly through Honey's fur. Kevin leaned back as well, propping up on a pillow and tucking a hand beneath his head.

She wasn't sure what compelled her to do it—maybe it was the wine, maybe it was the smoldering looks of Viggo Mortensen, maybe it was how nice Kevin was being to her—but she wiggled her body closer to his and rested her head on his arm. She saw his glowing smile out of the corner of her eye, and in a single sweeping movement, he moved his arm to tuck it around her shoulders and pull her closer. They lay like that the rest of the night, Honey snoring softly between them.

Chapter Twelve

Living in a suffocating small town did occasionally have its perks. For Jess, Haverfest was one of them.

This particular day had been a special one for her growing up, always starting with a stroll down Main early in the morning. Her father would take her and Dakota hand in hand to the different tents as vendors set up for the crowds that would swarm Haverport. Dad caught up with the townies as she and Dakota watched seafood skewers sizzle on grills, cotton candy spun into cones, sugary kettle cones stuffed in plastic bags. They would dance past the tents hosted by the local radio stations and duel each other in games like the water blaster or the ring toss. Everything was offered to them for free, all in thanks to her father's kindness to this town. His constant desire to *give, give, give,* and never ask for anything in return.

After their stroll, they would make their way down to Cap's for the massive beach bash, and then end the night in Dad's boat watching the fireworks as they floated down the bay. It was always the perfect day.

Getting her job at Scoops changed their tradition; a

quick skewer or a cotton candy before she had to report for her shift scooping cones. When she finally got the chance to take that day off the summer before her senior year, giving the other newbies at Scoops the honor of working that horrific shift, she pretended like she still had to work and snuck off with Charlie for the day. At the time, she was happy, care free, in love. She had no idea that day would be the beginning of the end.

So it didn't surprise her that she was anxious setting up the booth with Jan, Dan, and Kevin that morning. She kept quiet as she placed pastries in the small display case they set up on the table, Jan setting up a tower of jam jars beside her.

Kevin curled a hand around her wrist. "Everything okay?"

She exhaled, her eyes darting back and forth along Main, wondering if her father was making his rounds. "Fine," she said tersely. "Just...on edge."

He rubbed his thumb along the inside of her wrist. "Anything I can do to help?"

She looked up at him. His hair was tucked back behind that bandana. He wore an old Port Wheels tank top, tucked into army green board shorts. Her eyes trailed down his tattoo, realizing that she'd never actually seen it before. Curly strands of ivy ran down his neck to his shoulder, wrapping around his bicep. She swallowed hard when she noticed his hazel eyes were drawn to her lips. He flicked them back up to her face in an instant.

Her gut reaction was to wrench from his grasp and shut him out. Yet she hesitated as the tracing of his thumb calmed her. She thought back to their movie night earlier that week, the softness of his touch, the ease of being in his company. She felt she could trust him with the soft parts of herself, the parts that felt unfamiliar after years of building a fortress around her heart.

"Do we need to do our breathing exercise?" he asked, his tone careful. There was no tease in his voice. He understood her in a way that no one else seemed to, and to her astonishment, she didn't mind.

Jan ordered Dan to help her grab something from the car and stepped away from them. Jess peered around Kevin and watched her step into the sun. She turned and winked in her direction, then walked away, giving them space.

"Yes," she replied.

"Close your eyes."

She did, concentrating on the warmth of the July heat and the calloused hand on her wrist as he guided her through three breaths. She fluttered them open when they finished and glanced up. His eyes were still closed.

"I'm nervous I'm going to see them," she admitted. "I don't think I'm ready yet, Kev."

"How come?" he asked, his eyelids blinking open. "What's holding you back?"

Her shoulders dropped. "My disappointment in them... Their disappointment in me."

"Jessica, you're going to have to knock off that last item on your list at some point."

She attempted to pull her arm from his grasp, but he tightened his grip.

"Don't push me away, sweetheart. Please. Talk to me. You don't have to do this alone."

Familiar voices traveled from a couple of tents down from theirs. Jess whipped her head around, and for the first time in five years, saw her father.

Her dad was doing his usual rounds, a lobster roll in hand. He cocked his head back and laughed at something the artist who was talking to him said. He looked exactly like she remembered; the same suede sandals, the same cargo shorts, the same frayed Cap's hat with the original logo on his head.

Dakota stepped out from the tent, holding up an embroidered pillow to him, face beaming. Dad smiled, his shoulders melting as he reached into his back pocket and pulled out a bill, handing it to the artist in front of him.

The whole scene made her want to cry.

They waved goodbye to the artist and scanned the tents ahead of them, Dakota hooking an arm through their father's.

Jess ducked behind the booth and sat on the pavement, the tablecloth blocking her from view.

"*Jess*," Kevin hissed. Thankfully, he didn't look down at her, not drawing attention to her spot. "You can't keep running from this."

She scooted closer to him and threw her arms around one of his legs like a child. "Please. Do this for me."

He exhaled, and after a few torturous moments, she felt his body shift, his demeanor casual and at ease. "Mr. Valerie! Great to see you."

"Good to see you too, my boy. And please...call me Logan," he said.

Jess watched as Kevin reached out a hand and shook her father's.

"Interested in a pastry? A jar of jam? If you buy a bike, you can get all three!"

"Now that's a deal." He chuckled. "Where are the Fletchers?"

"Either fighting or making out by their car, who knows," Kevin joked.

"Is Jess around?" Dakota asked. The sound of her

sister's timid voice made her heart twist to a painful degree, like play dough in rough hands.

"She's hard at work making more of these raspberry croissants back at the bakery," he lied. "We're expecting to sell a lot of them today."

Jess ran her fingers down Kevin's calf. He knocked her softly with his other foot.

A sad sigh was her father's response. The silence was excruciating. She squeezed her eyes shut.

"I'll take ten croissants, please," he said.

Ten?!

"No bike to go with that?" Kevin teased, opening up a paper bag in front of him. He snatched the tongs and counted the croissants as he went. The bag wasn't big enough for all of them, so he opened up another.

"You of all people know I already have one," he said. "Thanks for helping me out the other day, by the way. It's no longer making that god-awful squeaking noise."

This time Jess squeezed his calf hard, digging her nails into his skin. *He was at the shop?*

Kevin coughed in response to her tight hold.

"A little oil always helps with that," he replied. "Happy to give it a tune-up whenever you need it."

"And will my daughter be hiding when I stop by?"

Her gut dropped. *Oh shit, oh shit, oh shit.*

Kevin froze. "She's not hiding."

"That's not what she's doing over at the bakery right now?"

She let out a quiet breath in relief.

"Okay, maybe she is hiding," he grumbled. "But give her some time. I really think she's going to come around. Soon."

Jess dropped her hands and scooted away from him. Far away.

Another throaty, weighted sigh from her father. "I hope so, son."

She curled in on herself and shoved her face in her knees.

"Tell her we love her, will you?" Dakota asked.

"Absolutely. Have a great day, both of you."

The two of them remained like statues, up until Kevin finally shifted to her, looking down.

"Fuck you," she grunted, standing up. "How dare you not tell me that my father came to the shop. You promised me you would not lie to me anymore."

For the first time in her history of knowing Kevin, he looked livid, and all his anger was directed at her. It was unsettling. "Jess, how else would you have liked me to handle it, huh? Did you want me to tell you he was standing outside the shop and pull you out there with me?"

She wrung her hands. "The customer the other day... with the kanelbullar and the caramel macchiato."

He nodded, his face still stony. "Yes, that was him."

She crossed her arms and held them tight to her chest, tearing her gaze from his. Her father and Dakota were no longer in sight, swallowed by the growing crowds.

"Also, I did not lie," Kevin said, his tone defensive.

She sniffed. "Did he say anything to you then?"

He exhaled. "He asked how things were going, and how you were."

She gazed back at him. He no longer looked angry, but his expression was dim. She shifted back and forth, waiting for him to continue.

"I didn't lie to him, Jess," he admitted. "I told him that the shop was getting more business and we needed to keep up that momentum. And I told him that you seemed happy, despite everything."

She frowned. "What does that mean?"

"I think he knows you left Charlie."

"Dakota probably told him. I admitted it to her and Jasper when they stopped by."

Kevin nodded and shoved his hands in his pockets.

"I'm sorry," she huffed. "You're right. You made the right call. I'm sorry you had to get in the middle of this."

"I sort of knew I would be, though, with the list and all."

She nodded and looked down at her clogs.

Kevin stepped forward and wrapped his arms around her, tucking her tight against his chest. "Whenever you're ready, however long it takes, I will be here for you."

"I'm sorry," she mumbled back. "Thank you for being my friend. For being patient with me. Even when I'm a complete and total bitch."

"I'll accept your apology, only if you promise never to call yourself that again."

"But I am..."

"No, you're not," he said. He stretched his arms out and placed his hands in his favorite spot—at her shoulders. "You may be stubborn sometimes, Jess, but you're also resilient. I don't know much about what happened between you and your family, but I can see how much pain you're in because of it. There's probably a lot to process through, and it's okay to be patient with yourself as you do it."

He brushed at the tears streaming down her cheeks.

"Why can't I stop crying these days?" she grumbled.

"Is Kevin making you cry?" Jan asked as she approached the tent. "Need me to call Calvin to beat him up?"

"*Calvin?*" Dan balked as he trailed closely behind his wife. "What about me?"

"You can barely lift a crate of jam, my love. We need arms. And Calvin has those."

"Tyler might have him beat," Jess teased. She wiped at her tears and tied her denim apron. "And no, he did not make me cry. He makes me smile."

Kevin grinned from ear to ear, and if she wasn't mistaken, his cheeks were painted pink.

THE REST of the festival went by in a blur of sticky pastries in paper bags and boisterous laughter—mostly from Dan and Jan. The strawberry danishes were gone in a couple hours, and the raspberry croissants an hour after. Jess had to run back to the bakery and grab extra inventory to sell to the hungry summer people in Haverport who, even after they had their fill of fried clams and funnel cake and freshly squeezed lemonade, couldn't resist heading to the beach or Hillside Park with paper bags full of pastries.

Tired and pink from the sun, Jess finished up taking down the booth with Dan and Jan while Kevin attempted to close another sale.

"Aw, you guys are out of croissants?" the young woman pouted. She brushed her curly hair over her shoulders, blinking her long lashes slowly up at Kevin. "You sure you have none left for me?"

Dread coiled around Jess's ribs as she watched Kevin grin at her. *That's my grin.*

She shook her head and snapped her attention back to the table she was folding. *Her grin?* Since when did she own anything of his? Since when did she get *jealous* of a girl flirting with Kevin? It was a rogue thought that needed to be squashed like a bug.

He laughed, low and deep. She hated how much she loved that sound. She hated that it wasn't directed at her.

"Um, Jess, we don't have any extras, right?"

"No," she snapped, not looking in their direction. "All out. Sorry."

"Maybe you could make it up to me then?" said the curly-haired woman. She lifted a finger and traced it down the tattoo on Kevin's arm.

Jess was five seconds away from standing up and breaking that delicate finger.

Kevin stepped away from the woman's touch. "Sure, stop by the shop sometime and you can have any pastry you want, on the house." To Jess's surprise, he turned to her. "We still have that thing tonight, right?"

Jess shook her head. *Unbelievable.* "Yes, we do. We should probably get going soon."

The woman frowned, grasping the handlebars of her new bike. "Well, if you change your mind, I'll be at Wilson's Pub later with some friends."

"Thank you for the invite, but I committed to something with my friends months ago. Sorry."

Jess chuckled, then lifted the table and walked away. She heard him jogging up to her.

"What's so funny, Jessica?" He grabbed the other side of the table and helped her lift it into Jan's car.

She put her hands on her hips. "You know you're not invited to the bonfire. It's a Scoops tradition, and you're not a Scooper."

"Oh come *on*, I'm an honorary Scooper," he said. "Pleeeeease!"

She scowled at him. "If you go, you have to eat the biggest slice of the cake."

Kevin grinned, and she relaxed. Yeah, that was her grin.

She wanted to put it in her pocket and keep it for herself. "I have been hearing about your gross cakes for years, I desperately need to try one. I'll beg on my knees if I have to."

It was a long-standing tradition with the Scoopers to have a beach bonfire the night of Haverfest, and as a special treat to the people who worked the gruesome shift that day, they had to watch the rest of the Scoopers eat the weirdest ice cream cake in their honor. Tonight was her fifth year of making the cake, and she had something extra devious up her sleeve.

She smirked. "Begging on your knees wouldn't hurt."

Kevin kneeled on the pavement in one swoop.

She rolled her eyes and pulled him back up. "Stop, I was kidding. You can come."

He kept his hand clasped in hers and squeezed. He stepped closer. "Tell me, are you allowing me to come because you saw me get hit on and you don't want me to go to the bar?"

She scoffed. "*No.*"

He booped her nose. "Jess, I thought we promised each other we wouldn't lie."

"I am not lying!"

He laughed as he walked away from her, his head held high.

FOLLOWING THEIR USUAL TRADITION, Jess showed up to Scoops, this time with Kevin in tow. After much back-and-forth debate between Calvin, Jess, and the rest of the Scoopers, Kevin was formally invited to join in on the bonfire. It only seemed fair at that point to invite Zach. On the verge of a hissy fit, Jay said he should be allowed to bring someone if they were all coupled up—despite Jess's insistence that she and Kevin were *not a couple*—and stepped aside to call some girl named Vanessa. Whoever that was.

Then they got to work. Calvin and Melanie continued to serve customers at the windows as she and the rest of the Scoopers cleaned and closed up the shop for the night. Kevin chipped in, drying the dishes Jay washed and singing along with him—both of them poorly out of tune. Tyler, home from football camp for the weekend, assisted Rory with restocking the candy, cones, syrups, fudges, cups, and spoons. She only had to pull them apart once from their aggressive make out in the walk-in fridge, which felt like a victory given the two never stopped touching each other. Blake and Zach cleaned and vacuumed, the former looking sunburnt and utterly elated after spending the day with his boyfriend, stealing longing looks at him like he was the moon and the stars.

Jess smiled to herself as she opened the freezer and picked up her cake, the rest of the Scoopers surrounding the desk in The War Room, waiting with bated breath. She may have discarded many of the traditions that mattered to her most as a kid, but at least she had this one to look forward to every year. At least she had these people she considered family.

She placed the cake down and with a smirk, lifted the lid.

The dramatic inhale was collective. No one spoke.

Compared to last year's cake, made with the atrocious Blue Bombshell ice cream Ron insisted on selling that season, this cake's flavor was obscure. Mysterious. And completely covered in black frosting.

"It looks like death," Blake gasped as Zach slipped an

arm around his waist.

"Is the secret ingredient...poison?" Jay chaffed.

"Oh my god," Rory coughed, "don't tell me you put squid ink in the frosting."

Tyler bent over. "That's it, this year I really am going to get sick from this thing."

Jess kept smiling at them, not revealing a thing.

"Jess, I'm dying, please just tell us the flavor," Blake cried.

She cocked a brow, crossing her arms. "This year we're going to do things a little differently. You won't know what it is until you cut into it at the beach."

Jay frowned. "Not even a hint?"

"Let's just say the theme is...savory."

Rory covered her face with her hands.

"This is so intense." Kevin clasped his hands together, looking giddy. "I love it."

"I kind of feel like we should leave the top blank," Melanie chimed in. "I know Calvin and I are supposed to add whatever gross topping we want, but..."

"I agree," he said. "It looks like the depths of hell already."

Jess nodded, closing the lid. "Off to the beach we go."

The group piled into cars and drove to Scallop Shell Beach. Jess parked her car at the dirt lot across the street, a bonfire already blazing in the distance. Kevin sat in the passenger seat, the cake box in his lap.

"Do you ever miss driving?" she asked as she unbuckled her seat belt.

"Honestly? No. Taking the bus is easy, and I like to walk. I also have my bike."

She held the box as he unbuckled his belt. "You know, if you ever need it, you could borrow my car."

Kevin smiled. "Yeah?"

She nodded. "Yeah."

"Jessica, not sure if you realize this, but you willingly offered to *share* something with me," he teased. "We're one step closer to 'what's mine is yours' and all that."

She rolled her eyes. "And there you go, making it weird. In record time, I might add."

He laughed, then ran around the car to open the door for her. "I appreciate the generosity, and may have to take you up on it soon, if that's okay."

She nodded. "Okay, yeah, just let me know."

They followed the rest of the rowdy group to the bonfire, taking seats on towels and blankets. Everyone silenced when Jess placed the cake down in front of Calvin, handing him the knife.

"Calvin, in honor of you working the Haverfest shift five years in a row, I would like you to cut and reveal the cake," she said.

Calvin frowned. "I couldn't take the spotlight from you. You've worked just as hard the past five years."

She sat down next to him, Kevin on her other side. "And this is why you need to do it. You care for all of us before yourself. So please, for the love of god, be selfish and cut the damn cake."

Melanie placed a hand on his shoulder. "Do it, babe. It's okay to be appreciated. We all love you."

"Not *all* of us," Jay squawked at the other end of the fire, sitting next to a girl donning a headband with velvet cat ears atop her short curly hair. She kept a respectable distance from him, Rory on her other side.

Calvin's eyes were lined with silver as he sliced into the cake. He placed the first piece on a plate, his eyes wide at what was at the center of her death-like creation. Then he tipped back and laughed so hard, it startled the rest of the group.

"Fuck I'm nervous," Tyler whined. He shifted toward Rory and buried his face in her neck, curling his arms around her waist.

"Aw, is big boy Tyler *scared?*" Rory teased.

"Menace," he growled.

"Come on, Cal, spill the tea...or in this case, the cake," Kevin said.

Calvin sat up, wiping tears from his eyes. "This year's cake is certainly savory."

Brows furrowed as they all looked at Jess.

She smirked. "The top layer of the cake is vanilla, mixed with ketchup," she explained. "The bottom layer is the same, but with Worcestershire sauce. And in the center is—"

"Meatloaf," Calvin answered for her, holding up a slice.

The group screamed and gagged. Kevin laughed along with Calvin. He took the slice from Calvin and a cotton-candy-colored spoon from Melanie. Everyone watched in horror as Kevin dug into the slice and took a bite.

He coughed, swallowing slowly, then grinned at Jess. "Tastes just like Gram's."

The group lost it, and Jess loved every second. She kept her eyes on Kevin, his gaze playful as he took another bite, then winced. She chuckled and passed slices out to the rest of the group before taking her seat next to him again.

He shimmied closer to her. "Hey, Jess?"

She took a bite of the meatloaf, surprisingly not hating the taste of it. The caramelized shallots were actually a nice touch. "Yeah?"

His eyes darted back and forth as he scanned her face. "You make me smile, too."

Chapter Thirteen

THE SUN PEEKED through the bakery's back window, the deep purple sky getting lighter and lighter as Jess rolled croissants for the morning. Honey snored on the dog bed by the door, belly up, paws in the air. She made a mental list of what she needed to do while they proofed—spoon the muffin batter into the tins, brush the tops of the scones with cream, and fill the danish pastry with jam. Customers had been coming into Port Wheels asking for the strawberry danishes and raspberry pastries from Haverfest, only to leave empty handed and disappointed. So Jess had Rory come in and add both treats to the colorful menu.

She slid the croissants into the proofer when the door swung open.

Without saying a word, Kevin placed the two mugs in his hands down on the counter, then snatched one of their energy drinks out of the fridge. He cracked it open, pouring half into each mug.

She stepped up to him and took the mug he handed her. "I'm usually more of a coffee-in-the-morning person."

"I figured it wasn't a good idea for me to try to tinker with that fancy machine you have out there."

"That's fair." She took a sip. "Why are you up so early?"

"How would you know my morning routine? Maybe I'm always up at five."

She cocked her head and he laughed.

"Fine, you caught me. I actually came down here to ask a favor."

She nodded and placed her mug down, reaching for the clean muffin tins on the shelf.

Kevin stepped to the sink and washed his hands, then rolled up his sleeves. He knew by this point if he wanted to hang out in the kitchen he would have to lend a hand.

He placed paper wrappers in the tins while Jess scooped the batter.

"My mom's birthday is tomorrow. My family and I have always done a big brunch for her in the morning, and I've yet to miss one."

She reached for the sparkling sugar and topped each muffin. "You need the car."

"Is that okay? Just for tonight and tomorrow, I'll be back by Tuesday morning."

Her heart sank into her stomach. "So you're skipping our Monday."

"That's right, you'll be off the hook. How will you spend your day of freedom?"

Her face felt tight. She transferred the muffins to the oven, then went to the fridge for the pre-baked scones, not bothering to look at him.

"Jessssss..."

"Hmm?"

"Look at me, please."

"What? You can take the car. Go see your family. I'll see you on Tuesday."

She listened as his breathing grew heavier. She dipped the pastry brush in the small bowl of cream.

His hand enveloped her wrist as he guided her to put down the brush.

"Do you want to come with me?"

She dropped the brush in the bowl, cream splattering onto the counter.

He grinned. "Come with me to Vermont. Meet my family. Are you okay with tofu scramble? Mom's vegan."

"I—but the bakery—" she sputtered.

"Will survive. You have enough stock to miss a day of prep. We could ask Zach to close up this afternoon and we'll leave after the morning rush."

She blinked, unable to string words together.

He kept smiling, as if her inability to form a sentence amused him. "We could even camp tonight, if you wanted. There are so many campgrounds on the way up to Burlington."

"I don't have any camping gear..." she mumbled.

He scoffed and placed his hands on his hips. "Jessica Valerie, I come from a long line of hippies. Do you really think I don't own any camping gear? We can share."

She shuffled back and forth. "Your family won't find it weird that I'm just...showing up with you? It's not like we're together or engaged or anything..."

He laughed at that. *Laughed.* Her cheeks flushed. She felt nauseous.

Kevin must have realized her reaction because his laughing slowed, his mouth forming a silent O. "Sweetheart, that is—"

"Don't call me sad," she whispered.

He hesitated. "Is that really why you didn't hang out with his family? Because he never gave you a ring?"

She nodded. "They only allowed partners to join in on holidays and trips if they were engaged. I waited *years* for Charlie to pop the question, waiting for the day that I could finally be part of his family. But he never did, which I guess is a good thing. After a while I wanted nothing to do with them. They're a brood of vipers."

He scowled. "What an absolute piece of shit."

She hummed and checked the croissants. "What's your family like?"

"The complete opposite. It's all good vibes and mantras and mary jane. Mom always told me marriage is a business transaction and I should focus instead on finding a soul connection with someone. I'm honestly not even sure if my parents are married."

She smiled. "She sounds wonderful. I can't wait to meet her."

He perked up, hopping back and forth. "So you're in?"

"And we'll bring Honey?"

The puppy flipped from where she slept at the sound of her name and noticed Kevin. She charged for him.

He scooped her up and planted kisses on her furry head. "*Duh.* Camping with my girls? Sounds like a dream."

She shook her head, not bothering to fight him on his use of *my girls*, riding on the high of being included in his family's traditions. She spent the rest of the morning mulling over his words, liking the idea of finding a soul connection with someone else. It felt far more approachable than hopping into another relationship and losing herself all over again.

"Favorite road trip snack?"

Jess scrunched her nose and patted Honey in her lap. "I haven't been on a road trip in forever so I have no idea."

Kevin leaned back in the driver's seat, one hand placed casually at the top of the wheel. "All right, imagine this; we take a pit stop somewhere for gas. What is the food you want to get?"

"Cheetos."

Kevin cheered. "Now *that's* what I'm talking about."

Jess smiled as she kicked off her shoes. Kevin offered to drive the first leg of the trip to Burlington, but after three hours in the driver's seat, he hadn't asked her to switch, and she didn't mind. It was nice being able to sit back and simply pet the pup on her lap, watching the sun lazily set among the hills and the trees that only grew taller as they drove north.

She kissed Honey's head. Her ear perked up from the touch, then she melted into Jess's lap and began to snore. "What's your favorite road trip snack?"

"Chocolate milk and gummy worms," he said unashamedly.

"That sounds repulsive together."

"Jess, you put a literal *meatloaf* in an ice cream cake. I feel like nothing should repulse you."

She chuckled. "Yeah, but the intention was to be disgusting. You're choosing to do it of your own volition."

He grinned, his eyes on the road. "I like that you guys have that tradition. It makes me wish I had coworkers."

She brushed a hand through Honey's fur, her pale-yellow locks longer than when they first picked her up. "You have coworkers now."

He rubbed a hand across his face, then rubbed his neck, his cheeks pink. "Yeah, I guess I do."

Jess liked his rosy cheeks, his hazel eyes sparkling against the golden summer sun. "Maybe we should make our own traditions."

"Yeah? Like what?"

"Hmm...annual camping trip?"

He hummed. "Let's see how tonight goes first."

She scoffed. "You think I can't *handle it?*"

"Oh, I do," he said. "But I'm not sure how you're going to feel after sleeping in a tent with me."

She fidgeted in her seat. "Oh."

"Sorry, I only realized as I was packing. But it does sleep four people, so there's plenty of room."

She exhaled. "That's fine, Kev. Don't worry about it."

He nodded. They remained silent as he turned around a bend and down a road veiled in trees. He slowed the car at the entrance for a campground and pulled in. Honey perked up as he stepped out of the car, but Jess kept a tight grasp on her pup as Kevin spoke with the attendant, then grabbed a stack of firewood and a bag of ice. He hauled them in the trunk and got back in the car.

"I told him it was your first time camping and he gave us the best lot on the grounds," he explained. He rolled the car down the dirt road, past campsites with couples and families building fires and setting up tents for the night. Kevin turned and parked next to an empty spot. Jess stretched her legs and stepped out of the vehicle, holding Honey firmly in her arms as she walked toward their small fire pit in the center of a clearing overlooking a lake behind them. The water glistened as the sun set, the sky streaked with soft peachy pinks.

"Wow," she breathed. She felt Kevin step up beside her. "He wasn't kidding. This is the best lot."

Kevin hummed. "Come on, let's get set up. First rule of camping: never wait to set up camp until the sun goes down."

Her eyes widened. "Why? Bears? Are we going to get eaten?"

He barked out a laugh. "No, silly, we're safe here. It's just a pain to set up a tent in the dark."

She relaxed. "What's rule number two of camping?"

"S'mores must be consumed."

"I like that rule."

"Me too," he said, swinging an arm around her shoulders as they walked back to the car.

They set up the tent and tossed sleeping bags and mats and pillows in, then focused on dinner. Honey remained tied up with a long leash that gave her enough room to run around, but she seemed content sitting next to Jess as she tossed sliced peppers, onions, and sausage in a bowl with oil and seasoning, then dumped them in sheets of aluminum and wrapped them up tightly. She noticed Kevin standing over her as she finished folding up the packets.

"Jessica, camping means hot dogs on sticks, condiments not always necessary. This is fancy."

"You really think I'm going to settle for a hot dog on a stick?" she quipped.

"At this point, I don't think you'll settle for *anything*."

"Damn straight," she mumbled to herself, heat trickling up her neck.

Kevin set down two camping chairs as she carefully tossed the packets on the grill, then took a seat next to him.

Honey jumped up on his lap and licked his face, then dropped down with an exhausted *foof*.

"You know, for someone who's never been camping before, you sure look like you know what you're doing," he said, gesturing toward their foil pack dinners.

She pulled up her legs and sat crisscrossed, getting comfortable. "My dad has this obsession with making foil pack dinners on the grill. Or...he did. I guess I don't know if he's into it anymore."

Kevin nodded. "I bet he still does. Logan doesn't strike me as the kind of guy who likes change."

Jess's mind flashed to their days at Cap's, remembering the way her father bristled at everything Charlie's father suggested they do. She knew he hated it, but he'd kept it to himself—mostly. The space was in dire need of saving, and Charlie was willing to make the investment. So her father nodded along, and watched his precious boatyard transform before his eyes.

"Yeah," she breathed. "Not really his thing."

"What kind of foil pack dinners did he make?"

"Clam bakes, with corn and sausage and potatoes and lemon. We always made them when we got back from our days clamming."

"You used to go *clamming*? Jessica, that's so cool."

Jess gripped her knees tightly. "Yeah, we would go every summer. Sometimes multiple times. Just me and Dad... Dakota hated how messy and muddy it would get. But I always loved those mornings with him. We'd get up early and eat donuts on the beach and wait for the tide to get super low, then we would dig for a couple hours. We would come home reeking with buckets and buckets of clams. Mom always complained how his truck smelt like clams for weeks after, but I never minded. The smell of seafood never bothered me. It just...smelled like home."

She paused, realizing how much she'd admitted, and felt a flash of embarrassment. There was something about Kevin that made her comfortable enough to share things, comfortable enough to let him in on those parts of herself she tried to push away or forget. Everything about her family had felt too raw with Charlie, so she never spoke about them, never admitted how much she missed them. But with Kevin, things felt...safe. He gave her space to share her thoughts and feelings, to talk through what was going on in her head without any judgment. It reminded her of what he said weeks before, about how friends liked to do things for each other without asking for anything in return.

Her eyes lingered on him, the way his mouth quirked up on his left cheek always, how his wavy hair curled around the flat-brim hat on his head. The navy sweatshirt he wore looked soft, the sleeves pushed up to his elbows, the muscles in his forearms flexing slightly with each stroke of Honey's fur.

His smile widened, letting her know he was *very* aware of her lingering gaze, and her cheeks flushed.

"What's going on in that mind of yours, my dear Jessica?"

She broke her gaze and stared hard at the fire, listening to the oil sizzling in the packets, the smells of fatty sausage and onion wafting toward them. "I was thinking about your tattoo."

"Oh yeah? What about it?"

"What it means, why you have it."

"Does a tattoo always have to have a meaning?"

She pursed her lips. "I...guess not."

A gust of wind rushed past them. Jess shivered,

burrowing deeper into her seat, and crossed her arms tightly to her chest.

Kevin stood up, keeping Honey tucked in his arm as he opened his duffel bag on the table. He pulled out another sweatshirt and tossed it her way.

"Thank you," she said, shimmying it on. It smelt like cinnamon and sand with a hint of metal. She wondered if he wore it while working at the shop, tinkering away at the bikes.

Kevin stepped in front of her and placed Honey on her lap. Before she could protest, he shoved a thick beanie on her head, pulling it below her ears. He patted her cheeks with an amused smile, then sat back down in his chair.

"I could have grabbed my own sweatshirt, you know," she muttered.

"Jessica, you clearly wanted one of mine," he jested, motioning toward the sweatshirt he was currently wearing.

Her face flushed. "That's—that's not true."

He grinned and crossed a leg over his knee. "You know, for someone who's against sharing, you've let me share with you. *A lot.*"

She grumbled to herself and ignored his comment.

They ate in a contented silence, listening to the crackling fire and the buzzing cicadas. Honey stood on Jess's lap and attempted to nip at the fireflies floating around their camp. She felt herself drifting off in her chair, the sounds of the forest and the trees so different from rolling waves and cawing seagulls. It sounded like magic.

She felt a warm, calloused hand on hers. "Want to call it a night?"

"But what about rule number two of camp?" she murmured.

"We'll do it another time."

"Promise?" she whispered.

Gentle, featherlight fingers brushed the line of her jaw. "Yeah, sweetheart, I promise."

She stepped into the tent and slipped into Kevin's extra sleeping bag, zipping it up to the top. Honey nuzzled under her arm and curled into a ball. She dozed off to the sounds of Kevin stoking the fire, waking briefly when he crawled in next to her. She sighed at the comforting smell of cinnamon and the warmth of his body next to hers as she fell into a dreamless sleep.

Jess woke to the sound of birds chirping and the whistling of trees overhead. She blinked her eyes open and was welcomed by the sight of Kevin sprawled out next to her, one arm stretched toward her, the other curled around Honey's belly. The pup was in her usual sleeping position; on her back, paws in the air, snoring. She must have ditched Jess at some point to cuddle with Kevin instead.

"Player," she whispered.

Honey's ear twitched, which made Jess's heart swoop. Her hearing still wasn't great, but little things here and there seemed to catch her attention. She wondered if her hearing would fully heal and made a mental note to take her to the vet.

She let out a soft sigh as she slipped out of her sleeping bag. She carefully crawled over Kevin so she wouldn't wake him, then unzipped the tent and stepped into the warmth of the glowing dawn sun. The lake behind them was breathtaking, the waves shimmering with light. A herd of ducklings followed their mother along the water, dipping in and out of the water and ruffling their feathers. The whole scene felt innocent, almost untouched. It was hard for Jess to fathom that such peace could even exist.

"Morning," said a gruff voice.

Jess turned toward Kevin. She sniggered at the way his hair stood up straight on one side of his head. His cheeks were covered in a light dusting of stubble. He rubbed his eyes, his sweatshirt lifting in the front. She dared a glance at his tan skin and the dips at his hips.

Honey pattered up to Jess and licked her ankles. She tore her gaze from his golden skin and scooped her up, looking back out at the water.

"Well, there you have it. You camped. Four down, six to go."

She smiled. "Which one should we tackle next?"

"Don't worry, I have a plan for the next four. But there are two that I will not touch with a ten-foot pole."

Her smile shifted into a smirk. "Not gonna help me find a stranger to hook up with, huh?"

"Nah, sweetheart, that's all on you," Kevin said, his voice gravelly.

A squirrel ran past them and climbed up a tree. Honey let out one of her hoarse barks, then began squirming in Jess's arms. She clicked on her long leash and let her down, the pup running for the tree and taking a seat, like she expected the squirrel to come back for her.

"I've never kissed anyone else," Jess admitted, keeping her eyes on Honey as she said it. "It's only ever been Charlie."

She saw him shift in her periphery. "Are you nervous?" he asked

"I don't know. Maybe a little?"

"Do you need to practice?"

She snapped her gaze to his. He licked his lips and smiled at her, his eyes bright with amusement.

Jess glared. "That's awfully bold of you."

"Oh come on, just one kiss. I can even give you notes, if you want them."

The idea isn't horrible, she thought. If anything, Kevin was the most comfortable she'd felt with a guy (besides Calvin, who was basically her brother). So, kissing him? That didn't seem so bad.

He wiggled his brow at her. "Come on, you know you're curious."

She frowned. "You're acting *way* too eager."

"Can you blame me? Jess, *I'm* kind of curious."

She looked down at her clogs and kicked at a rock. "I—I don't know."

He took a step closer. She let her gaze trail slowly up his body, thinking it through. She *was* curious. And after years of having someone to kiss constantly, going over a month without that intimacy felt weird. She would like to be kissed. She wondered what it would be like to kiss someone who wasn't her ex-boyfriend.

Her eyes landed at the faint freckle near his bottom lip. Her nerves thrummed, her body felt warm.

Just one kiss.

"Okay," she whispered.

"Holy *crap*."

Her breath hitched as strong arms wrapped around her waist and pulled her close.

"Holy crap what?" she murmured. She fisted his sweatshirt, the cotton soft between her fingers.

"I didn't actually think you'd say yes."

She scowled. "Don't make me regret it."

Kevin pressed his forehead to hers. "Trust me, I won't."

He dipped down and nuzzled her nose with his, then he leaned in and kissed her.

Butterflies soared in her stomach at the feel of his lips on hers. He tasted like cinnamon sugar and golden sunrises and good decisions. She leaned her head back, allowing him to deepen the kiss. He groaned, his soft lips gliding against hers as he slipped a tongue into her mouth. She shivered, moving her hands to his stubble-dusted cheeks. She followed a trail to his neck and dug her fingers into his sleep-tousled hair. He sucked in a shocked breath, then nibbled at her lip and plunged in again, her fingers in his hair rousing him to another level of intensity as he kissed her deeply and thoroughly. His arms remained wrapped tight around her waist, his hands curled at her hips.

Honey barked.

They broke apart, breathing heavily. She cracked open her eyes, noticing his were still shut, his face anguished.

He dropped his hold on her and stepped back, then scratched the back of his head.

"I take it back," he muttered, not looking in her direction.

"Take what back?"

"I take what I said back," he breathed. "I can't practice with you. I'd lose my damn mind."

Chapter Fourteen

They rode in silence the rest of the way to Burlington. Honey panted on Jess's lap as Kevin drove. He kept his eyes on the road as he gripped the steering wheel with white knuckles. He pulled off the exit and down windy roads with small houses tucked behind evergreen trees. Minutes later they turned into a dirt driveway in front of a brick house that was barely visible, hidden behind hundreds of winding strands of ivy.

"Are you sure your tattoo doesn't have a hidden meaning?" Jess jested, trying to lighten up the thick tension that lingered between them.

Kevin gave her a smile and unbuckled his seat belt.

She crossed her arms. "You told me you wouldn't make me regret it."

He hesitated, then let out a defeated exhale. "You're right. I'm sorry."

"Is it going to be weird if I go in there with you? I can drive somewhere and pick you up later..."

"Jess, no, it's fine. Really."

She expected him to reach out and touch her hand or

her shoulder or *something*. But Kevin kept his distance as he cut the ignition and leaned back in his seat.

"You don't seem fine."

He sighed, then unbuckled his seat belt and got out of the car. Honey bolted after him, then instantly found interest in the bed of lavender planted by the front door and ran for that instead.

Jess jumped out of her seat and chased Kevin as he circled the car, stopping him with a hand at his chest. "If you don't talk to me then I'm not going in there."

"Well, that would be very rude of you. Mom made a special batch of her sourdough banana bread so she could impress you."

Her chest tightened. *She made something special to impress me. Charlie's mother would never.*

She glared at him. "Then it would be *especially* rude if I skipped out on it all because you wouldn't talk to me."

Kevin cupped her hand at his chest with his own and squeezed it delicately, then dropped it back to her side and let go. "Jess, you got out of a really big, really serious relationship, and I know you're not interested in any of this right now."

"That doesn't mean I have to be celibate," she said, her words clipped and tight.

"Yes, but...you're looking for a rebound, sweetheart. A one-night stand. No strings attached. And I am nothing *but* attached."

She felt like an entire apple was lodged in her throat.

He took a step back and traced a rectangle between them. "Here's the table." He threw his hands to the right. "I can be your friend, your comrade, your coworker, your partner in summer bucket lists. Or..." he continued, shifting his hands to the other side of their metaphorical table. "I can be the other thing. Much more. The 'we're partners but sleep in two beds' kind of more. But I can't be anything in between. It's one or the other."

"I can't do more right now, Kevin. You said that yourself."

He sighed and shoved his hands in the pockets of his jeans. Like he was restraining himself from touching her. "I know. I can be patient, Jess. I'll wait until you tell me you're either ready or that there's no possible way this would work. But I can't be dangled in between. I told you I'm a commitment guy. I stand by that."

She nodded, her eyes on the invisible table. "I get it. I do. I'm sorry."

"Dear lord." Kevin finally reached for her and pulled her in for a tight hug. "You don't need to apologize. It was me who instigated this, remember? You did nothing wrong."

"Then why does it feel that way?" she mumbled.

"Because I'm an idiot."

"You're not."

"No, I am. I couldn't help myself. I had to know."

She looked up at him, resting her chin on his chest. "Had to know what?"

His breath hitched as he tucked a strand of her hair behind her ear with gentle fingers. "What it would be like if you were mine."

Her stomach dipped.

"Is that my Kevvy Bear??"

Jess peeled herself out of Kevin's arms and turned around, watching as his mom approached. Her skin was deeply tanned like his from the summer sun, and she wore a denim vest with a floral skirt that flowed down to her bare feet, her left ankle covered in anklets.

Kevin smiled as he dipped down to wrap his arms

around his mother's waist and lift her off the ground. "Hi, Mom. Happy birthday. Stop calling me that."

She jumped down and flicked his ear. "Never."

A pang sat deep in her belly as she watched their comfortable greeting. She stepped away and looked for Honey, finding her attempting to nip at a bumble bee sitting on a stalk of lavender. She scooped her up and scratched the backs of her ears.

"Mom, you remember Jess, right? We went to school together."

Jess stepped toward them and held out her hand. "It's nice to see you again, Mrs. Perkins."

"*Bleh*, Mrs. Perkins. Call me Arielle." She nudged Jess's hand away and wrapped her up in a hug instead. Honey wiggled out of Jess's grasp and licked Arielle's face.

"Oh now isn't this the sweetest little one," she said. Arielle cooed as Jess handed the pup to her. "What's the name?"

"Her name is Honey," Kevin explained, and to Jess's surprise, he swung an arm around her shoulder. "We're dog parents!"

"Dog parents, huh?" she teased, winking at Kevin.

Kevin bristled, ignoring his mother's coy smirk as he released Jess and looked back at the house. "Where's everyone else?"

"They're setting up on the back patio." She placed Honey back on the lawn and stood to face Jess. "How's your father doing? Last I heard he gave up ownership of the boatyard. Has he been up to anything new since we left Haverport?"

Jess felt like an overly baked muffin inside of Kevin's sweatshirt as they stood under the sun. She shoved the sleeves up and wiped her sweaty hands on her shorts, trying hard to make her breathing sound steady and normal.

"He—he's—he's good," she stammered.

The front door swung open then, and a tall man with wavy gray hair half tied up into a bun stepped out. "Arielle, my love, your birthday brunch will go cold if you keep us waiting."

Kevin beamed and stepped up to his father, clapping him on the back.

Arielle looped an arm through Jess's and squeezed. "Can't let the tofu scramble get cold. Shall we?"

"You okay?"

Jess didn't have to turn much to face Kevin. The patio table was barely big enough to fit six chairs, so they all sat close, knees grazing and thighs bumping as they passed plates and poured steaming cups of coffee from carafes. Kevin's younger sisters were recalling the previous week's high school drama to his parents, giving the two of them a reprieve after their endless questioning about the new bakery at Port Wheels.

Kevin pressed his leg up against Jess's and whispered to her again. "I'm guessing my mom's question about your father threw you off."

She toyed with the berries on her plate with her fork. "Yeah, it did."

He slid a hand on her knee and rubbed back and forth, then froze. He swiftly removed his hand, like he'd thought better of it.

"You know what's sad? I have no idea what my father is

up to," she reckoned. "I screwed up so badly with them that I don't even know how he spends his days anymore, or if he's working at all."

Kevin placed down his fork. "Jess, are you ever going to tell me what happened with them?"

She sucked in a breath.

"We're friends, right? You can trust me. I'm here whenever you're ready to talk about it."

"What if I'm never ready?" she confessed.

He turned his head and leaned in, his words barely a whisper. "You see, you made a grave mistake, Jessica. I know that working things out with them is the last thing on your bucket list. And I *really* don't think you want to start collecting unemployment."

"You wouldn't—"

"Are you sure about that?" He cocked a brow.

She glared at him. "Glad to see you're back to being your insufferable self."

He looked at her with a devilish grin. "Glad to see you're back to hating me."

"I don't hate you."

He stretched up, reaching for a plate of sliced banana bread. "Don't worry, sweetheart, I certainly know that *now*."

She kicked his shin under the table, causing a slice of banana bread to tumble off the plate and hit the wooden patio floor with a dramatic *plop*.

Kevin laughed and cleaned up the mess as Jess shook her head.

"Jess, you can tell me if you don't like the bread, no need to throw it," Arielle teased.

"Oh gosh no, that's not—"

Kevin pinched her calf as he finished cleaning up the mess. She yelped.

She fumed. "Arielle, please tell me why you call your son Kevvy Bear."

"Traitor," Kevin growled as he sat back up.

"It's what he used to call himself," Arielle explained with a teasing glint in her eye. "He carried around his teddy bear and said he was the Kevvy bear."

Jess shot him a wicked grin. "Brilliant."

Kevin pointed a fork at her. "You are going to regret this."

"Oh I don't think I will."

His family laughed at their banter. Jess asked for more embarrassing stories, and his mother and father entertained her with tales of Kevin covered in scabs from crazy bike rides and coming home with lonely animals that needed a home.

"My Kevin has always had a soft spot for collecting lost souls," Arielle mused.

Jess felt a pang in her heart. She snuck a glance at Kevin and noticed his flushed cheeks, his eyes on his plate.

THE REST of the afternoon went by in a blur of sunshine, lawn games, and tall glasses of iced tea. Honey chased every Frisbee Kevin threw into the can at the opposite end of the lawn, attempting to intercept it with a jump and a swipe of her little teeth, only to tumble back down into the grass. His sisters squealed every time at "the cuteness" and willfully ignored Mr. Perkin's pleas for them to help clean up.

Jess stacked plates in her hands. "Let them play, I can help."

Arielle planted her hands on her hips. "Put those plates down, you are our guest."

She gave her a warm smile. "And you are the birthday girl, so let me do this."

Arielle loosed a resigned sigh, wrapping up leftover bread and pouring cold coffee in her potted plants as Jess carried dishes to the kitchen. She turned on the spigot and began washing, peeking a glance out the window every so often and smiling as Kevin teased Honey with a dog toy, making her chase him around the lawn to grab it. She liked his parents and the girls and this brick house covered in ivy.

Arielle stepped up beside her and dried the dishes she cleaned.

"He looks happy here," Jess admitted. "I don't really understand why he didn't move back here with you after graduation."

"He loved Haverport too much. The idea of leaving didn't feel right to him. I couldn't fight my son if his heart was connected with that place more than this one."

"Yes, but...he's so far from family. If my family was like this, I would never want to leave."

Arielle rubbed a hand on Jess's back. She noticed the way Kevin's mother was constantly soothing with her hands and arms. It made it very clear where Kevin's need for physical touch came from.

"Is everything okay at home?" Arielle asked, her tone even.

Her throat felt dry. She swallowed a couple of times before responding. "Not really. My parents and I...we're not on speaking terms right now. Well...my sister and I are a little bit, but my mom and dad..."

Her voice caught in her throat as tears lined her eyes. She wiped at them with her wrist, sudsy water from her fingers dripping down to the floor.

Arielle kept rubbing her back. Jess flushed as she continued with the dishes, too embarrassed to look Kevin's mom in the eye.

"No matter where I go or what happens in my life, I always seem to find myself with two options," Arielle started. "Either live in fear and never try, or choose to be brave and live in your truth. Putting ourselves out there can feel scary because there's always the chance of failure. But what would be worse? Living without knowing what could have been, or living knowing you gave it your all?"

She had the sneaking suspicion that these words weren't only meant for her situation with her family. Jess's gaze instinctively linked to Kevin outside the window, admiring the grin on his face and the sound of his laugh as he chased his sisters around the yard.

"Now tell me...has my son been brave with you?"

Jess whirled around and faced Kevin's mom. "Huh?"

"Has my son shared his feelings for you?"

Goose bumps flecked her skin. "Did he tell you he has feelings?"

Arielle shrugged. "I have a sense for these things. I also know my Kevin. It's written all over his face."

It was practically identical to what Gram told her a month ago. *The look.* Were his feelings really so plain for everyone to see?

Arielle rubbed Jess's arm, patiently waiting for her to respond, almost like she was waiting to see whether she needed to give her son a scolding.

"He's made it...clear," Jess murmured.

His mother smiled and tucked a strand of Jess's hair

behind her ear. "And how about you, my dear? Will you be brave with him?"

Her chest tightened to an unbearable degree at her question. She stared at Arielle with wide eyes, unable to speak, unable to take a full breath.

Arielle must have caught on because she gave Jess a reassuring smile. "Don't make him wait too long, okay? He deserves your bravery, too."

"I'm not very good at being brave," she whispered.

She cocked her head, a warm smile still on her lips. "Sweetheart, I don't believe that for a second."

Honey snoozed by her feet as they made the five-hour drive back to Haverport, two loaves of sourdough banana bread tucked safely in the trunk. Jess didn't want to leave the warmth and closeness of his family, but they didn't have an option; summer season was in full swing back at home, and they had a shop to save. She'd done her best to contain her tears as she hugged Arielle goodbye, her words dancing around in her head.

He deserves your bravery, too.

Jess looked over at Kevin, a bright smile still on his face, even an hour after leaving the house.

She couldn't help it; she had to ask. "Why would you not want to be near them?"

He shrugged. "I like my life in Haverport. I like being near the beach and helping build parade floats for charity and working at the bike shop. I like hanging with Calvin... with you. It feels harder to leave that than to drive away from my family in Burlington. I can drive up whenever I want to see them...or, well, used to. I'll have to get a new car eventually."

"I already told you to take mine whenever you need it."

"I know, sweetheart. I would hate to be a burden though."

"You're never a burden," she said softly. "Also...does your mom call you sweetheart, too?"

He blushed. "Yeah, sorry, it's what we say to each other in my family. I can stop if it makes you uncomfortable."

She wiggled in her seat. "No. Keep calling me that. I like it."

"Good. Me too."

She drew her gaze out the passenger window to the blur of trees and mountains surrounding them. "Kevin?"

"Hmm?

She sucked in a breath. "Am I a lost soul you felt you needed to save?"

She heard him sigh.

"I watched you sacrifice so much of yourself for a man who couldn't do the same for you in return," he replied. "I know I came across strong at first with my offer, but it's because I've always known you deserve better than that. You deserve more."

"And do you think I'd find that with you?" As the words left her lips she froze, but Kevin didn't even bat an eye.

"Not if I don't make you happy," he confessed. "I want you to be happy, Jess. If that's not with me, then so be it."

Jess wondered if the life lesson Arielle gave her in the kitchen was one that Kevin had heard before. He wasn't just being brave, he was being honest. He put everything out there on that metaphorical table, making his intentions clear, knowing that it might not work out for him in the end.

What would be worse? Living without knowing what could have been, or living knowing you gave it your all?

Her heart twisted at the thought. She flicked on her pop punk playlist, letting the music fill the space between them as she processed what she was feeling. Being with Kevin was the safest she'd ever felt with someone. She trusted him with her deepest vulnerabilities and he still chose to spend time with her, to be her friend, even when she was the worst version of herself. Despite how hard she tried pushing him away over the years, he was always a constant. A friend who cared enough to ask and to want more for her. To have what she deserved.

Maybe I need to be brave.

She shut down the thought immediately. Why would she do that to herself when she finally had her freedom? Why was she incapable of being single and independent? She needed months—maybe *years*—before even considering another relationship. And Kevin made it clear he was not going to be a rebound.

She closed her eyes and rested her cheek on the cool glass of the window, hoping to drift off and mute these new, raging, unwelcome emotions.

Chapter Fifteen

Jess nibbled on the blackberry hand pie in front of her, then paused. It wasn't *right* yet—the filling didn't taste as sweet as she hoped, and she felt it needed something else to give it that special zing. *Maybe more lemon juice?* She bent over her table and made a note to try that in her next batch.

Kevin stood at the other end of the shop with Calvin, their heads bent, mumbling something she couldn't hear.

"Are you going to share with the class or are you going to keep ignoring the fact that I'm here?" Jess barked.

Kevin grinned, looking between her and Calvin. "She's such a charmer."

"If that's what you want to call it," Calvin jested.

Jess's mouth fell open. "Did you just *sass* me, Ball?"

"You deserve it sometimes," he chafed, following Kevin as the two of them made their way to her counter. He crossed his arms in that familiar military-like *I now mean business* stance. "Okay, do you want bad news or worse news first?"

She rubbed her face. "Just tell me."

"The breakfast rush you have is great, but it's not

enough to make up for the lull in the afternoon. You guys are behind."

"And the worse news?"

"Even if you do find a miraculous way to get customers in here during the afternoon, you may find yourselves needing another investor or a new owner."

She perched her elbows on the counter and placed her head in her hands.

"It's all right, Jessica, we'll figure it out," Kevin said softly.

The tiny bell at the door made a cheerful ding as someone entered the shop. Jess stood up straight, recognizing the platinum blonde hair and the round belly.

"Dakota, hi!"

Her sister smiled, waddling her way over to the counter. She was in her seventh month now, yet she still looked radiant as always; glowing skin, hair shiny and silky, freckles dotting across her nose and cheeks. She looked down at the half-eaten hand pie on the counter. "Whatever that is smells amazing, do you have another?"

Jess pushed the plate to her. "Finish it and tell me what you think, I can't seem to figure out what's wrong with it."

"There's probably nothing wrong with it," Kevin bantered.

Dakota smiled, taking the plate. "You know Jess, always a perfectionist."

She rolled her eyes. "Everything okay?"

"Yeah, do you—um—have a minute?"

Jess nodded, making her way around the counter. Kevin pulled a chair out for Dakota at one of the tables by the window and held out a hand, assisting her into it.

He took a step back and bumped into Jess, then held out his hands in apology. "Sorry, didn't mean to—"

Jess sidestepped and took a seat. "All good."

Kevin gestured for Calvin to join him outside, the two of them mumbling to each other again as they exited the shop.

Dakota cocked her head. "That was weird."

"Yeah, weird is an understatement," Jess grumbled. "Let's not talk about it. What's up?"

Her sister raised her brow, but she obliged. "I have something for you."

Dakota slipped a sage-green envelope across the table. Jess picked it up timidly, noticing the way her sister was beaming again at her, like she was the damn sun. Jess ripped open the envelope and pulled out an invitation.

Come shower Baby Carver with lots of love!

Jess gulped, reading the rest of the invitation details. It was two weeks from now, and it was being held at the house. *Their* house. Her childhood home.

The RSVP was to her mother, Whitney Valerie.

Jess froze, eyes on the invitation, not daring to make a move or a sound. She felt like her brain short-circuited as she remained in that spot, thinking through what she should do next and never coming up with a solid plan.

"I...I know it's a lot," Dakota hedged after their bout of silence. "But I can't imagine not having you there, sissy. I need you, and I need you in this baby's life."

Jess remained silent, eyes on the invitation.

"It's probably cruel for me to ask you to come and to face them, but I—"

"It is cruel, Dakota. They kicked me out. They wanted nothing to do with me."

She finally looked up at her sister and watched as

Dakota pursed her lips. "Jess, you were so single-minded then. You only had your focus on *one thing*—being with Charlie. You broke their hearts. You broke *my* heart."

"Is that why you sided with them? Because you were angry that I chose Charlie and his father?"

"Yes," Dakota admitted, face firm, brows knitted together. "You know how much Dad loved that place, and Mr. Sullivan ripped it right out from under his feet. He was in pain, and your words rubbed dirt in the wound."

"What did he expect me to do, huh? Break up with Charlie after four years because our fathers were fighting? I was a teenager and deeply, *deeply* in love with him. The idea of being forced to break up with him felt like ripping out my own damn heart. I couldn't do it. I had to sneak out and see him."

"It's messed up, I know. He made some dumb decisions. He regrets it."

"But when is he going to say that to *me*? Buying ten croissants at Haverfest isn't the answer. He has to say it...*to my face.*"

She pursued her lips again. "You heard about the croissants?"

"I was under the table."

Dakota rolled her eyes. "Dammit, Jess. You could try too, you know."

"How do I when the last words he spoke to me were 'I never want to see you again. You are no daughter of mine.'"

Her chest squeezed tight, like firm hands around a soft fruit. She sucked in shallow breaths but couldn't get enough oxygen. She bent over, holding her chest.

"Jess, sissy, oh my god—"

Dakota bolted out of her seat, reaching around the counter and snatching a white paper bag. She flicked it open and placed it over Jess's mouth, then reached for her hands and helped her to hold it steady as Jess kept trying to suck in air.

"I'm here, I'm here," Dakota reassured, rubbing a circle on Jess's thighs.

Jess finally got control of her breathing. She sat back and tossed the bag to the floor.

"Jess, how often does that happen?"

"Probably too often," she admitted.

Dakota was still on her knees in front of Jess. She should have helped her sister up, but she felt boneless after her panic attack. *A panic attack.* Even thinking about the fact that she had one didn't seem real.

The bell on the door chimed. "Everything okay in here—?"

Kevin noticed the paper bag on the floor, the way Dakota was kneeling before Jess, then ran over to them. "Did it happen again?"

Dakota's eyes widened. "Ye—yeah."

Kevin brushed a palm on Jess's cheek. "Are you okay?"

The warmth of his hand felt like a nostalgic comfort after days of not being touched by him. Ever since coming back from Vermont, Kevin had kept his distance. He didn't touch her wrist when she gave him his daily kanelbullar or put his hands on her shoulders when they talked or give her a hug at the end of the day. She knew it was his way of guarding his own heart, and she hated how selfish she felt for wishing he would stop enforcing those boundaries. Especially now that she couldn't deny the feelings that were taking root inside of her.

She leaned her cheek into his palm. "I'll be okay."

At some point Calvin entered the shop and helped Dakota up from the ground, but Kevin kept his hand on her.

He brushed it down her face and cupped the back of her neck.

"I'll—uh, I'll just go then," Dakota said. She reached for the invitation on the table. "I'm sorry for putting this on you."

"Leave it."

Dakota looked up at her sister with big, elephant-sized tears in her eyes.

"I'll think about it," Jess croaked.

Dakota's bottom lip quivered. "Th-thank you."

Calvin offered to walk her out, keeping a steady hand on her back as he guided her outside. Jess glanced out the window and watched as Jasper hopped out of the truck and ran for Dakota, his face full of concern and, from the looks of it, anger. She tore her gaze away before Jasper could notice her. She knew who that anger was meant for.

Kevin crouched down and tugged on Jess's neck, forcing her to look at him. "Jess, what do you need?"

What did she need? She needed to scream, maybe throw the plate and the half-eaten hand pie across the room. She needed to blast her music in the car and sing at the top of her lungs until her voice went so hoarse she wouldn't be able to make a sound for days. She needed to get her hands in dough and knead the emotions away, bake until the sweet smell of the shop drowned out her senses. She needed to curl up on her bed with Honey and sleep for a day. Maybe two. Maybe a week.

She needed to feel loved, cherished, adored. She needed to bend down and kiss those lips again, feel his confidence and joy, run her hands through his honey-brown hair.

She jerked out of his hold and stood up. "I need to figure out how we're going to get afternoon customers."

"Jess—"

She didn't stop to hear what he had to say and escaped into the back of the bakery, tying up her apron.

JESS SAT on the couch at the Balls' cottage, Honey snoozing by her feet. She had her notebook open in front of her as she furiously took notes, doodles of pastry concepts and potential recipes covering the pages. Nothing she put together seemed to click, nothing seemed to be enough to keep the crowds coming. How could you compete with places like Pop's Seafood or Penny's Pizzeria or Seabreeze Café during the lunch hour? Sandwiches on leftover croissants did sound like a solution for lunches, but Grampy's already sold grinders during the afternoons and the last thing she wanted to do was seem like a copycat *again*. She needed something fresh. Something these businesses weren't already doing.

She heard the spinning of bike wheels and the click of pedals as someone approached the cottage. Loud footsteps climbed the stairs, then Kevin was standing outside the door. He had on that soft sweatshirt he wore when they went camping, paired with his signature board shorts and sandals.

Her heart skipped at the sight of him. She cursed to herself as she moved, squashing those feelings deep down back into her belly until they practically disappeared.

She opened the door. "Yes?"

"Jessica, hello, it's a lovely evening."

She squinted her eyes. "Why are you here?"

"For number seven on your list."

She felt her face go warm. *Which one was number*

seven? There's no way he would be bold enough to offer a hookup, especially after throwing everything on "the table."

He gave her a beguiled smile and ticked his head toward the ocean. "It's the one where we get butt naked and dive into the Long Island Sound."

Her face felt much warmer now—scalding, actually. "You don't have to join me for that one. It would be...weird."

"We're adults, we can handle it," he said with a wink. "Come on, grab a towel and let's go."

She didn't move an inch.

He groaned. "Jess, come on. I know things are stressful right now, but I also think this will set you at ease."

She charged back into the cottage, Kevin close at her heels. "I can't think about anything else but the bakery right now, Kevin. We need a solution, and *fast*. How are we going to bring in afternoon customers? What else can we be doing? What am I not seeing here?"

He sighed. "I actually have an idea."

Her brow raised. "You do?"

"But I'm only going to tell you if you follow me outside and take off your clothes."

She covered her face in her hands, mumbling *insufferable* to herself a few times.

He must have picked up on what she said as he chuckled in response. He walked to the hallway closet and snatched a towel, then assertively walked out, as if he expected her to follow. She did.

She walked behind him down the windy road and to Scallop Shell Beach. The night was too cold for lingering late-night beachgoers, so it was only the two of them standing on the sand, looking out at the black waves that softly rippled a couple of feet in front of them.

She glared at him. "All right, Perkins, strip."

"So bossy," he teased. He peeled off his sweatshirt, and Jess couldn't help but sneak a glance. Even in the darkness she could see the outline of his toned abs. She wanted to dip her pinky down the crevices at his hips.

"Jessica, if you get a peek, I get a peek. It's only fair."

She whipped her head back toward the ocean. "No peeking."

"Not even *one?*"

Without looking in his direction, she reached over and grabbed his arm, squeezing his tricep as she shoved him hard. He laughed, feigning a fall as she peeled off her T-shirt. She quicked a look at him and noticed he *was* peeking, his cheeks pink as his eyes grazed over the lace of her bralette at her shoulders.

"KEVIN."

"Sorry, *sorry!*"

"I thought you said we could be adults about this!"

"We can! Okay, we both got a peek. Now, no looking."

She unzipped her shorts and dropped them to the sand, and before she could lose her nerve, she removed her bralette and her underwear. Her skin felt ice cold, but the back of her neck felt like someone set it on fire.

Kevin also paused, the two of them standing there completely naked, looking straight ahead.

"On the count of three," he started. "One, two—"

She ran and didn't wait for three, listening to his howling laughter as he chased after her. She held up her arms and dived into the ocean. Her body sliced into the sea as her hands brushed against strands of seaweed, the taste of briny seawater on her lips.

Everything about being in the ocean felt right to her. She thought back to the last time she actually *dived* into the ocean, and realized it was when the Scoopers jumped the thirty feet off Sunset Rock to celebrate Rory, Melanie, and Tyler's graduation. She'd been so busy she almost forgot that the sea was even *here*, so close to the cottage around the corner. Coming back to the waves was like coming home, and as her head broke the surface and she breathed in the salty, sea air, she realized she wouldn't want to be anywhere else. Even if her adventurous soul wanted to camp in forests or go to grungy rock concerts, her heart belonged here. And to her surprise, the thought didn't scare her. It left her with this deep feeling of fulfillment—something she had yet to feel in her twenty-three years of life.

Kevin's head popped out of the water a few feet away from her. He pushed his long hair back with his hand, his tattooed torso bobbing in the water. "This is probably the most exhilarated I've felt in my entire life."

"Your life must be pretty boring then," she jested.

"On the contrary, my life is perfect," he said. "I just never realized how much I needed my boys to be free in the ocean."

"Your...boys?"

He winked at her. "My *boys*."

"Oh...oh dear god," she grunted.

He laughed. "Jessica, look at us! We're halfway through the list."

She plunged her head into the water and exhaled, big bubbles coming out of her nose. She came back up for air. "Kevin, I think we should put a pause on the list. We have to focus."

"No can do, sweetheart," he said. "We finish the list by Labor Day. That's the rule."

"How in the world are we going to—"

He held up a hand to stop her. "Jess, I've already come up with solutions. Are you ready to hear them?"

She frowned. "Fine."

"Next weekend I have a plan to tackle the rest of the list. Give me twenty-four hours, and it will be over."

She furrowed her brow. "How?"

"You're just going to have to trust me, sweetheart."

She huffed. "Whatever. What's the second thing?"

"You should serve your focaccia at lunchtime."

She drifted in the ocean for a beat, thinking it through. "The focaccia I made you?"

"Yes, not only with tomatoes—although that one will probably always be my favorite. You could also experiment with different flavor combos. Sell big fat slices, maybe have batches of fancy flavored iced tea and lemonade."

"That's actually not a bad idea."

He grinned. "I told you I have good ideas sometimes."

"Few and far between."

"But when I *do* have them, they are epic, right?"

She rolled her eyes, but conceded. "Okay, yeah, you're right."

He gave her a wolfish smile. "Now should we talk about the fact that you gave me a clear shot of your ass by running to the water early?"

She dipped her mouth into the salty water so he couldn't see the grin on her face. She didn't want to admit to him that she may or may not have done that on purpose.

Chapter Sixteen

"Kevin, I swear, if you don't tell me where we're going, I'm turning this car around and we are going back home."

He sat in the passenger seat, fiddling on his phone. "You're going to love it, trust me. Keep driving."

She sped the car along the highway heading west, with absolutely no idea what their destination was. He told her to get in the car after a surprisingly busy day at the shop— the townies flooded Port Wheels after a local foodie influencer featured the new focaccia on her page—and they were now heading off to god knew where. She'd been driving for twenty minutes now, with still no idea when the end was in sight.

"You know, I think at this point, I'm okay with getting fired," she said. "I mean, I don't think you'll actually do it since I'm single-handedly saving your business—"

His laugh sounded like a squawking bird.

"—but I'm willing to take my chances."

He looked up from his phone. "Pull off at the next exit."

She grumbled but did as she was told, following the exit

and the rest of the directions he gave her, until they pulled into a train station.

Jess parked and stared up at the train tracks, flabbergasted. "Where are we going?"

"Oh my god, can you really not handle surprises?" He picked up the flat brim hat balancing on his knee, then tucked his hair and placed it backward on his head. The way his wavy hair curled around his ears and trailed down his neck made her want to reach over and *tug*.

She frowned—half at him, half at that warm feeling simmering in her gut. "It's like you don't know me or something."

Kevin rolled his eyes, a grin still painted on his face. "Sweetheart, look at the sign on the platform, where does it say the train is going?"

She looked where he pointed and watched the flashing electronic sign hanging above the track.

Grand Central Station, Boarding in 15 Minutes.

She gasped. "New York?"

"If we're going to a grungy underground concert, we might as well do it right, yeah?"

She slowly turned to face him. "Y-yeah."

He opened the passenger door. "Let's go."

Two hours later, they stepped off the train and into Grand Central. Jess paused when they hit the main terminal, eyes glazing over the turquoise ceiling covered in gold constellations. The station buzzed as people swerved in and out, dancing around each other as they entered and exited trains. The constant movement made her feel frazzled, and on instinct, she grabbed Kevin's hand.

He squeezed. "Are you all good?"

"Overwhelmed," she breathed. "But—a good over-whelmed."

"I've got you, sweetheart, don't worry."

She looked over at him, his eyes also on the ceiling, duffel bag slung across his shoulder. The motion made her realize a very, very big problem. "Kevin, you didn't tell me we're staying the night! I don't have any clothes!"

He smirked. "Don't worry, I've got a plan."

"And what's that?"

"You'll see. We're staying at a hotel near the station, but we won't have time to check in. Our first thing closes soon, so we need to go straight there."

He tugged her arm, keeping his grip firm around her hand as they weaved through the station and out onto 42nd Street. A melody of honking horns filled the air as flashes of yellow cabs zipped by, the setting sun casting glimmering hues on street signs and sleek buildings.

Jess kept close to Kevin, their hands still clasped, as he followed him block after block down Park Avenue. He turned right when they hit Madison Square Park, and after another few blocks, be paused in front of a distressed wood door, a rugged brown awning overhead that read *Thrifty City*.

Before she could comment he pulled her inside, down a flight of stairs, and through an archway that opened up to reveal a massive basement. The space looked like it spanned an entire city block and was lined with racks upon racks of clothes.

She stood there flabbergasted as Kevin unzipped his bag and handed her a second folded duffel. "Everything here is five dollars or less. The place closes at nine, so that gives us two hours to find you—"

"The perfect pair of jeans," she finished for him.

"Exactly. And a few other things, you know, to replace those high school tank tops you say you don't care for. Maybe you'll even find something fun to wear to a concert."

She looked up at him. He *remembered*. Even if it was a small comment about a tank top she didn't care about, he remembered it and found a place where she could do a complete wardrobe overhaul. One that even fit her budget. "Th-thank you."

He smiled that perfect golden boy smile. Under the flickering fluorescent basement lights, he still glowed. He walked backward as he made his way down the racks. "Come on, sweetheart. Let's find you a pair of jeans that perfectly accentuate that amazing round ass I now know you have."

She rolled her eyes and followed him farther into the thrift shop, then they got to digging.

THEY RODE the elevator up the 18th floor of their hotel, duffel bags stuffed with Jess's new wardrobe. They'd found soft cotton T-shirts and comfy oversized sweaters and dressier tank tops and linen shorts that actually made her feel like an adult—a far cry from the distressed cut-offs of her high school days. She even bought new chunky sandals and Boston clogs that made her squeal with delight, a small pleather crescent bag, and of course, the *perfect* pair of jeans. Light wash, no rips, straight leg that cut right below her ankle, stretchy enough around her curves, the denim at her hips no longer cutting into her skin.

The entire haul made her feel giddy. "I forgot how much of a rush shopping can be."

The elevator dinged as the door opened. She followed Kevin down the hall.

"And all for under fifty bucks! It's like your dream come true."

"You have *no* idea."

Kevin tapped the key on the door of their room, and it finally dawned on her. Panic rose in her chest. "Wait, we're sharing a room?"

"Figured paying for two wasn't in the budget?"

Damn, he's right, she thought to herself. If he'd gotten two rooms she would have definitely given him shit for being so frivolous. But...*still.*

She followed him in, then exhaled. The space was small, but it was big enough to squeeze in two queen-sized beds.

"You got two beds."

Kevin placed his hands on his hips, looking vexed—but in his usual, playful way. "Did you really think I wouldn't? You're so *adamant*!"

She smirked. "Come on, admit it, sleeping in your own bed is really nice."

He grumbled something she couldn't quite catch as he plopped his duffel bag on the bed and unzipped. "The concert is at ten. I was thinking we could grab a dollar slice somewhere on the way?"

She plopped her own bag on her bed, rummaging through her goodies, that giddiness bubbling up in her chest again. "I have so many options now. This is awesome."

"Your ass deserves to be in those jeans tonight."

"Which ones? I found four pairs."

His head dipped, his pupils dilated. "You know which ones."

She smirked, pulling them from the bag. "Pizza sounds great. Give me five minutes to get changed."

Jess kept close at Kevin's heels as they walked up to a crowded dive bar, booming music flooding through the open floor-to-ceiling windows. Patrons poured out the bar holding plastic cups of foamy beer.

After a bouncer checked her ID and stamped her hand, Kevin snatched it and pulled her in, keeping his grip firm as they snaked their way through the crowd and close to the stage. He didn't let the small clusters of people stop him as he pushed his way forward until they made it to the front, then pulled her to the stage and stood behind her, like a guard.

"We don't have to be *in the front,* you know," she teased. "I wasn't even expecting to see the stage."

"Oh trust me, we need to be in the front," he quipped. "Is the vibe good? Floor sticky enough for you?"

She lifted her new chunky sandals, delicate straps buckled around her ankles. It was certainly sticky, and it made her grin. "Vibes are immaculate."

The lights dimmed and the crowd screamed. Jess cheered along with them, even though she had no idea who was about to hop on stage. When the band stepped up the screaming grew louder, her ears ringing and popping from the sound. But when she saw the singer with hot-pink hair approach the microphone, everything in her vision felt like it slowed, the cheering and the screeching from the amps dulling.

"Kevin..."

The singer with hot-pink hair snatched the microphone. "NEW YORK, MAKE SOME NOISE!"

More screaming. Jess watched in awe as the bassist fiddled with the amp, the drummer trilled the bass pedal, and the guitarist held up rock signs to the crowd.

"We're Definitely Maybe, and you're going to need a drink in your hand for this one."

The guitar started to tick as the lead singer unhooked the microphone from the stand and began to sing. The bass dropped, the drums cracked, and the band rolled into the first chorus of "You + Me." Jess didn't stop the tears that flowed down her cheeks as she watched her favorite band perform live. She turned to face Kevin behind her, his eyes on the band, his arms in the air.

He was singing along. He knew every single word.

THE BAND ROLLED through all of her favorite songs, and she sang along without abandon, not caring if her ears would be ringing for days after standing so close to the speaker, or if her voice was hoarse from singing the lyrics she knew so well—the songs that'd brought her back to life. Full of hope for people like her; who felt dark, lonely, anxious, disappointed, abandoned. The entire moment was magical, and she never wanted it to end.

After the band thanked the audience and promised one more song with a wink from the singer, they rolled into the one that the entire crowd seemed to know by heart. Fans jumped and threw arms in the air as the band tipped over into their final number for the evening.

A small mosh pit formed at the center of the bar, crushing fans aside as they pushed and danced. One fan lifted his hand in the air to protect the plastic cup of beer in his fist. But another shove had him stumbling back, his beer sloshing and tipping as he headed right for Jess.

Kevin jumped between them, shielding her in his arms, and hunched. Jess peered up and watched in horror as the entire beer slipped out of the fan's hands, pouring over Kevin's hair and pooling down his back. Her body tensed as she watched him wince at the cold liquid, but then he beamed, a wide full-mouth grin of delight, his eyes squeezed shut.

"Oh my god, man, I am so sorry," the guy said, the plastic cup crushing beneath his sneaker as he stepped up to Kevin.

Kevin brushed his beer-soaked hair back and peeled an eye open, a smile still brushing his lips. "As long as you didn't get any on my girl and her perfect jeans, you're all good."

Instead of feeling irritated like usual, Jess's cheeks bloomed with pink at being called *my girl*. She took a step back, examining her jeans, her sandals, and her new white sleeveless bodysuit. Miraculously, she was dry. No splotches of beer in sight.

The guy exhaled in relief as the song petered out, the band wrapping up for the night. "Can I buy you both a drink to make up for it?"

"Dude, you lost your entire beer. I should buy *you* a drink," Kevin joked.

"That's ridiculous, no. What are you drinking?"

Kevin eyed Jess, brow cocked.

"Tequila soda with a lime, please," she answered.

He smirked and looked over at the bar. "I'll take something on tap. Mind if I go up there with you?"

"Not at all."

Kevin looked in her direction, and held up his thumb. "You okay here?"

She nodded, watching Kevin as he weaved through the crowd, joking with his new friend. Only Kevin would have an entire beer poured on him and find himself laughing with the culprit. It's like he never got angry at anything; he always found the good in people, and made everyone happier and brighter around him. Even herself. Even when she was at her lowest point in life, he bottled sunshine and handed it to her in the shape of a snarky joke, a compliment, a subtle praise.

She smiled to herself as she leaned against the front railing, watching the band exit, the stage hands already cleaning up the equipment. Music blared through the speakers as the lights brightened, the sweet ringing in her ears reminding her of how amazing all of it was.

"Here alone?"

Jess looked up to find a tall man next to her, wearing an all-black ensemble—T-shirt, tight jeans, and a pair of black suede boots that felt impractical for the muggy August evening in the city. He leaned against the railing, his arm brushing against hers.

"Um, no, my friend went to get a drink at the bar."

"Friend or...?"

Her face felt hot, her hands clammy. "Friend."

His smirk was heart melting and beautiful, his straight jaw and five-o'clock shadow the kind you wanted to trace with your hands. "Can I buy you a drink then?"

"Tequila soda with lime, sweetheart," Kevin said,

thrusting a plastic cup in her direction. She watched as he paused, looking back and forth between Jess and tall, dark, and handsome. He froze.

She took her cup from Kevin's hand, her fingers brushing his slightly. "Thank you."

Handsome pushed off the railing, his height towering over Kevin by at least half a foot, maybe more. "If you want another, come find me."

She watched him step away, a little dazed at being hit on for the first time in, well, *ever*. He was everything a girl could dream of, and yet...even if his looks made her insides melt, she wasn't interested in more than a lingering look. Not in the slightest.

Kevin shuffled around her and lowered down into the bar seat next to him, resting his head back on the poster-covered wall as he took a sip of his beer. "You still have number eight, you know."

Jess took a sip of her drink as well, shifting on her feet. "Not like this."

He squinted his eyes. "What do you mean *not like this*? That was the perfect setup, Jess. You're in a city where no one knows you. You could have your pick."

She scanned the crowd with a slow turn, her heart sinking lower and lower. He was right; she could do it if she really wanted to. She could pull tall, dark, and handsome into a corner and have her way with him, and Kevin would let her do it. To make her happy. To give her what she deserved.

But it wasn't what *he* deserved, and deep in her gut, she knew this wouldn't make her happy. It would leave her feeling hollow.

There was really only one person who left her feeling whole.

She finished her circle and faced him, his hair slicked back and sticky from the beer. He placed his beer down on the table and threaded his hands, resting them casually in his lap.

Be brave, Jess.

She took a long gulp of her drink and placed it on the table as well, then stepped closer to him, right between his legs. She brushed her index finger down his neck, trailing his tattoo along his collarbone and down the opening of his button-down short-sleeve, following the ivy until it hit the center of his chest. She pinched the first button and flicked it open. "I've made my choice."

He hummed, his hands still loose in his lap, not giving in to her touch. "Jess, I told you, I can't practice with you. It...it would destroy me."

"Maybe it's not practice," she whispered.

He let out a guttural sound as he leaned his head back again, slamming his eyes shut. "Sweetheart...please."

"Please what?"

"Please don't do this unless you're absolutely sure you're ready."

She played with the next button of his shirt, tucking it in and out of its hole. She let out a shaky breath. "I can't give you what you want," she admitted. "I'm not sure when I'll be ready for a big commitment. This...this is all I can give you right now."

Her stomach twisted after she said it. She knew she was hurting him, and she hated herself for it. But she needed to be honest. She wasn't sure what the "right" steps were after breaking off a nine-year relationship. But there was one thing she *did* know, and it was a step she was ready to take.

"I want you," she breathed. "More than anything I think I've ever wanted in my life."

He looked at her, his eyes dark and intense, his pupils dilating like they did when he saw her in those jeans at the thrift shop...when he spoke about them in the hotel room. She wanted to know how big they would get if he saw her fully naked. Her toes curled at the thought.

She released her hold on his shirt and took another sip of her drink. She broke her gaze from his and tucked a strand of her hair behind her ear, then slowly trailed her fingertips down the deep V of her bodysuit, landing at the tip right above her navel.

"Oh for fuck's sake."

She yelped as he gripped the belt loops of her jeans and pulled her in closer with a forceful yank. He curled his hands around her hips, his palms roaming down to the curve of her ass.

She bit her lip as she pressed her nose against his. "Maybe you're the one who needs to watch your mouth."

He slithered a hand around her neck and cupped the back of her head. "I don't think you'll be saying that after tonight."

Then he crushed his lips against hers. She dipped her tongue in his mouth and tasted him, sweet and tangy from the beer. He groaned and slipped a hand down her spine, tucking it in the back pocket of her jeans. She ran her fingers through his sticky hair and pulled. He chuckled into her mouth as they broke apart.

He gently traced her jaw and pinched her chin, then rubbed his thumb against her lips. "Tell me when it's too much, sweetheart. I don't want to do anything you don't want."

She nuzzled in closer and wrapped her arms around his shoulders. "I want everything," she breathed.

They couldn't get out of there fast enough.

Chapter Seventeen

THEY FAILED three times to hail a cab, distracted by their hands and mouths and teeth. Eventually the bouncer cursed and hailed one for them, opening the cab door and pleading for them to *please take that somewhere else.*

Kevin pulled Jess into the cab by her waist, telling the driver the address of the hotel before pressing his mouth back to hers, extracting soft moans from her lips like they were candy.

The cabbie chuckled. "Looks like someone is having a good night."

Kevin grinned wildly. "The best night of my life, actually!"

Jess licked down his neck and sucked on his tattoo.

He mewled. "Jessica, you're killing me."

Her lips curled into a smile. She nipped on his ear. "Good."

The cab pulled up to the hotel moments later, and after an elevator ride where they miraculously remained clothed, they were at the front door of their room. Kevin pressed her up against it and sucked on her bottom lip as he reached into the back pocket of his jeans for the key.

"Are you on the pill?" he mumbled. "If not, I need to go to the store..."

She smirked wickedly at him. "Why, thought you wouldn't get lucky?"

"Never in my wildest dreams did I think I would get *this* lucky."

She rolled her eyes, a smile still on her lips. "Yes, I'm on the pill."

He unlocked the door with a tap and a soft click. He cradled her waist and guided her deeper into their room, his kisses wild and hungry. "I've thought about this so, so much."

"And is it everything you imagined?"

"My imagination didn't even scratch the surface."

Jess rocked to her tiptoes and ran a hand through his hair again, wanting to tug it, like *she* always imagined. But her fingertips got caught in knots, his hair unruly and sticky from the beer.

She pulled back and loosened her grip, watching his cheeks flush.

"Maybe I should take a quick shower first," he whispered.

Her back straightened. She planted her feet back on the carpet. "Yeah, okay sure."

He pushed her to the wall and kissed her neck. "Two minutes. Don't change your mind, okay? This is a good thing."

He stepped back and snatched one of the clean towels, then disappeared into the bathroom.

She sighed and plummeted backward onto one of the

beds, arms stretched wide. *It is a good thing*, she thought. *He is a good thing.*

Jess sat up and began unbuckling her sandals as her phone made a chirpy *ding* next to her. She paused her unbuckling and flipped her phone on the bed to see the screen, then froze.

CHARLIE

> Jessie, I can't do this anymore. This is too hard. I need you.

A chill rippled down her spine as she stared at Charlie's name at the top of the thread. It was her first time hearing from him since she walked out. She couldn't help feeling disappointed that he'd never stopped in at the bakery, didn't try to show face or text her congratulations or *something*. But she also wasn't surprised. Charlie didn't think much beyond himself and his needs. She learned that long ago, when he left for college and stopped by to see her only when it was convenient for him.

"Everything okay?"

Jess looked up at Kevin. His face was twisted with concern, probably at whatever shocked look was currently on her own. She scanned his face, her eyes landing on a lock of wavy wet hair curling at the center of his forehead, tiny droplets trickling down his nose.

"Y-yes," she lied, her voice cracking. "All good."

He brushed a hand under her chin, guiding her gaze to those hazel eyes. "Did you change your mind?"

The Jess before would have said *yes*, would have never put herself in this position in the first place. She would have run to Charlie, given him what he needed, sacrificed for him...then sacrificed some more. Because it's what you did in a relationship. You gave yourself up for another.

But this Jess was different. A little selfish. New. *Brave.*

She silenced her phone and tossed it to the other bed, then tugged on the towel at his waist, letting it fall to the floor. "No," she purred. "Like you said...this is a good thing."

Kevin removed her clothes at the speed of light, his hands roaming her body and his mouth tasting her like she was the dessert he'd been craving. When he was done ravishing her, her body quivering with desire, they finally came together. And *oh my*, Jess thought. *This is, in fact, a very, very good thing.*

IT WAS FAR TOO late to be up; Jess was used to early nights and early mornings now that she ran her own bakery. But a single time with Kevin didn't quell the deep hunger she had for him. So they kept thoroughly exploring one another with their hands and their mouths.

Jess lay in bed, lazy and content, her hand splayed on his chest. She kissed the tip of an ivy leaf on Kevin's pec and rested her chin there. "Tell me about your tattoo."

He twirled a piece of her hair with his fingers. "It's a reminder that home isn't just a place, that I can find it anywhere. As long as I'm brave enough to seek it."

She smiled. "Your mom taught you a lot about bravery."

"She gave me the confidence to say what I feel. To allow myself to be soft when the rest of the world tells me I need to be hard."

She traced a finger up the vines to his neck. "I like that. I like her."

"I like *you.*"

Her chest expanded with joy. "I think I might like you, too."

He grinned and pulled her closer, skin to skin. "Looks like someone is learning how to be brave, too."

"Trying to be," she whispered, a soft confession only for him. He was the only person she felt like she could be brave with.

He planted a soft kiss on her temple.

She hummed. "Okay I'm exhausted. Get out of my bed."

"*Dammit!*"

She smirked. "Thought you could change my mind with your hot body and naughty mouth?"

"Told you I wouldn't need to watch it." He smirked, nuzzling his nose in her neck.

She wiggled her toes, a smile on her lips thinking about *his mouth.*

He looked at her with puppy-dog eyes. "Please don't make me get into a cold bed."

She sat up and gave him a playful little wave.

"You suck," he grumbled, throwing his legs over the edge. He tore the duvet off the other bed and climbed in.

"I certainly did."

He choked at her comment, then turned off the light.

JESS BLINKED her eyes open the next morning, listening to the sounds of rumbling trucks and distant honking horns and sirens. She rolled over and glanced at Kevin, who was starfished on the bed—legs and arms wide, head turned to the side, smiling in his sleep. She snickered and snatched her phone to take a picture of how blissful he looked in that bed *alone*, and made a note to make fun of him later. But when she tapped her screen, her heart sank. Three missed calls and another text.

CHARLIE

Please call me. Let's talk about this. I want to make it work. I'll do anything, Jessie.

Her chest tightened as she thought about Charlie, probably all alone in Garrison in a new apartment doing whatever fancy new job his father lined up for him. His family was probably *thrilled* that Jess was no longer in the picture, but she realized then that she hadn't put a ton of thought into how Charlie was doing. That maybe it wasn't all on him to reach out; she was just as guilty for not checking in on him.

She waited for the guilt to come, waited for that gnawing feeling of doubt about leaving him and starting a bakery and hooking up with someone else. But that feeling never came; she still felt content in her choices. She still felt content after taking Kevin up on his offer and leaving Charlie behind.

Then her mind reeled back. *She hooked up with someone else.* It felt monumental for her, a huge new step into claiming her life again.

Except if she was being honest with herself, being with Kevin didn't feel like a hookup. It felt like joy. It felt like comfort. It felt like that first bite of a sugary pastry or slicing into freshly baked bread. He made her feel elated, excited, inspired. He made her feel seen. He made her feel—

Movement from the other bed pulled Jess from her thoughts. She peeked over her phone screen and watched as

Kevin stretched with a big, satisfied yawn, then relaxed again in the bed, hands perched under his head.

She smiled and placed her phone down, then rolled out of her bed and peeled back the cover of his. She crawled in and swung a leg across his torso, kissed up his neck to his ear. "Good morning," she whispered.

Kevin's smile grew bigger at the sound of her voice. He traced lazy hands to her hips, then in one swift movement he tightened his hold and flipped her over so he was on top of her, making her squeal. He brushed the hair away from her face. "Good morning, my dear Jessica."

She shook her head, willingly let the smile bloom on her face. "Can't you think of a new nickname?"

"*Never.*"

She rolled her eyes. "I feel like I need a nickname for you, then."

"I like when you call me Kev," he admitted, kissing her cheek. He brushed a hand up her side, goose flesh dotting her skin from the feel of his fingers on her.

"Not Kevvy Bear?"

"*Stop that.*"

She grinned. "Kev doesn't have the same ring to it, though."

"Fine, then you can call me *daddy*."

"Anddddd you took it too far."

He cackled, sliding his body next to hers and curling his arm around her waist. "As much as I would love to fully explore the fact that you crawled into my bed without clothes on, we do have things to do this morning..."

She pouted. "But those things aren't as fun."

He smiled, kissing her neck. "Then I guess if you would rather stay here instead of getting a New York bagel then learning how to make egg tarts at a culinary school—"

She ripped off the blanket and jumped out of bed.

Kevin chuckled. "Yeah, that's what I thought."

AFTER DEMOLISHING bagels with lox and large cups of coffee, Jess followed Kevin as they ventured through the subway down to the financial district.

He held her hand the entire time.

They walked through the doors of Brookfield Place and up the stairs, leading to the entrance of the Institute of Culinary Education. Her mouth dropped open as Kevin showed the concierge the tickets on his phone, and they were led over to a set of elevators.

He curled a hand around her waist and kissed the top of her head. "Is touching you like this okay?" he whispered.

"Why wouldn't it be?"

"Because I wasn't sure how far we were taking this whole hookup game."

She looked into his eyes. "Who said it was a game?"

The elevator dinged and the doors flew open. Jess stepped out of his grasp with a smirk, watching the way Kevin rubbed his neck and dipped his head low to hide his smile.

A student near the door pointed them to their classroom. Jess snatched Kevin's hand and pulled hard as they stepped into the industrial kitchen.

The instructor stood by the door with a big smile. "Welcome to the Institute of Culinary Education! Please take a folder and an apron and find an open seat."

Jess froze when she looked down at the aprons. "Oh."

She felt Kevin place a hand on her shoulder, his lips grazing her ear. "Don't worry, sweetheart, I didn't forget."

She turned to him and looked down at a familiar denim apron in his hand.

Jess grinned, and without thinking about who was watching or what they thought, she got on her tiptoes and kissed him on the lips. "You know me so well."

He blushed as he unfolded her apron and placed it over her head.

THE TWO WALKED side by side in the early afternoon sun hours later. Jess took a bite of the Portuguese egg tart in her hand, the other wrapped around Kevin's waist. His arm was slung around her shoulders, and he was holding a paper bag with their leftover pastries from class. She held up the pastry to his mouth and he took the last flaky bite, licking her fingers and humming in approval.

"Think you'll want to sell pasteis de nata at the bakery?" he asked.

"Maybe, we'll see," she said. "This feels like a treat that would be great for fall or winter. I have more things I want to do with fruit before they're out of season."

"Like what?"

"Peach streusel muffins, triple berry crisp, lemon tartlets—"

"I love it when you talk pastry to me."

She bumped his hip. "Where are you taking me now?"

"Lunch. There's this place in Little Italy that apparently sells the best meatballs in the city, but there might be a line...if you don't mind getting back home a little later."

She leaned her cheek on his shoulder as they came to a stop at an intersection, waiting to walk across the street. "I don't mind."

Kevin stepped aside from the bustling city goers and slipped a hand behind her neck. He pulled her close, brushing his nose against hers. His thumb traced behind her ear and down her neck. She sighed and hooked a finger through the belt loop of his jeans, pulling his body closer.

"I'm usually not one to crave physical touch, but I missed this," she admitted. "I missed your hands."

"I missed touching you," he whispered back, pressing his forehead against hers. "Can I touch you like this when we get home?"

She looked into his eyes. Her head screamed *no*, running through the ticker tape of all the reasons why she shouldn't allow this. She finally felt independent, making decisions for *herself* and no one else. She had a bakery to run and a dog to take care of and a car to repair and money to save so she could eventually get her own place. For the first time in nine years, she felt free.

And yet...her heart was telling her *yes*. To take hold of what felt good, to be with a person who made her feel alive.

"Yes," she exhaled. "Yes, I want that."

He grinned as he leaned all the way in, then pressed the most precious kiss to her lips. This kiss wasn't desperate with want like last night, but slow. Caring. Patient. Lovely.

He pulled back, planting soft kisses on her lips before wrapping her up in a hug, resting his chin on the top of her head.

She glanced at their hotel up the block. "Do you want me to send you some money for the room?"

"Nah, sweetheart, I got it."

She hesitated, then took a step back. "You know, I am curious. How *did* you afford this trip?"

He shrugged. "Don't worry about it, I have it under control."

Jess bristled. "I don't like that answer. You promised no secrets."

Kevin lifted his brows, then put his hands on his hips. "Okay well, if you must know, I put it on my credit card."

She felt the world slow around her at the sounds of those three very, *very* familiar words. *My credit card.* Suddenly everything around her was spinning—the hot dog cart and the dog walker with ten different leashes and the yellow cabs. Her body tilted to the side. She felt like she was going to faint.

"Whoa whoa whoa," Kevin said. He grabbed her elbow and held her steady. "Jess, breathe. In and out."

She did. In and out. In and out. But the dizziness didn't go away, the crushing feeling in her chest tightening.

He squeezed her elbow. "What's wrong? Talk to me."

"Do you have the money? Can you afford this right now, or are you going into debt?"

Kevin puckered his lips, then frowned.

She scoffed, stepping out of his reach. "You broke *both* of your promises to me. You said no more debt."

"Jess, it isn't that much! I will be able to pay it off in a few months."

"A few *months?*" She was reeling. Was this really happening all over again?

"I don't understand why you're upset about how I handle my money."

"He did this all the time," she admitted in a rush. "*All the time.* He didn't worry about money or savings and charged his card, never worried about where the money would come from or who would pay. Never thought about how much I was struggling to keep up with it all."

"I am not Charlie. And it's not fair for you to compare me to him."

"But it *is* fair for me to consider all of this if I'm going to get involved with someone," she spat, the sound of her voice causing tourists to turn their heads. "I can't be with someone who is financially irresponsible again."

"*Irresponsible?*"

"You know what, I'm not hungry," she said in a huff. She turned and started up the street toward their hotel. "Let's get our bags and go home."

"You can't walk away from this conversation, Jess. We need to talk this out."

She flicked her hand. "No need, I already made my decision."

They didn't look at each other for the remainder of the day, from the train ride back to Connecticut and the car ride to Haverport. He didn't even say goodbye as he got out of the car when she dropped him at his apartment, the slam of the door the only sound shared between them.

Chapter Eighteen

"ARE you going to tell me what happened between the two of you, or are you planning on moping the rest of the shift?"

Jess flicked Calvin off, bending over the ice cream cake in front of her with a bag of sky-blue frosting. "I'm not moping."

"You're certainly moodier than usual, and that's saying something," he quipped, taking a seat at the desk as he counted out the stack of bills in front of him. "I'm assuming based on how he's acting that whatever happened was *bad*."

She stiffened, the bag of frosting in her hands hovering over the last dollop she just made. "How's he acting?"

"Like it's the end of the world."

She rolled her eyes and returned to piping. "That's dramatic."

"I've never seen him like this, Jess."

She didn't answer him at first as she finished off the line of frosting, then slid the ice cream cake in the box and sealed it up. She placed it back in the industrial freezer behind her. "He's a grown man. He'll get over it."

"But do you *want* him to get over it?"

She huffed and placed her hands on her hips. "For someone who can be such a hard ass, you really are nosy when it comes to people's personal lives."

"Only the people I care about."

Jess tapped her foot, looking down at her sneakers. They were the new pair, or at least new-*ish*, that she found at the thrift store last week. She didn't plan on wearing them to work, but when Calvin asked her last-minute to help him catch up on cake orders, she agreed to pop in after closing the bakery for the night. She breezed past Kevin without a word when he locked up, only briefly glimpsing back before getting in her car to watch him slink around to his apartment and escape inside. He hadn't said a single word to her since their fight. He didn't even bother to look at her.

Desperate to change the subject, Jess cocked her head toward the freezer. "Are you always this behind on cakes?"

Calvin groaned. "Yes. Melanie does her best, but we're not as speedy as you are."

She tapped her finger to her lips. "What if we partnered up somehow? Maybe I could make cakes and a portion goes to Port Wheels?"

Calvin frowned. "Sorry, Jess. I can't. The cakes bring in a significant amount of revenue."

"Eh, well, I tried." She shrugged. "Wish we had something like that to bring in steady business."

"I heard you added focaccia to the menu."

"For the afternoons, yeah." She shifted side to side. "Do you think it's helping?"

He sighed. He placed his elbows on the desk in front of him and steepled his hands at his chin before gazing up at her. "I think it's time to consider finding another financial partner."

Her heart sank down to her belly. She leaned against the back counter for support, squeezing her hands against the edge where the wood and the cool tile met. "Does he know?"

"We talked about it last night."

She blew out a shaky breath. "I feel like I failed him."

"Jess..."

Crossing her arms, she glanced away.

Calvin moved from his seat and slid next to her. He placed a hand on her shoulder and squeezed. "You didn't fail him. You kept that business going for longer than we expected."

"But it wasn't good enough."

"But it *was*. We knew going in that opening a bakery would be challenging. Trying to compete with Grampy's and Seabreeze that have steady, loyal customers wasn't going to be easy. Yet you still brought in business each day. You should feel proud of that."

She said nothing, not returning his gaze.

But he didn't seem to mind as he continued. "Plus, we're not giving up. We're just going to consider some options."

"Why are you so invested in this? What's in it for you?"

"Seeing my friends happy is enough for me." He squeezed her shoulder tight, dropping his voice to a murmur so Blake and Rory wouldn't hear as they scooped cones at the front of the shop. "Will you let yourself be happy? With him?"

"I'm scared, Calvin," she whispered, cracking open the depths of her heart and allowing him to see it for the briefest moment. "I can't go back to the way things were. It was too hard."

"Or maybe things would be different. Maybe being with him would be like nothing you expect."

She exhaled, looking up at the popcorn ceiling above them, tears sliding down her neck and collecting at the collar of her T-shirt. Calvin released his grip, then tapped a knuckle to her elbow. She looked down at the pink napkin in his hand. She mumbled a thank-you and took it, then wiped her face.

"Go home. Thank you for your help," he said. "I'll see you back at the cottage."

She crumpled up the napkin and tossed it to the trash. "You should consider training Rory to make cakes. If she's around she can be another set of hands. She should be doing them anyway, being an artist and all that."

"Can you come in and train her for me?"

Jess agreed, setting a date that worked, then grabbed her bag and left.

Jess pulled into the driveway at the Balls' cottage. A familiar black Lexus was parked on the street. She ripped off the seat belt and stumbled out of the car, locking eyes with a pair of blue irises.

Charlie bolted out of the plastic chair on the porch, making his way down the creaky wooden steps and over to her.

She slammed the car door and stormed up to him. "What in the hell are you doing here?"

"Jessie, please," he begged, reaching a hand out to grab her.

Jess stumbled away from his grasp, squeezing an arm around her stomach. "How'd you know I was living here?"

He dropped his head, staring at his loafers. "Our phones still track each other. I've been watching—"

"That's so fucking creepy," she spat, stepping around him. She seized her phone in her bag and opened the app, deleting him as she made her way to the house.

He followed. "You were in Vermont? *New York?*"

"Again, really fucking creepy."

"I'm sorry, I'm *sorry*—" He bounded up the steps and reached for her again, his hand firm on her arm as he pulled her closer. "Please, can we talk about this?"

"No."

His expression crumbled. "Why not? What did I do to make you upset and leave me?"

"It's what you *didn't* do, Charlie!"

Charlie froze, his eyes wide. "What do you mean?"

She wormed her way out of his grasp, stepping beyond his reach. "You didn't really *try*. You never fought for me when it came to your family. You saw me struggling with money all the time and didn't try to meet me halfway unless I *begged*. You watched me wither away into this shell of myself and didn't give me the opportunity to *live*."

"I thought we had a good life."

"Did you really? For fuck's sake, Charlie, be honest with me. Did you really think I was happy?"

He didn't respond.

"Going to Vermont or New York or *anywhere* besides maybe the Cape once a year would have never been an option," she continued. "Spending your own money was never an option. You relied so much on your father and you were so deeply tangled up in his toxic web to see that I was getting smaller and smaller. I forgot who I was—"

And he helped me remember.

The thought came to her so easily. A memory of Kevin flashed in her mind, the way his hazel eyes sparkled as he made notes on that scrap piece of paper, creating a list of things to do together that would make *her* happy.

We're doing this, he'd told her. *You deserve this.*

She gazed at her past standing in front of her, realizing he would have never done those things for her. Maybe surprise Chinese takeout, or burnt pancakes in the morning, but it was never really about her. With Charlie, it was about his needs. With Kevin, she rarely ever considered his needs. And she'd compared them, as if they were one and the same. When, in reality, Kevin was the opposite. A spark of golden sunshine on a bleak, cloudy day.

"This will never happen again, Charlie," she explained to him, keeping the tone of her voice calm and collected. "We tried, probably giving this more years than we should have. But it's not going to work. We aren't compatible."

Thunder boomed in the distance as Jess swung open the screen door, quickly latching it closed. Honey jumped off the couch where she sat in Gram's lap and ran after her, jumping on her back feet as she pawed at Jess's knees.

Rain came down in sheets. Lightning crackled in the sky. Honey yelped, her hoarse bark drowned out by the rumbling thunder.

"Living without you is so hard. Jess, please. *Please*. Tell me what I need to do." Charlie reached for the door and opened it wide.

"NO! STOP—"

Honey bolted, sprinting around Charlie and down the stairs, disappearing into the inky night.

Jess chased after her, pushing Charlie out of the way as she ran. "HONEY STOP!"

She kept her eyes on her golden fur as Honey ran down the street and to the beach. Lightning ruptured again in the sky, the sound causing Honey to pivot from the sand toward the wall of boulders at the end of the beach, vanishing into a forest of evergreen trees.

"Shit!" Jess screamed. Her hair was plastered to her face. She looked back at the porch and stalled. Charlie stood there in shock, his eyes wide. But he didn't bother to run after her, to help her.

It was enough of a confirmation as any.

She stormed up to the steps, her drenched clothes dripping on the porch as she pointed at his car. "Get out of my sight."

"Jessie—"

"Don't call me that," she demanded. "We are done, Charlie. I'm not going to let you rely on me anymore. Enjoy your life in Garrison. Do not contact me again."

She didn't care to watch him leave as she swung the door wide and snatched her phone from her bag. She dialed a number and hit Call, pressing the phone to her ear. Violent shivers ripped through her as she paced the linoleum floor. Gram was up and at her heels, her eyes full of worry.

He answered on the second ring. "Yes?"

She let out a sob. "Kev, it's Honey. She ran away. Charlie was here and he opened the door and the lightning scared her and she—"

"I'm on my way," he interrupted.

Her shoulders shook as she held a hand up to her mouth. "What if she can't hear us and we can't find her and—"

"We will find our girl, Jessica," he said. "Take a deep breath."

She did as she was told, listening to the sounds of jingling keys on the other end of the line.

"Now another."

She obeyed.

"Go, I'll be there in ten."

She hung up, handing Gram her phone and running back out into the rain. Charlie was already gone, the black Lexus turning the corner as he exited the neighborhood. She hustled down the beach and scrambled up the boulders, standing on the cement dock as she screamed Honey's name over the sound of the wind howling and waves crashing. Nothing. She weaved through the trees and kept shouting, stepping through a clearing that backed onto a curved road. She jogged down the street, swiping at the rain that pelted down on her, unable to see anything clearly.

Clicking from a bike wheel sounded as she rounded the corner back toward the cottage. Kevin dropped his bike in the lawn and ran up to her, his sweatshirt and board shorts sticking to him like a second skin. He stopped a few feet from her, keeping his distance. "Any luck?"

Her bottom lip quivered. She shook her head.

"Tell me exactly where she ran."

Jess motioned for him to follow as they retraced her path, down the beach and toward the boulders, then up into the trees. She followed Kevin as he stepped toward the evergreens, the branches partially shielding them from the rain.

"I already looked here," she shouted as thunder boomed again. "I couldn't find her."

The sound from the thunder faded. Kevin lifted a finger and tapped his ear. "Do you hear that?"

She frowned. "Hear what?"

He pointed to her. "Exactly. It's quieter around the

trees. She hates the noise, so she probably wanted to find somewhere quiet."

They weaved through the trees slowly, turning every corner, looking around every rock. Jess kept sneaking glances at Kevin yards away, his face twisted tightly with worry and determination. He was soaked from the rain, his flip-flops squishing underneath him.

The complete opposite, Jess thought. She hated herself for the words she said to him in New York. She needed to tell him—needed to fix it.

Fifteen minutes later, she saw that face soften with relief. He bent over and scooped up a very wet, shaking Honey. The puppy burrowed into his arm and whimpered.

Jess sobbed as she ran up to them, nuzzling her face in Honey's drenched fur. She peered up at Kevin, noticing he too was openly sobbing, his cheeks crimson, his hair clinging to his forehead and grazing his eyes. She lifted a hand and slicked his hair back on instinct, then brushed her palm against his cheek.

"I'm so sorry," she wept. "I said awful things. You didn't deserve that. You are nothing like him."

His forehead creased as he squeezed his eyes shut. "You're right. I don't deserve it. You keep pushing me away."

She dropped her hand and stepped back, watching as he slowly blinked his eyes open.

Lightning cut across the sky. Honey dug her snout in the crease between his arm and his chest. He gripped her tight as he took a tentative step toward Jess, then paused, reeling back.

"Jess...I've had a crush on you since that day we met in tenth grade biology," Kevin admitted. "But this summer? This summer I fell in love with you. I am so head over heels that it *scares* me. I need you like I need air, and every time we're apart I feel like I'm cleaving myself in two."

He wiped at his tears with his free hand. "I know I don't deserve how you've been treating me, but I can't stop coming to you. I can't seem to control myself. Because I want *you* to be my home, Jess. I want to be wherever you are, always."

She closed the distance between them, balling his wet sweatshirt in her hands and pulling him close. "I don't want to push you away anymore. I want you to be my home, too."

Jess waited patiently and listened to his ragged breathing, feeling the beat of his heart pounding in his chest. Then, in one swift movement, he laced his free arm around her waist and pressed in. He pushed her lips open with his and slipped a tongue in her mouth as he guided her back and pressed her against a tree, the pressure of the bark on her back igniting something deep inside her belly. Her hands roamed down his chest and hugged at his waist. She slipped them inside the back of his sweatshirt and dug her nails into his skin. He moved his hand from her waist and pressed it on her ribcage below her breast, extracting a moan from her mouth the same moment thunder rumbled above them.

Honey squirmed in his other arm from the sound.

Kevin parted his lips from hers, his breathing heavy. "Jess, I don't want to drop her."

She nipped at his lip, sucking on it gently before responding. "Stay the night."

His eyes brightened. "In your bed?"

She nodded. "Yes. Don't go. Please."

He grinned, planting one last lingering kiss before pressing his forehead to hers. "I wouldn't dream of it."

GRAM WELCOMED them back to the cottage with warm towels and cookies. Jess sat down on the floor and bundled Honey up in a towel, patting her dry. She yelped and jumped out of her grasp, shaking violently and scattering water droplets across the floor.

"Well, that's one way to do it," Kevin teased, wiping up the water as Honey tottered over to her fluffy dog bed. She plopped down with a defeated *thump*, then closed her eyes and fell asleep.

Gram yawned as Kevin stepped into the bathroom. "I'm glad you found her."

Jess, still sitting on the floor, squeezed her wet hair with a towel.

Gram leaned down and pressed a soft, wrinkly hand to her cheek. "Do you believe me now?"

Jess frowned. "Believe what?"

"That everything will be okay?"

Kevin opened the bathroom door, his gaze full of longing and love and delicious heat.

She glanced up at Gram and nodded. "Yeah, I believe you now."

Gram patted her cheek then scurried up the stairs, escaping into her room.

Kevin held out his hands to Jess and helped her up, wrapping her in his arms before kissing her deeply. A hand roamed down the small of her back as he cupped a cheek and squeezed.

She giggled. "You really like my butt, don't you?"

"It certainly is my favorite," he teased. "But I like everything about you, Jess. Every single bit."

Jess threaded her fingers around his neck, rubbing her thumbs along his jawline. They lingered in each other's arms as the storm relented, the rain softening against the porch steps, the gray clouds drifting apart.

"Promise me something?" he whispered.

"Okay."

"Don't say it back unless you mean it. I'm not expecting a response. I needed to tell you how I feel, why this means so much to me."

She nodded, then pulled him into her bedroom.

He released his grip on her hand, then with careful fingers, peeled the wet shirt off her body. She did the same for him, wet layers discarded to the floor until it was only cold skin and warm sheets. The way he held her felt different than New York. Like having her in his arms was the missing piece of a puzzle finally fitting into place. He murmured confessions in her ear as he touched her with gentle, unhurried hands, his soft words of devotion playing through her head long after they finished. Kevin cradled her in his arms, his lips at her temple, her back pressed against his chest.

She felt like love was a word that had lost all meaning, a phrase used to reassure the other that they were still committed, that they weren't planning on going anywhere.

Yet here, in Kevin's arms, she felt a spark of something she hadn't felt in a long, long time...and wondered whether she ever knew what it meant to truly be in love, and be loved in return.

Chapter Nineteen

Her phone chirped on her nightstand at 5:30 the next morning, like it did every work day. Jess seized it and switched off the alarm, then silently began to slither her way out of Kevin's grasp.

He tightened his hold around her waist, pressing her back to him. "You really thought you could get away that easily?"

She huffed out a laugh. "As Zach says, I have to keep making that bread."

"Do you mean that literally or financially?"

"Um...both?"

He laughed, his breath warm against her neck. He kissed her shoulder. "Five more minutes?"

She groaned. "Then five minutes turns into ten and then I'm late and rushing to walk Honey before heading to the shop—"

"I'll walk Honey with you."

She pried his hand from her stomach and shot out of bed before he could grab her again. She slipped on a sweatshirt. "It's okay, you sleep, I'm used to the early mornings—"

Kevin flipped the sheet over and moved to sit at the end of the bed, wrapping his hands around the backs of Jess's knees and pulling her body flush with his. "Jess, you're doing it again."

Her shoulders melted at how quickly he realized her tendency to push him away, even before she realized she was doing it herself. She ran a hand through his tousled hair, his morning bed head making her heart twist in her chest. "Walk with me then."

He smiled up at her, teeth and all, and it made her want to crawl back beneath the sheets and stay there with him the rest of the day. She watched as he stood up, slipping on his sweatshirt and shorts he'd laid out on her armchair in hopes of drying them out, then grasped her hand and followed her out of the house. Honey tugged on the leash, pulling them closer and closer to the beach.

"Seems she didn't get enough yesterday," Jess teased, following the puppy onto the sand. "Usually we walk a lap around the block."

"Maybe she's feeling brave to try new things, too," he rumbled.

She peered up at him, watching his eyes roam her face. His skin glowed from the early morning sunlight that broke across the horizon, the rising sun waking up the bay around them.

Honey pulled on the leash again, aiming for the water, causing Jess to practically topple over into the sand. Kevin laughed as he caught and steadied her, then took hold of the leash. "I think she'll be okay if we let her run free for a few minutes."

Her eyes widened. "I don't want to lose her again."

"I won't let that happen, I promise" he reassured her. He unclipped Honey's leash and let the pup run for the edge of the shore. The two of them chuckled as she pressed tentative little paws into the water then yelped from the cold and jumped back.

Fingers brushed her chin as Kevin guided her to look him in the eye. "Do you want to tell me why Charlie was here last night?"

She frowned. "Do I have to?"

"I think at this point I deserve to know what's going on, yeah?"

She loosed a breath. "Okay, yeah."

Honey growled at a hermit crab close by, then laid her belly down in the sand, her eyes intent on the crab as it scampered across the broken shells.

Jess kept her eyes on the pup and took one of her deep breaths, avoiding his gaze. He taught her what it meant to be brave, to go for the things you wanted even if it seemed scary, even if there was a good chance everything would fail. The past twelve hours she let herself do the same, let herself open up and be vulnerable. So she held on tightly to that new kernel of bravery in her soul and swung the door open wide.

"When my dad took on Mr. Sullivan as a business partner at Cap's, everything about my life changed. Cap's was no longer going under, and for the first time that I could recall, we had money to spend. We moved into a bigger house and we got a second car and I no longer had to wear Dakota's hand-me-downs. And we hung out with the Sullivans—a lot. They came over every week for family dinner, and I always sat next to Charlie. We became best friends, and then, we became something more."

The smell of freshly baked shortcakes and bright strawberries came to mind as Jess thought about her first kiss with

Charlie, tucked away next to the kitchen. Even in the beginning, they were hiding.

"At the time things felt off between my dad and his. They bickered constantly and at some point, the Sullivans stopped coming for family dinners. I was afraid that if we told them about us we would make it worse, so we didn't say anything to our families. We kept it a secret for a little while, sneaking away when we thought no one noticed.

"We finally decided to tell them when junior prom came around, but had no idea about what was going on behind the scenes. Apparently Mr. Sullivan was slowly writing my father out of the business. He'd started taking business meetings without him, brought on vendors and employees without his consent, made deals with high-paying clientele, and had all these plans for expansion. My father was technically still the owner, yet he only found out about these things through word of mouth in town, so he fought Charlie's father on it constantly. Then...they had the meeting."

She sighed, curling a hand into a fist. Kevin brushed his knuckles against hers, his touch reassuring. She linked her pointer finger with his, her eyes drawn to their hands.

"Mr. Sullivan decided to go through the books, dating all the way back to when dad opened the place in 1997. He hired some lawyers to make a case for ousting my dad, and it was a strong one. My dad was more of a people person, not a business person, and Charlie's dad used all this legal jargon to essentially deem him irresponsible and unfit to run a business. They offered my dad a hefty sum to buy him out and leave Cap's for good."

Kevin exhaled audibly, shaking his head. He squeezed her finger with his.

"When I told my family I was dating Charlie, my

father...he sort of lost it," she breathed. "He said the Sullivans were manipulative and he didn't trust Charlie to take care of my heart, so he refused to let me go to junior prom with him. Banned me from seeing him again."

She shook her head, looking out at the horizon. "We had to get more creative about sneaking around, sliding out of windows and down trees late at night, faking being in after-school clubs so we could have a few hours to drive off and be free. The more we did this, the more *angry* I got with my father. The only side of the story I was getting was from Charlie's perspective, who told me what his father said: that my dad was running the business into the ground, that it was for the best that they went their separate ways. I believed him. I believed *them*. I truly thought it was all my father's fault."

Honey bounded over to her and nuzzled her wet, sandy nose at Jess's ankle. She dipped down to wipe off the sand, then dug her face into Honey's golden fur, letting the salty smell of her pup ground her for the next excruciating part of her story. The night that changed everything.

She stood back up and faced her golden boy, shining in the soft morning sunlight. "Toward the end of my senior year, my mom caught me sneaking out. Dakota was home from college at that point and...it was the night from hell. The three of them were screaming at me, so disappointed that I would go behind their backs, that I had been lying to them for over a year. I said nasty things to my father about how this was all his fault, that none of this would have happened if he'd just been better at his job. He said nasty things back...he—he said I was no daughter of his, that he never wanted to see me again. So I left. I lived with the Sullivans for a week, and then Mr. Sullivan said I could move into one of the apartments he managed in town after graduation."

Anger heated her cheeks. "Charlie was so stoked, he made it sound like it would be *our* place, that we finally had our freedom. But it wasn't really. I was his plaything when he was home, when he was not required to be with his parents. It was always them first, me last. By the time he *really* moved in after college, I felt neglected. But I dealt with it, thinking that's what it meant to be in a relationship with someone you love. Yet now..."

Kevin reached up and cupped her face, drawing her close. She quivered from the softness of his touch, the way his thumbs brushed against her cheekbones.

"Now I realize that I don't think it was love, I think it was dependency," she whispered, her body shaking as she shared a truth that was finally dawning on her, like the midnight moon breaking through a cloudless sky. "I had no one else, and nowhere to go. I was too proud and stubborn to go back to my family, because deep down, I wanted them to come to me. I still want my father to apologize for the things he said, to make things right. But I know I hurt him, too. And that's what scares me the most. That I lost five whole years with them all for a man who didn't take care of my heart, just like Dad warned."

She wrapped her hands around his wrists, leaning into one of his palms. "Last night, Charlie came to me begging again to get back together with him—"

"*Again?!*"

She winced. "Yeah, he tried contacting me while we were in New York."

Jess watched as Kevin worked to school his features, trying to act calm when he clearly wasn't. "And what did you say to him?"

"I turned off my phone because I had other, more important things to do."

He snorted, then pulled her close and placed a gentle kiss on her lips. "And last night?"

She smiled, her lips brushing against his. "I called the one person who has always been there for me, and he came to my rescue."

He sealed his lips to hers, running his hands through her hair. She wrapped her arms around his shoulders and stood up on her tiptoes as his hands slid down and gripped her waist, holding her up so he could kiss her thoroughly.

The jingling of Honey's tags as she pattered up to them pulled Jess from the spell. "I have muffins to bake."

"Fuck the muffins."

Kevin pressed in again, slipping a hand inside her sweatshirt and up her spine, sliding it around to her chest.

She laughed into his mouth and stepped away, shaking her head as she began walking back toward the cottage. "As hot as it is to listen to you swear when you want to get it on with me, I do not want to fuck the muffins."

"Okay fine...then want to fuck me?"

"*Kevin!*"

He laughed, clicking Honey's leash back on her collar and bounding up the sand, sliding an arm around her waist and tucking her close to him. He kissed her temple. "Thank you for telling me all of that, sweetheart."

She beamed at him. "You're the only person I trust right now."

He hesitated before he gave her that golden smile and squeezed her hip.

Jᴇss sᴡᴜɴɢ the door open with her hip, balancing a large tray of peach streusel muffins in her hands.

Zach handed a customer a light green matcha latte, a new menu offering he'd insisted on. Jess had been skeptical when he suggested it a few weeks back, but it seemed everyone loved matcha—hot, iced, even in their baked goods. She attempted a batch of matcha latte cookies last week and they sold out in a matter of minutes.

He waved as the customer left, then held out a piece of paper to Jess. "You got a call about a cake order."

She cocked her head as she placed the tray of muffins down on the counter, then reached for the note. "We don't make cakes."

"This customer said they used to get them from you at Post Road. I think they're hoping you'll make an exception."

"They could go to Scoops?"

"If they want an ice cream cake, yes...but they were insistent on a regular cake. From you."

She looked down at the slip in her hand, not recognizing the name. But the order was simple enough—red velvet, cream cheese frosting, red frosted trim, happy birthday written on the top. "I haven't baked a cake in a while. I kind of miss it, to be honest."

Zach gave her a genuine smile. "Then it looks like you made your decision."

The bell at the front door jingled as Blake stepped in, nose pink from the blazing August sun. He walked up to the counter and leaned against it. Zach curled a hand around his neck and gave him a kiss. Blake's freckled cheeks flushed at the gesture.

Jess smiled as she placed the baked muffins into the display case.

Zach pinched Blake's chin, pulling his face up to meet his gaze. "Hey, want to see a magic trick?

"Mmmm."

Zach chuckled, then cocked his head to the side. "Hey, Kevin, come here for a second?" he called.

Jess stood up, then glared at Zach. Blake's brows pinched together in confusion as Kevin jumped up from where he was crouched in front of a bike. Kevin wiped his hands clean with the rag hanging from his back pocket as he approached, toeing his way around the counter.

Immediately his hands were on Jess, one tugging the belt loop of her jeans, the other at the nape of her neck, drawing circles on her skin.

Blake's eyes widened.

"Did our shipment of cups come in yet?" Zach asked casually, his eyes dancing with mischief.

Jess continued to glare at Zach, who looked mighty proud of himself.

"Not that I know of, but I think Jess can track it down? She places all the orders."

Zach gave her a devilish grin, a dimple tucked into his left cheek. "Right, my bad. I forgot."

Kevin chuckled, then tightened his grip on her neck and twisted her head up to face him. The tension in her shoulders melted away as she scanned the smile across his lips.

"Hi," he whispered.

"Hi back. Want a muffin?"

"Me and the muffins are currently not on speaking terms."

She chuckled as he leaned in and kissed her, smiled, then kissed her again before letting go and returning to the bike he was fixing.

Blake sputtered, unable to form a full sentence.

The bell at the door jingled again. Rory chased Honey into the shop as Calvin held the door open for Melanie.

Blake jumped, pointing a finger at them with a stupid grin on his face. "I know something you don't know!" he singsonged.

Rory froze. "Hot gossip?"

"*Steaming* hot."

"Blake..." Jess warned.

She watched Calvin as he turned to Kevin. A knowing look passed between them, then Calvin smirked and fist-bumped his friend.

"Mmkay I'm not doing this," Jess snipped. She slid the glass display case closed and beelined for the kitchen door.

"*Jessica*, come here!" Kevin pleaded, jogging in her direction.

"Nope."

She was halfway through the door when he caught her wrist. He pulled her back and right into his arms, then rubbed his nose against hers. "They were going to find out eventually."

She growled, which only made him laugh. He cupped her face and kissed her, and everything melted away again.

Squeals came from the other side of the shop. Jess opened her eyes and saw Melanie and Rory clinging to one another as they jumped up and down, ecstatic.

She coughed and stepped around Kevin. He caught her waist before she could get too far and stepped right behind her, wrapping an arm around her stomach.

"So you guys boned, right?" Rory asked.

Jess shook her head. "I'm not answering that, you're a child."

"Hello I am *eighteen* and dating a hot football player, do you really think I—"

She cut her off. "Please, for the love of god, do not finish that sentence."

Rory smirked. "But in all honesty...your one-night stand? Was it..."

Kevin tucked a flyaway behind her ear, his eyes burning into her. "She couldn't help but come back for more."

"*Oh my god,*" Jess groaned, slapping his hand.

The rest of them howled with laughter. Jess felt her face go hot as she attempted to squirm out of his reach, but with no luck. He steered her right back in and gave her another mind-melting kiss that practically had her forgetting her own name.

"Wow, okay, yeah, you definitely boned," Rory teased.

"I am *such* a big fan of this," Melanie swooned.

"And I knew before you did!" Blake cheered.

Jess gave them a shy smile and gave in to the moment. She leaned the back of her head against Kevin's chest. "Why are you all here? I didn't know it took four of you to walk a dog."

"Tyler's coming home this weekend," Rory said. "I forced Mel into planning a bonfire with me so we could all hang tomorrow."

Melanie handed Jess the leash. "Do you guys want to come? We'll be at Sandy Cover after Scoops closes."

She flicked her eyes to the small cork board hanging on the back wall and surveyed the sage green invitation tacked to the center.

Kevin must have noticed where she was looking, his hands rubbing up and down her arms.

"I think—I think I need to go to this family thing tomorrow," she answered timidly. "Not sure how long it will go, so...maybe."

Zach asked Melanie if he should bring anything and the

group launched into bonfire details, but Jess's chest was too tight to pay any attention, her gaze still hyperfocused on that piece of paper.

Kevin dipped his head down to her level, placing his chin on her shoulder. "You okay?"

She took a deep inhale, then let out a slow breath. "Will you go with me tomorrow?"

"To the shower?"

She nodded.

His voice wavered at her request, but she was patient. She knew asking him to hop into her family drama with her was *a lot*, to say the least. She tried telling herself she would be fine without him, that she could face it alone. But she was sick of being *fine*. She didn't want to be afraid of asking for what she wanted, and right now, she wanted him. And she really didn't want to be alone.

"Are you sure?" he finally whispered in her ear.

"I'm sure."

He sighed, then kissed her cheek. "Okay, my dear Jessica. I'm in. Let's finish this list of yours together."

She grinned, not caring if the Scoopers were watching as she turned to face her golden boy and folded her arms around him in a fierce hug.

JESS SAT in the passenger seat of her car the following afternoon, her legs bouncing as Kevin drove them closer to the house she hadn't seen in five years. She wrung her hands and tried to do her breathing technique, but nothing calmed her. Her nerves had her sweating through her sundress, the fabric sticking to her skin and the bottoms of her chunky sandals sliding against her feet.

A warm hand glided against her thigh, then squeezed.

Kevin was awfully quiet after they left Port Wheels earlier, wearing his collared short-sleeve and khakis. She expected him to make jokes or say *something* to make her feel better. But he remained silent as he drove to her childhood home.

He turned onto her street and inched forward. Cars were parked along the road leading up to the house. Jess peered through the windshield and saw an arch of green and yellow balloons fastened to the porch, a glittery *Oh Baby!* sign above it.

Kevin parked the car at the end of the line and killed the ignition. He leaned back and sighed, closing his eyes.

Jess crossed her arms. "What's going on, Kevin? I'm shocked you saw that sign and didn't immediately scream *oh baby!*"

He sighed. She watched as he rubbed his neck, which was a dark shade of red.

Is he embarrassed? Nervous? she thought. *Was it wrong of her to ask him to come?*

"If this is too much, I understand," she whispered. "I can go in there by myself...I can do this alone."

"I know you can, sweetheart," he muttered back. "But I want to be here for you."

"So then what is it?"

He rubbed his face, then *finally* looked at her, his hazel eyes dim. "Jess...there's something I need to tell you."

Chapter Twenty

"You're making me nervous, Kev."

She attempted to reach for his hands, but he pulled back.

"Please," he said. "Let me get this out first."

She huffed and crossed her arms. "Spill it already."

He ran a hand through his hair, his eyes trained on the fabric of her dress at her knees. "Earlier this year, during the offseason, a man came into the shop and asked me to fix his bike. So I did, and we got talking."

She felt her stomach sour. *Why does he have to tell me a story right now?*

"He asked me how business was going, and I was honest. I said that things weren't great and I needed to figure out something new or I'd have to give up the shop. As I fixed his bike, I explained to him about this idea I had for a bakery and a bike shop in one, and he liked it. He said he wanted to help."

"The mystery investor."

Kevin nodded, still not looking her in the eye. "The man said he would invest his money into the shop for a very small percentage of the revenue, but said he would only do this if I did him two favors."

She froze, her heart feeling like a shriveled rock thudding to the floorboard below.

"He told me he would give me the money if his daughter was the one to run the bakery...and if I could get her to leave her boyfriend."

She swore, placing a hand over her mouth.

"Jess..." Kevin begged, finally looking at her, finally reaching for her.

But she tore away from his grasp. She unbuckled her seat belt and flung open her door, then stormed down the street away from the house with the balloons.

The other car door slammed and the slapping of sandals followed behind her. "Sweetheart, please, wait—"

"How *could you*," she fumed.

"I was *desperate*, Jess. And his offer was so good...and a part of me wanted to do it because I really, *really* wanted you to leave Charlie."

"So you partnered with my father," she spat. "He paid for the renovations, the new espresso machine, my tablet..."

"I told him the tablet might have been a bit much, but he wouldn't listen after I told him you were still using your high school laptop."

She stopped her march and spun around to face him, then glared. "You *told him that*?! How much more does he know? Were you feeding him information this whole time?"

"No, after the tablet, I told him that I'd held up my end of the bargain, and if he wanted to know more about you, he would have to reach out himself. I promise, Jess."

"Your promises mean nothing." She forcefully kicked away a rock on the sidewalk.

"Sissy!!"

Her back went ramrod straight at the sound of Dakota's voice. She looked up at the house and saw her standing there in a flowing green maxi dress, her feet bare, soft waves of blonde hair tumbling down her back. Her face was bright with hope as she beheld Jess, waving her over to the porch.

"I can't believe you thought that *this* was the best moment to tell me the truth."

"He asked me to not tell you, not until you were ready to talk to him yourself. And then you asked me to come to the shower and I—"

"You thought you were off the hook," she finished for him. "How many more secrets, Kevin? Why are you always holding things back from me?"

"Because I'm afraid you'll push me away."

"You can't always be afraid of that."

"Oh yeah? Then explain to me what you're doing *right now*."

She glared. "I'm taking a walk."

"And not running away from what's going on in front of you? Not trying to create as much distance as you can from *me*?"

"You just told me you've been secretly in cahoots with MY FATHER," she yelled at him. "What do you expect me to do, huh? Kiss you and say it's okay? That I still love you?"

His eyes widened. "You...love me?"

Jess felt her face go hot, her breathing jagged after those words slipped right out of her mouth.

He reached for her, his hands on her elbows.

"I—I can't do this," she croaked, wrenching away. She ran down the grassy slope next to the house and to the dock attached to the backyard. The wood creaked under her feet as she jogged, then she stopped at the edge and let out an ear-piercing scream. Tears finally fell down her cheeks.

Tears for how much had changed and how much time she'd lost. Tears for having said those three words to Kevin when she wasn't even sure if she was ready to say them. Tears for a life that felt equal parts beautiful and terrifying and frustrating.

She sat on the dock and looked out at the river that led into Haverport's bay and out to the Atlantic. She wasn't sure how long she sat there, but at some point, she heard the boards creak as someone approached from behind. She sucked in a breath and whipped her head around, ready to unleash again.

But it wasn't the golden boy approaching her.

Jess's father held up his hands in mock surrender. He wore his usual "dressed up" getup for Dakota's shower—cargo shorts, his T-shirt swapped out with a polo, and a pair of boat shoes on his feet.

She exhaled as she continued to stare. There was so much she needed to say, and yet, she was unable to form a concrete sentence.

He slid his hands into the pockets of his shorts, then cocked his head toward the boat floating in the water next to them. "Shall we go for a ride?"

Her eyes flicked up to the house. Dakota was standing there with her mother, Jasper rubbing her shoulder. Nosy guests were also watching them, probably wondering who the crazed blonde girl was screaming bloody murder down by the dock.

Jess got to her feet. "Sure."

EVERYTHING ABOUT BEING on her father's boat felt exactly the same. He untied the ropes as she stepped in and opened up the dock box, pulling out her life vest that was still waiting for her. Like she never left. She clicked it on and took a seat as he revved the engine, then steered the boat down the river and out to the bay.

Jess kept her eyes on the water as they rode in silence for five minutes, ten minutes, fifteen. The sound of the waves and the rumble of the boat below her feet calmed her anxious heart. She unfurled her tightly wound hands in her lap and inhaled, the salty sea stinging her nose and watering her eyes.

When they finally reached a patch of relatively calm water, her father killed the ignition. He swung his chair toward her and gave her that crooked smile, the same one he used to give her those early mornings clamming on the beach or walking down Main Street before Haverfest or working the docks with him at Cap's. It somehow all felt familiar yet so foreign to her, and for the briefest moment, she wondered if it was all a dream she would wake up from.

He cleared his throat. "You look good, Jessie."

She crossed her arms. "I look exactly the same."

He shook his head. "Nah, you look settled. Happy."

"And apparently I have you to thank for that."

"I—" He grimaced. "He told you, I'm guessing."

"That wasn't fair of you to make him keep it a secret."

"You're right, it wasn't fair. But if he'd told you the truth, would you have said yes?"

She squeezed her hands into fists and looked away.

"There's so many things I've wanted to say over the years," he confessed. "So many ways I wish I could have fixed it."

"Why didn't you?" she muttered. "I—I thought—"

I thought you would come after me. She spent years hoping and dreaming they'd finally "come around," when everything would go back to the way things were. But he never did. They never tried. She never tried.

"You know that stubborn pride you have, the same one that makes you so determined and so good at running your bakery?"

She looked his way and arched a brow.

"You get it honest, my love. Every time I thought about coming after you, I felt hurt all over again. I let it consume me and take me away from what I should have been doing."

"And what should have you been doing?"

"Rescuing my little girl."

Jess shook her head. "I don't need rescuing."

He chuckled. "You're right, you don't need anyone to do *anything* for you. You've had that independent streak since you were little. But I knew deep in my gut that Charlie was not the man for you, and I should have done something about it."

"You did. You kicked me out."

She watched as her father blew out a breath and looked down at his boat shoes, pink coloring his cheeks.

"You also told me—"

"Don't. I know what I said. Those words haunt me every minute of every day."

She tucked her legs underneath her and made herself small, shielding herself from the pain she knew was inevitable, hoping it would hurt a little less this time.

"I didn't mean it, Jessie."

"Then why did you say it?"

"Because you were my pal and your words broke my heart. I wanted you to hurt like I was. I was foolish. I am your father and it is my job to protect you, and I failed miserably. I let you down. With Cap's, with how you felt about Charlie, with everything."

"You didn't let me down with Cap's," she exhaled. "I eventually put the pieces together and figured out that none of it was your fault. I know he ousted you."

He nodded, lifting the worn ball cap on his head to brush his hair back before fastening it back on. "My life's work, taken away, like that." He snapped his fingers.

"I'm sorry," she whispered.

"I know you are, love."

They waded in silence for a little while, the waves swaying the boat as the sun peeked out from the clouds in the sky.

"Dakota really misses you," he murmured. "Your mom really misses you."

"And I miss them."

"...I really miss you."

She refused to give him that sliver of hope. At least not yet. "Have you gone clamming?"

"Not since you left."

"That's incredibly stupid."

He chuckled. "I tried once, but I ended up crying the entire drive there, so I turned the car around and didn't try again."

"So many clams just sitting there."

"Then maybe we could go sometime."

She pursed her lips. "I'll think about it."

His lips curled into a smile. "Good."

Jess nodded.

"How's business going?"

"Figured you would already know that."

"Kevin refuses to tell me anything, says I need to fix my problems before I can see the books."

She huffed. "At least he got one thing right."

"I think that boy got *a lot* of things right."

Jess scowled.

Her father chuckled again. "Don't be mad at him. He was saving his business. And I think he also really wanted to save you. I barely had to ask before he screamed an enthusiastic yes."

"He probably did a dance when he said it."

"He did, actually."

She began to smile, then caught herself, schooling her face back into a frown.

"Business is steady, but we need more," she explained. "We're not making enough to support ourselves through the offseason. I might have to consider letting Zach go, which I *really* don't want to do. We might have to sell and hope the owner doesn't want to demolish the place."

"I could invest more."

"Excuse me? With what money?"

He shrugged. "Getting bought out of your own business does have its perks. I have a lump sum in the bank, enough to allow me to go into early retirement. Plus some."

She felt flustered at how willing he was to simply solve her problem. "No. That's way too much to ask of you."

"You didn't ask. I offered."

"And I'm refusing."

He smirked. "Still as stubborn as ever."

"Did you think I wouldn't be?"

"No. But I did hope that maybe you'd want to work with your old man."

She glowered at him. "You really think we can make the jump from not speaking to one another to being in business together after one conversation?"

"We're already in business together, Jessie."

"Against my will," she grumbled to herself.

"I know it's a lot to consider, and you're right, it's one conversation." He revved the engine. "But I would like to keep having more conversations."

She eyed him, his face full of hope. Hope for what they could be, for what they could return to. Jess nodded once in his direction. He returned one with a smile, then drove the boat back toward the dock in comfortable silence.

JESS TENTATIVELY FOLLOWED her sister into the house she thought she would never step into again. Despite the throngs of people and the pastel shower decor, everything about her childhood home felt the same, and she was thankful for it. Thankful she could count on this place to be a constant when everything else in her life was changing by the minute.

Dakota snatched her hand and pulled her down on the leather couch next to a mountain of presents. She handed her a notepad with a smile and asked her to take notes as she opened gifts. Jess was thankful again that her sister still knew her so well, knew that she would want something to do with her hands and keep busy instead of shifting uncomfortably.

Thankful. It was a feeling she did not expect to experience today.

Jess took notes with a smile, watching her sister glow and laugh as she opened each onesie and pacifier and bib. She was joy and sunshine and goodness, a beacon of happiness in the living room. The same exact spot Jess'd had her last conversation with them on a dark, dreary, horrible night.

Dakota held up a breast pump with a grin. Jess shook her head at her sister's amusement over a *breast pump*, then scribbled it down.

Her sister placed it carefully back in the bag and handed it to their mom, who was looking at Jess like she was a ghost that would disappear if she glanced away.

Jess cleared her throat and leaned close to Dakota. "Any chance you know where Kevin went?"

Dakota's face fell a smidgen. "Calvin picked him up. I tried to get him to stay, but he told me he didn't want to be the cause of any more of your pain. Something about how this is your true home?"

She frowned deeply, his words from the other night in the storm ringing in her head. *I want you to be my home, Jess.*

She'd said those words right back, without hesitation, after he told her how he truly felt. Yet, when she told him how *she* felt, she let those three words tumble from her lips without being completely honest. Then she did what she does best. She pushed him away.

But this time he let her. He didn't fight it. He simply got in the car and left.

A soft hand squeezed her own. "I can hear you over-thinking."

Jess gave her sister a tight smile. "Not much has changed there, huh?"

"No, maybe not." Dakota smiled. "But a lot *has* changed, and I think for the better."

Jess leaned her head against the couch as guests mingled, piling food on plates and pouring cups of sweet tea. "Like what?" she asked.

"Like you being here." Another squeeze. "Like you spending all summer being challenged by a man who only wants what's best for you."

"I hardly think going skinny dipping or shopping for clothes would be considered a *challenge*."

"Things you probably wouldn't have done last summer," Dakota countered. "Everything on that list challenged you in some way, and I really like him for that."

"Why?" she whispered.

Dakota placed a hand on Jess's cheek. "Because it was good practice for facing this final challenge and coming home."

WHY IS BRAVERY SO MESSY?

It was the thought that ran through Jess's head throughout the rest of the shower, and the hours after as she helped clean up. Her father didn't say much to her after their talk on the boat, her mother also equally as quiet as they worked side by side wiping down surfaces, doing dishes, wrapping up leftover food, and tying up trash bags. When the house was finally cleaned she mumbled her goodbyes, leaning down to hug Dakota sitting on a porch chair, Jasper massaging her feet propped up on his knees. She didn't make a move to hug her parents, and neither did they. Timid smiles, cordial waves, and Jess was off, driving away from her home once again. But this time with the promise of coming back.

She pulled the car onto the main drag and slowed as she made her way down the road, past a crowded Wilson's Pub and Pop's Seafood and Penny's Pizzeria, a classic Saturday night in

Haverport unfolding before her eyes. It was only a matter of weeks before the summer people packed up and left town, and it all felt like it was going by too quickly. They were running out of time, and she had no idea how to fix it or what to do.

Jess drove slowly past Grampy's, glancing into the dark window and noticing a faint glow coming from the back kitchen. Without thinking about it too much, she pulled over and parked, then walked to the back door and knocked three times.

The door creaked open and a hand shot out, holding a brown paper bag. "Five bucks. Cash only."

"Need a hand?"

He opened the door further, his gray beard twitching into a grin when he noticed it was Jess. "Got your apron?"

She reached into her purse and pulled out her denim old faithful. "Always."

He stepped back to make room for her. Jess fastened her apron and looked around the cramped kitchen. Cartons of blueberries and flour and brown sugar sat open next to square silver takeaway trays that lined the entire counter. She peered into the oven and saw it was already full with trays on trays of blueberry coffee cake.

Before she could say anything, Grampy thrust a piece of paper at her. She took it from him and scanned the top.

Grampy's Blueberry Coffee Cake

Her eyes widened as she continued to read the recipe in her hands.

"What...did you just...are you serious—" she sputtered.

"Chop, chop. I don't have all night," Grampy interrupted. He handed her a whisk.

She walked up to the counter and placed the prized recipe down, then, still completely shook, began to follow the most coveted recipe in Haverport. Beat the butter and sugar, add an egg and vanilla. Sift the flour, salt, baking powder and soda, then add it to the wet ingredients. As she got to the part where she was folding in sour cream (*sour cream*, she thought, *of course*), Grampy handed her a small bowl of freshly washed blueberries. Adding it in, she spread the cake batter into prepared pans and handed them off to Grampy to top with his signature sugary crumb and slide into the oven.

They kept at it for another hour, preparing one cake after another after another. Her hands were cramping from folding cake batter, but she was beaming as she took a seat on a nearby stool, watching Grampy pull the last few batches of cakes from the oven.

"So you do your baking the night before," Jess commented.

"The early mornings were becoming too much, especially for the demand," Grampy explained. "I can't have this many cakes ready by seven."

"Have you ever thought about opening later?"

"And disappoint the town? No, never."

Jess smiled, swinging her feet. "You let me see the recipe."

Grampy shrugged. "Yes, well, I figured it was time to let someone see it."

Her jaw dropped. "Are you telling me I'm the *first*?"

He grinned. "Sure are, kid."

"*Why?!*"

Grampy crossed his arms. "For the same reason you knocked on my door and offered me a hand. You're dedicated. I see how hard you've been working to make your bakery into something in town, despite all the odds."

"It doesn't seem to be enough, though," she grumbled.

"Tell me more."

She did. She explained about the different changes she'd made, like adding focaccia to bring in afternoon customers and matcha to bring in a younger crowd and their date-day bike rental deal they finally implemented. She briefly told him about the numbers Calvin meticulously laid out for her and Kevin recently, and how much they would need to stay afloat the rest of the year.

"We failed," she concluded.

To her shock, Grampy rolled his eyes. "You did not fail. I don't want to hear that."

"Then what would you call it?"

"A learning curve."

"A learning curve that ended up curving right into failure."

He shook his head. "Not if your next move is a smart one."

She cocked a brow. "Got any ideas?"

His mouth twitched. "Potentially."

She frowned. "You're scaring me, Gramps."

"Ha! *Gramps*." He shook his head then pulled out another stool and took a slow seat. "As you can see, I'm getting old."

"No, you're not. You're going to live forever."

Another laugh from him. Jess grinned.

"Here's a thought...What if I buy Port Wheels?"

Her eyes widened. "What? *Why* would you do that?"

"Because it would work well with my retirement plan."

"And that is?"

"To hand down this place to you."

Chapter Twenty-One

JESS FELT like she blacked out for a moment as she stared at the man in front of her, the commodity in town who felt more like a legend than a chef.

Grampy gestured toward his kitchen and the storefront. "I've had this shop for decades. I'm proud of it, but I'm not banking on my kids wanting to take on the business when I finally decide to throw in the towel."

Jess was still speechless, so she simply nodded, leaving him space to continue.

"My kids are happy with their jobs and their lives and kids of their own. When I started feeling ready to give this place up, I knew I'd need to find the right hands of someone I could trust. Then, I went grocery shopping at Post Road."

Her eyes widened.

"There were discounted boxes of pastries by the front door, so I grabbed one, and I haven't stopped thinking about that— Oh, what was that one with the cinnamon and sugar pearls tied like a knot?"

"Kanelbullar," she choked.

"*Yes*, it was exquisite. I saw you're selling them at the bakery, too."

"Y-yes."

Grampy smiled. "A month later I caught wind of you leaving Post Road and found out you were opening up your own spot, so I kept a close eye. I wanted to see how you handled things. Not just the long lines and the grueling early hours, but the negative press and the slower days when everything feels doomed."

She coughed. "And...what did you think?"

"I think I found my set of hands."

Jess blew out a shaky breath. "This is insane."

"Quite the contrary, my dear. I think it's perfect."

"You want to hand me your prized bakery and deli, where customers line up *down the road* every single goddamn day? They're going to be so upset when they find out who's running the place. Everyone in the Port will think I'm ruining this town."

He shook his head. "When we make it clear that I chose to hand it down to you, they'll be fine. Especially if you keep selling the coffee cake out the back door."

She stood up and paced the length of his kitchen. "Okay, so explain this...if you're handing it down to me, then why buy Port Wheels? Those seem like opposing business decisions."

"You can't work in two kitchens, now can you?"

"Obviously...?"

"So you move your baking here, and treat the bakery at Port Wheels as an off-shoot of this business. Make it more of a café, a sit-down spot instead of a counter like this place. You could get rid of the back kitchen and expand seating."

Jess tapped a finger to her lips. "Grampy's Café at Port Wheels?"

He shrugged. "I'm not attached to the name. You can change it, if you'd like."

"I can see the torches and pitchforks now."

"Oh, who cares," he grunted. "All I want is for my name to remain on the blueberry coffee cake. That's my legacy. The rest does not matter."

"It *should* matter."

He shrugged. "I'll leave that up to you."

She pinched the bridge of her nose. "So you buy Port Wheels and...then what?"

"I'll be the owner of both establishments, but I'll make you my business manager. I'll step down from the day-to-day and eventually I'll transition out, but stay on as a silent partner. We can have weekly meetings to work all of this out when the summer season is over. You and the bike boy."

"He's going to freak," she muttered.

"I'm guessing that's a good thing?"

"A *very* good thing."

"Is that a yes?"

Jess blew out a breath and scanned the bakery, a place so iconic, she felt like an imposter even *being* there. Yet the man before her looked at her like she was the solution, like *she* was a bright hope for his future.

She closed her eyes and sucked in a breath. *Be brave, Jess.*

So she was.

Jess was buzzing as she turned the corner onto the sandy road and parked her car behind Calvin's truck. She hopped out and tripped over herself as she made her way toward the roaring bonfire on Sandy Cove Beach.

"MOM'S FINALLY HERE!"

The Scoopers cheered at Jay's announcement. Jess rolled her eyes as she approached the circle. She scanned each of them and noticed one familiar face was missing. "Where's Kevin?"

"He took Honey for a walk," Calvin answered. Melanie sat between his legs, her head leaning against his chest, his hands playing with her wavy hair. "How'd it go today?"

She scrunched her face. "It was...fine."

"What was today?" Rory butted in.

Jess was on the verge of telling her to buzz off, but the look on the girl's face made her pause. Rory looked *happy*, a smile curled on her lips, color in her cheeks. She was wrapped up in Tyler's arms, his fingers tracing her right arm lazily. The look of them together and happy after all the drama this past year made her soften her attack.

Instead, she shrugged and took a seat next to Calvin and Mel. "I went to my sister's baby shower."

No one said anything at that, which made perfect sense to Jess. *I wouldn't know how to respond either*, she thought. *I've never spoken to them about my family.*

Melanie coughed. "And it went...fine."

Jess nodded once. "Yep. Fine."

Silence again.

She looked over at Calvin, giving him a *Please make this stop* look.

He seemed to catch her drift and cleared his throat. "We were just discussing the next summer season."

"It's going to be so different," Blake cried. Zach was beside him, an arm slung around his shoulder.

"Aww, Blakey boy, you gonna miss me?" Jay teased.

Blake frowned. "Do you really have to move to *Japan*?"

It'd been a shock to all of the Scoopers when Jay revealed his big plans of studying abroad in Japan, but for the first time in probably ever, Jess noticed how happy Jay truly was. He wasn't pushing so hard for the attention of others anymore. Except for the girl with the velvet cat ears who always left him flustered when she stopped by the ice cream shop.

"And Tyler will barely be around," Blake whined. "He has to go off and be a famous football player."

Rory frowned as well and looked at her boyfriend. Everyone watched as he leaned in and brushed his lips against hers, then whispered something softly that had her smiling again.

Jay shoved Blake playfully. "At least you and Mel won't be the newbies anymore. Army boy will have to hire two people."

"Actually," Jess started. "Make that three."

Blake gawked at her, and Jay's mouth opened in shock.

"Are you...leaving town?" Rory sputtered.

"No," she rushed to explain. "But I think I'll be too busy to help out anymore."

"Too...busy?"

Jess jumped to her feet at the sound of that voice behind her. Kevin clutched the leash in his hand as Honey jumped up and down at the sight of her. She reached down to pet her pup, eyeing Kevin's disheveled hair and the dark circles under his eyes.

She scooped up Honey and stood. "Yes. I need to talk to you and Calvin for a minute."

Melanie shifted so Calvin could stand up.

"*No.*"

Everyone turned toward Blake. His face was red, his

arms crossed. "If this involves Port Wheels then this involves my boyfriend, and I think it's unfair that you keep leaving him in the dark."

"Yeah, you tell 'em, Blakey boy," Rory cheered.

Zach smirked and kissed the back of Blake's head, his hands twisted in his red curls. "You did promise open communication, Jess."

Jess looked between Calvin and Kevin. "It's...kind of big, and I'm still figuring out all of the details—"

"Then figure it out with us," Rory said. "We're a family, remember?"

She sighed and took a seat, eyes roaming over the group before her. Being with her sister and her parents today had felt awkward and foreign, but she knew deep down with time those feelings would change. Yet the group in front of her was familiar and, after years of working by their sides, she knew they were also safe. For as long as she could remember, she'd felt she had to hide what was going on in her life with the rest of them, because it was way too messy to bring to anyone else. Yet this summer, when she finally let her walls down and watched everything in her life change, she found Kevin was actually right after all: there's strength in being soft, even when the rest of the world says you need to be hard.

"Grampy plans on retiring," Jess confessed. "And he told me he wants to pass down his bakery to me."

"*Holy shit.*"

"ARE YOU KIDDING ME?!"

"But the blueberry coffee cake!"

"Retiring as in...like, *retiring* retiring? Done for good?"

So many responses from them all at once, Jess wasn't even sure where to start. She glanced at Calvin who looked shocked for the first time ever, his mouth hung open.

Melanie tipped his chin with her fingers to close it, giggling when it fell back open.

Zach shook his head, looking exasperated. "I'm so confused. So are you closing Port Wheels?"

Jess finally turned to look at Kevin, his face slowly crumbling with the emotion he clearly couldn't hold in.

She gave him a reassuring smile. "No. We are not closing."

Kevin choked out a sob and ran a hand through his hair, making the waves even more wild.

Jess faced the group and explained everything that happened that night, from the three knocks on the bakery door to practically falling out of her stool when he presented her with his offer. A new offer for her to consider, one that would irrevocably change her life. *Again.*

"He actually let you see the blueberry coffee cake recipe?" Calvin asked, still in shock.

Melanie covered her mouth with a hand.

"Yes," Jess exhaled. "Then we proceeded to bake dozens of cakes."

Calvin whistled. "Damn."

"Your bakery will close then?" Rory asked.

She shrugged. "Kind of. I'll still be baking, but things will shift at Port Wheels. We'll make it more of a café situation."

"And you'll change the name?"

Jess looked back at the golden boy. He rubbed his neck, not returning her gaze.

"I don't know," Jess replied timidly. "That's something we'll have to discuss as a team."

"A team?" Zach pried.

She dipped her chin. "Yes. A team. I refuse to let you leave us."

Zach let out a contented sigh, as if he was holding his breath this whole time and was finally able to relax. Blake beamed, turning to pepper his boyfriend's cheek with kisses.

"So when will all of this start?" Calvin asked.

Jess glimpsed at Kevin. He eyed her as well.

"He told me we can finish out the summer season, then we'll start having meetings this fall to discuss transitioning. He'll retire in a few years and stay on as a silent partner."

"You said yes?" Kevin asked softly.

She hesitated, then nodded. "Yes," she uttered. "I accepted his offer."

The *whoops* and cheers from the group had her beaming. Had her feeling satisfied after making the big decision less than an hour earlier.

Except for one of them, who remained silent.

Kevin stood up and wiped the sand from his khakis.

She got to her feet in response and stepped toward him. "Are you leaving?"

He nodded, his eyes on his sandals. "Yeah. I need to clear my head."

"But—"

Kevin smiled and looked into her eyes. His expression was kind, but she knew it well. He was putting on a front, the same face she saw in the car earlier, the one he used when there were thoughts swirling in his head. When there was something he was hiding.

"Tell me," she breathed. "What is it?"

He shook his head. "I'm happy for you, Jess. Really."

Before she could respond, he was walking toward the bike he'd left next to the beachgrass. He hopped on, then rode down the sandy road without another word.

THEY BARELY SPOKE to each other for a week. Nothing more than cordial hellos in the mornings or simple conversations about placing orders for supplies.

It drove Jess mad.

She tried at the beginning of the week, inviting him to take Honey on a walk with her during breaks or making a joke when she delivered his daily kanelbullar. But all she got in response was a shy smile and a shake of his head. It almost felt like he had given up on her.

So...she baked. Lemon blueberry scones and sticky buns and more matcha latte cookies. She enjoyed the predictability of baking the perfect recipe, especially when everything else in her life felt like it was falling apart. Sifting flour and creaming sugar were easy, achievable tasks that she couldn't fail at.

Jess had her headphones on, shuffling through her pop punk playlist on full blast, letting the music drown out her restless thoughts as she filled tart shells with a lemon curd.

The door to the kitchen swung open. Jess bolted upright and tore off her headphones, but her shoulders sagged when she saw it was only Zach.

"All right, everything is clean out there and ready for the morning. I need to refill the straws then I'll be on my way," he said.

She nodded, wordlessly pointing to the box above her.

Zach carefully lifted the box and grabbed a sleeve of straws, then gave her a nod and walked out.

Jess tossed her head back and sighed. *This is getting ridiculous.* She glanced over at the door and noticed a small blue plate with a kanelbullar on it, and realized she never delivered it to him, too distracted by her new lemon curd recipe to take a moment and walk to his side of the shop.

Almost as if her headphones had a mind of their own, she heard the music shift, the first verses of "You + Me" ringing loud enough to recognize from where they hung around her neck.

Jess removed her headphones and tossed them to the cabinet, then grabbed the plate and shoved open the door. The shop was quiet, which was to be expected—unless someone had a flat tire or some other bike repair need, no one popped into Port Wheels past four o'clock. She banked on that as she made her way around the tables and breezed past a small row of bikes, then turned the corner into Kevin's workshop.

Instead of working on the bike hanging on the stand behind him, Kevin sat hunched over at the computer, eyebrows knitted together as he scrolled through a spreadsheet, completely oblivious to her approach. She silently paced forward, squinting her eyes to get a clearer look at the screen. Rows upon rows of numbers were listed, with color-coded columns and sections. Kevin clicked on a new tab below and another spreadsheet popped up, with a whole new color-coded system.

"What is that?" she blurted.

Kevin minimized the spreadsheet, now hidden below a desktop picture of Honey growling at a crab on the beach. He swiveled his desk chair around and faced her. "Nothing."

She rolled her eyes, then aimed to turn and walk away. "Of course, why would I even ask?"

"You finally remembered to bring my kanelbullar?"

She paused, then shifted toward him and placed the plate on his desk. "Yeah, sorry, I was in the zone back there."

"How'd the lemon curd come out?"

"This is by far my best batch. The extra lemon zest really made a difference." She stopped herself, her eyes on the smile that curled his cheeks. She huffed. "What?"

"I love when you talk pastry to me."

She crossed her arms. "Surprised you even let me given how you've been ignoring me."

He hummed a sigh. "I have a lot on my mind."

"Care to enlighten me?"

Kevin hesitated, then shook his head. "It's nothing."

She rolled her eyes again. "Fine. Whatever."

Jess turned to walk away, ready to finish her tartlets and get them in the fridge before closing for the night. But the sight of Honey curled up in her dog bed made her stop, made her really think about that summer and everything that happened since taking their little puppy home. Camping in Vermont, skinny dipping late at night, opening the bakery, seeing her family again, *New York*...

It was the best summer of her life, and as she eyed the small sunbeam that turned Honey's fur into shimmering, shiny gold, she realized she wanted to have more summers like this one. And every other season in between.

"You know what, no," she said, spinning back around to face him.

His eyebrows raised in surprise.

She pointed to the screen. "You're clearly keeping something from me, and I don't like it. Why do you keep doing that, Kevin? Why do you keep secrets?"

"Because every time I tell you the truth, you run," he said.

"That's not fair," she rebutted. "You couldn't have expected me to take your hidden deal with my father well. I needed time to process it."

"You're right. You needed time to process it. You also needed time to heal and to fix things with your family. I was too selfish and stole all of your time this summer. And in the end, all I did was cause you pain."

"You know that's not true," she breathed.

"It *is* true," he countered. "I should have told you right away, from the moment I made you the offer. I should have told you *who* was behind it all. But then...but then things changed and you let me get close to you and I lost all of my control. So I didn't say anything because I *knew* as soon as you learned the truth that everything would be over and I—"

He rubbed his face hard, his eyes now red. "I'm so deeply in love with you, and I am *terrified* of losing you."

Jess took a tentative step toward him and brushed her knuckles against his. "You're not going to lose me," she whispered.

"Then why do I feel like I already have?"

"Because *it's me*," she confessed. Feeling bold, Jess climbed onto his lap. He closed his eyes and let out a shaky breath as she combed his wavy hair with her fingers, then angled his face to hers. When he blinked his eyes open, she gave him a smile, her stomach doing somersaults at the longing in his gaze.

She clenched on to that feeling, using it to fuel the words that she needed to finally say.

"You're right, I keep pushing you away. I keep pushing because I am so god damn scared to let someone in. I'm afraid I'll lose myself all over again and go back to sacrificing instead of letting myself focus on *me*. I'm afraid of falling in love then falling out of love and feeling stuck, to go back to living a life that felt stale and useless. I was in love with Charlie, but then that spark faded. What if it happens again? What if we fade and we hate each other and we feel—"

"Stuck."

She nodded.

Kevin reached up and rubbed her cheeks with the pads of his thumbs. "Can I show you what I've been working on?"

"Yes please," she whispered.

He pointed to the computer screen behind her. She stood up but before she could step away, he clutched her waist and turned her around, then guided her back down onto his lap. Kevin wrapped a tight arm at her waist as he pulled it up on his computer.

It was a massive budget for Port Wheels, sections separating costs for the bakery and the bike shop, areas with sunk costs that weren't getting revenue, and things to double down on that were making money. He listed out every meticulous detail—shipments, rent, utilities, labor. He clicked on the next tab and it was a similar spreadsheet, but with a completely new business plan. One that would get them through the entire offseason leading into next summer.

"Did Calvin make this?" she asked.

"Nope. I did."

She shifted to gape at him. "*How?*"

"I figured it was time to stop bothering Calvin with all of this and learn it myself. I took an online course for small businesses."

"But what about Grampy?"

"This was all before you spoke with him," he explained. "I thought I was going to have to sell the business. Fire Zach. *Lose you.* It felt like the kick in the butt I needed."

"When did you start this?"

"The night we got back from New York."

She shifted uncomfortably. "Oh."

Kevin set his chin on her shoulder, his cheek brushing against her ear.

"Do you not want to work with Grampy?"

"I think that's something you need to decide," he answered. "Do you want to take over his place?"

"Yes," she whispered, without hesitation. She couldn't stop thinking about those blueberry coffee cakes, and all of the things she could do with a new café space here at Port Wheels. Her notebook was so full of ideas, she'd had to buy a new one.

"Then that's what we do," he replied. "If you still want me here, of course."

"Why wouldn't I? We're business partners, remember?"

He hummed. "Yeah. We are."

She scanned the tabs at the bottom of the spreadsheet, noticing one at the end labeled *JKH*.

"What's this one for?"

Kevin didn't reply as Jess clicked on it, opening up a completely different kind of spreadsheet. It was all personal expenses. Her chest tightened as she read through the rows.

`Rent for apartment with two beds`

`Groceries for yummy food and weekly focaccia`

`Movie night snacks`

`Clothes for the ass I can't stop thinking about`

Honey's nibbles

Vet bills + insurance

ASL dog training?

Savings because #responsible

The list continued on and on.

"JKH," she breathed. "Jess, Kevin, Honey."

Kevin lifted his chin and tucked her hair around her other shoulder, giving him enough room to kiss her neck. "Our budget."

"Why would we need to share a budget?"

He tightened his hold around her waist. "Don't run, okay?"

She hesitated, then after an exhale, she nodded.

He sighed, his warm breath raising goose bumps on her neck.

"I was going to ask you to move in with me."

Chapter Twenty-Two

Jess immediately felt the need to bolt. She flinched. Kevin's arm tightened around her waist, his lips now pressed to her neck like a brand.

She snapped her eyes shut and took a deep breath. Then another. Then another.

"Good job, sweetheart," he murmured into her neck.

They remained silent for a couple of minutes, giving Jess time to sift through all of her complicated feelings. He drew circles on her stomach with his thumb, her T-shirt lifting with each stroke.

"M-move upstairs?" she finally asked, her voice cracking.

"I don't have enough room for two beds up there," he confessed. "We could save up and once we have enough, we move somewhere together."

"You want to wait?"

"No, I want to have you *now*," he confessed, kissing the soft spot under her ear. "But I also want you to be comfortable and have what you want. And if that means we wait to find you the perfect home, then I will wait."

Jess turned to face him, curling her legs up by his side. "If that's what you want, then why did you say you *were* going to ask me to move in with you. Did you change your mind?"

"After everything that happened last week with your family, watching all of the ways the four of you were hurting, I knew I couldn't do that to you again. I couldn't ask you to be ready for something that you so clearly told me you didn't want. And you'd just said all of that stuff about commitment and feeling stuck—"

"Do you think that? Do you think we'll feel stuck?"

Kevin tucked a strand of her blonde hair behind her ear. "I think it's normal in every relationship for those initial sparks to fade. We'll have to work hard to create new sparks, find new ways to bring excitement into one another's lives, to keep the flame ignited." He gave her a coy smile. "*But*, I also am absolutely certain of one thing, with all of my heart."

She blinked. "And that is?"

"That I will never, ever stop loving you. And I will never *ever* neglect you. You will always feel loved and cherished by me. Because I believe in us, and I will live out all of my days giving you a life that you deserve."

"But doesn't that scare you?" She whispered the question so softly, it felt like a secret. "Aren't you scared of having to sacrifice that much for another person?"

"Nope."

He was so sure of himself, his blunt refusal sucking the air from her lungs.

"I'm not afraid. I know my girl is going to take care of me, too."

She grunted and crossed her arms. "And what makes you so sure that I will?"

"Jessica, why do you bring me a kanelbullar every day?"

She gave him a *You have to be joking me* face. "Because you like it?"

"Even when you're pissed at me and we're not talking to each other, though? You *still* want to bring me a pastry?"

"Well, yeah." She shrugged, then hesitated as it hit her. The point he was trying to make.

Kevin chuckled, wiggling his hands into her elbows and prying her arms open, pressing himself as close as possible. He brushed his nose against hers with a smile, his hazel eyes dancing with mischief.

"We sacrifice because we *want* to, sweetheart. Not because we feel like we need to. We sacrifice because we love one another."

She stiffened at the use of *the big L word*.

"Did you mean it when you said it the other day?" he asked softly.

"It slipped right out."

"But did you *mean* it?"

She inched her face back, looking down at her golden boy. His tire grease-stained bandana tied at his neck, his deep tan and pearly white teeth, his wavy hair with streaks of blonde from the summer sun.

"Yes," she breathed. "I love you, Kev."

He wept. Jess smiled at his big, soft emotions after her confession and kissed away his tears as he held her tightly, then planted a lingering kiss on his lips. His hands moved fast, running through her hair and cupping her face, kissing her back with intensity and purpose. Like she was the answer to a prayer. Because that's what he was for her. It wasn't an apartment, a house, or even a bakery that gave Jess the freedom and the comfort she craved so deeply. No, it had always been him. With Kevin, Jess felt like she finally found the person who truly connected to her soul.

JESS NESTLED CLOSER to Kevin and kissed his chin. He purred, dragging his fingers through her hair slowly, the bedsheet sliding down her shoulders. She shivered from the chill in his bedroom. He lifted the sheet and tucked her in close, their bodies pressed together, his skin warm, his breath smelling like cinnamon sugar from the kanelbullar she'd watched him devour.

She peered around his room. "There isn't even room for a dresser in here."

"Yeah, my clothes are in the hall closet."

"Hmm," she rumbled. She traced a finger down his ivy tattoo. "We'd probably have to put a dresser in the living room then."

Kevin shifted and moved on top of her, bracketing his arms by her sides. "Are you saying what I think you're saying?"

She scrunched her nose. "I don't know. I'm thinking through the options."

He beamed. "Tell me the options."

"You have a pathetic excuse for a kitchen."

He barked out a laugh. "That's fair. We could use the kitchen downstairs?"

"Not if we change the space and move all the baking to Grampy's."

He shrugged. "We'll probably have some time before all of those changes."

She puffed out a frustrated exhale, which had him laughing again.

"Tiny bathroom," she continued. "Not enough room for the girly things."

He wiggled his eyebrows. "What kind of girly things?"

She swatted his arm. "Why must you always make it weird?"

"Because you set it up so easily!"

Jess attempted to shimmy out of his grasp but he pressed his body against hers, refusing to let her move. She sighed, running her index finger down his jaw.

"What else?" Kevin asked. "Does sleeping in the same bed really bug you?"

She sighed. "What if we compromise?"

"See, Jessica? You're sacrificing already. I'm proud of you."

Her face flushed. "Instead of *two* beds, let's just get one big one. California King. Enough room to spread out if I need it."

"But still the same sheets in case you need *me*."

She rolled her eyes.

"Anything else? TV too old? You hate my selection of shampoo?"

She shook her head. She felt a warm hand run up her thigh, fingers inching up the curve of her waist, his smile taunting.

"What are you doing?" she asked, her voice throaty and breathless.

"Giving you *another* reason to move in with me."

"Oh, I'm already well aware of this *reason*."

"And it's not convincing enough?"

She wiggled her toes. "It's pretty close."

His chest rumbled with a chuckle. He leaned down and

kissed her, his kiss transitioning from soft and sweet to hot and urgent in a matter of seconds, the press of his body on hers deepening the desire in her belly again.

In an instant he stopped and came up for air. "How about now? Convincing enough?"

She whined. "That was fresh."

"Oh you haven't seen how fresh I can be, sweetheart."

She growled at him. His bright laughter filled the room. Jess couldn't help the smile that bloomed on her face at the sound of it, at the way he rolled over and tugged her with him, her body now on top of his, his hands roaming down the small of her back and to his favorite...asset.

"So what's it going to be, my dear Jessica?"

She traced her finger down his forehead, around the curve of his nose, down to his lips. "I think I can handle a few months in this tiny apartment with you."

He grinned. "I take back what I said."

"Which time? You say a *lot* of things."

"About New York being the best day of my life." He cupped her face. "Because this beats it by far."

FOR THE LONGEST TIME, Jess thought being in a relationship with someone was similar to being locked up in jail. The kind of jail that didn't allow her to explore who she truly was and what she wanted in life, having to sacrifice so much in an effort to simply be together.

But with Kevin, those bars never came back, never sealed her back in. With him, she was *free*. He *encouraged* her to explore and to have fun. Instead of making her small, he challenged her to be bold and brave, to be a better version of herself. And he loved her with such a ferocious intensity. His laugh, his need to constantly touch her when she was close by, his words of adoration in her ear, his hands exploring her late at night.

As the last days of the summer season in Haverport breezed by, as they boxed up her few belongings at the Balls' cottage and moved them to the small apartment above the shop, she reminded herself of his words. Yes, the sparks might fade. Yes, she might not feel that same intense longing, that those feelings might evolve over time. But that didn't mean they weren't meant for one another.

I will never stop loving you, he'd told her. *I will never neglect you.*

Charlie neglected her, and if Jess was being totally honest with herself, she also neglected him. They fell out of love. They tried to stretch out their relationship for as long as they could, like taking a handful of dough and stretching it to the limit. But they hadn't tried to form it into something new, form it into something beautiful. That it snapped apart was inevitable.

Jess folded her jeans and tucked them gently into their new dresser, smiling at the framed photo of the three of them next to a pitcher of fresh flowers. It was a selfie from a couple of days earlier, Honey tucked into her arms, Jess tucked into Kevin's. They were laughing at some absurd joke of his before snapping the photo, and he'd framed it immediately.

"The start of *everything*," he'd said as he handed her the frame, a bouquet of sunflowers clutched in his other. The flowers had somehow ended up on the floor...and so did their clothes.

She slid the dresser drawer closed, then in an instant, felt those warm hands snatch her waist and spin her around.

Kevin pressed against her, dipping his chin and sealing his lips to hers. His hands slipped inside her tank top and slowly made their trail up her stomach.

Jess chuckled and broke apart. "If you keep doing this, we're *never* going to get things done."

He grinned. "Are we in a hurry?"

"Today? Yes."

He smiled at that, cupping her face and kissing her nose. "Are you still up for it?"

She closed her eyes and nodded. "Yes. I need to do this."

"Do we need to do our breathing exercise?"

Jess smiled, *really* smiled. At the boy who knew her so deeply. It didn't take nine years to get here. Time didn't seem to matter when it came to true love.

"No," she answered honestly. "I'm going to be okay, as long as you're with me."

He hummed as he curled his arms around her shoulders, pulling her into a hug. "With you is the only place I want to be."

Jess bumped the car door closed with her hip, balancing a tray of tomato mozzarella focaccia in her hand. Kevin reached for her as she made her way from the passenger side, and she interlaced her fingers through his. The tags on Honey's collar clinked against the metal clasp on her leash as she jumped up and down, exploring her very new surroundings as the three of them ambled up the steps of the porch.

Kevin squeezed her hand, released it to knock on the door, then threaded his fingers back through hers. She squeezed back, her heart pattering in her chest as she heard soft footsteps pad toward the door.

Dakota swung it open, rubbing her belly. "Sissy! You guys are here!"

Jess smiled. "We did say we were coming."

"Yes, but I almost didn't believe you when you said *we*." Dakota flicked her gaze down to their interlaced hands then back up to her sister. She winked.

Jess rolled her eyes as Dakota made room for them to step into the house.

"You look radiant, Dakota," Kevin said as she closed the door.

"I look like a whale."

"No you don't, stop that," Jess said. "Piglet would be offended."

Kevin made a *Did I just hear that correctly?* face. Dakota's bright laughter filled the hallway.

Jess grinned at her sister. "He's right, sissy. You are glowing with happiness."

"There's a lot of things to be happy about right now."

Dakota gave her a watery smile, and to Jess's surprise, she pulled her into a hug.

"Do I smell oregano?!" boomed a voice from the kitchen.

Kevin snatched the tray in Jess's hands and made his way to the kitchen. "What you smell is actually the best thing you're about to eat in your entire life."

"Kevin! My boy!"

Jess sucked in a breath, listening to her father and Kevin greet one another with cheers, hugs, slaps on shoulders, and all things focaccia.

Dakota gathered up Jess's hair and twisted it out of her

face, letting the strands fall softly to her back. "Are you going to be okay?"

"I think so." She nodded. "Taking one day at a time."

Dakota grinned. "I'm so proud of you."

"I'm sorry it took me so long to get here," she admitted. "I'm sorry we never spoke and I missed so much."

"I'm sorry, too," her sister whispered. She linked her arm with Jess's. "I'm ready to make up for lost time, are you?"

"Desperately."

"Then let's do this."

"For Piglet."

Dakota snorted.

"We should have made the baby shower pig themed, a missed opportunity really," Jess teased as they made their way to the kitchen. "Should I buy pig sheets for the crib?"

"I missed you too, Jess."

They stepped into the kitchen to the sight of Kevin and her father picking up slices of the focaccia, ready to devour. They both froze before taking a bite.

Jess frowned. "That's supposed to go with dinner."

"But can't it be an appetizer?" Kevin whined. "Logan is about to have his whole life changed!"

Jess eyed her father, watching the smile she'd missed for five years curl into his left cheek, new wrinkles crinkled at the corners of his eyes that she never experienced before. So much lost time.

And Jess was finally, *finally* ready to make up for it.

"Yeah okay, appetizer is fine."

They both took greedy bites. Her father groaned at the taste, shoveling another bite into his mouth.

"See! I told you!" Kevin cheered, his mouth also half full.

Dad swallowed and nodded fervently as he placed his slice down on a napkin, then patted Kevin's back. "I think *a lot* of my life is going to change today, my boy."

Jess shifted from foot to foot, unable to think of any kind of response to that. Her mother slid open the glass back door, the smell of buttery clams and potatoes and corn wafting into the kitchen as Jasper poked at the foil packs on the grill. "Dinner's rea— *Logan!* What are you eating?"

Dad frowned as everyone else laughed. "Jessie brought her focaccia! I've been dying to try it."

"Would you like a slice, Mrs. Valerie?" Kevin asked politely, lifting the serrated knife to cut her a piece.

"Thank you but no, I will be waiting for *dinner*. A concept my husband doesn't seem to understand."

Kevin and her father scoffed, then looked at each other and laughed.

"Oh god," Jess whispered to her sister. "Did I start dating...*Dad??*"

Dakota squealed. "You guys are officially *dating?*"

"Yeah," she admitted, twisting her mouth to contain her own grin. "Do you think it's too soon? You know...after everything?"

Her sister shook her head, then looked at her intensely, her brows knitted together. "Do you love him?"

She nodded. "Yes. Very much."

"Good," Dakota replied. "Because the way that boy looks at you...sometimes I think that gaze will melt every-thing in the room."

Jess peeked up at Kevin, and sure enough, he was looking at her with those bright hazel eyes, lingering on her lips. She blushed, then stuck out her tongue, which had him laughing as they were shepherded out to the porch.

"Am I allowed to know how the shop is doing now?" her father asked.

Kevin slipped a hand around her neck and rubbed a thumb down her nape. She turned to face his reassuring smile. He was already aware of the conversation she had with her father weeks prior. When Dakota texted her days before and invited her to dinner, Kevin encouraged her to say yes. Then declared he was going with her.

He nodded, his expression and his thumb stroking her neck soothing her soul. How she ever thought she could do this without him baffled her.

Jess turned back to her father and answered his question. "Someone offered to buy the shop."

Dad furrowed his brow. "Who?"

"Grampy."

The shocked expressions around the table were identical to the ones she'd received from the Scoopers on the beach. With a smile, Jess told her story again, then explained the beginning plans of their transition and renovations to the shop.

"This gives us the opportunity to have more tables for people who want to hang out with a coffee or a bite, and lingering bodies also mean lingering eyes—"

"And then everyone buys my bikes," Kevin butted in.

Jess chuckled and squeezed his thigh.

"But you'll be working at Grampy's?" her mother asked.

"I'll be *running* Grampy's."

"That's so cool," Jasper commented.

"Do you really know how to bake that blueberry coffee cake?" Dakota blurted.

Jess grinned. "Yes."

"How *wild*."

"So some of the inventory at Grampy's, or whatever you decide to call your bakery, will go to the new café at Port Wheels? Nothing will be baked there?" Dad inquired.

She nodded. "Precisely."

"Who's going to run the café then?"

Jess and Kevin looked at one another. He nodded, encouraging her to keep going, to follow through with the plan they'd discussed in meticulous detail.

She squared her shoulders and looked at the man she'd believed was lost to her, and did the one thing she never thought she would do.

She asked him for help.

"We were hoping you would step in as the manager for the café," she said. "If you still want to work with us, of course."

Dad arched a brow and leaned back into his chair. "Me?"

She and Kevin nodded. Everyone remained silent, eyes on her father, watching as he tapped his fingers on his knee, thinking it through.

Kevin coughed. "We don't need an answer now. We wanted to invite you to the shop first and hear our plans. We'll have dinner at our place and discuss."

"*Our place?*" Dakota chirped.

Jess felt her face get hot as four pairs of wide eyes settled on her.

"Y-yes," she replied softly. "I moved in with Kev."

To her shock, everyone around the table seemed *relieved*. Her mother beamed, curling a hand around her father's knee. Dakota held a hand to her mouth and tried to contain her excitement, Jasper kissing his fiancée on the forehead with a smile. Silver lined her father's eyes, his face full of joy. Like the storm was finally over.

Her chest tightened as she beheld her family, realizing how much hurt she'd caused them. How much hurt they'd caused *her*. How much history and feelings they had to sift through together. She knew this dinner and inviting her father to work with them wasn't nearly enough. But it was certainly a start. A new beginning.

And lately, as she sat next to her golden boy, she realized she really, *really* liked new beginnings.

Chapter Twenty-Three

"Now we lift and score."

Rory puffed out a breath, a strand of hair falling over her face. "And if it falls apart?"

"Then we try again," Jess reassured her. "But this cake is very cold so it will be fine. Don't think too hard about it."

Rory rolled her shoulders and leaned over the cake, then slowly lifted the metal mold off of the round vanilla ice cream cake in front of them. It came off clean, the cake still standing perfectly straight. She whooped, then tossed the mold into the sink.

Jess handed her the scraper. "Good, now score the edges."

Rory obeyed with a smile and scored the sides, then slid the cake into the box and placed it in the fridge to chill overnight, ready to be decorated in the morning.

She washed the dishes in the sink, handing them off to Rory to dry as Melanie and Blake finished serving the last customers out front. "See? You're going to be fine."

"It's going to be weird not having you here anymore," Rory confessed. "What are we going to do without you?"

"Wow, you make it sound like I'm dying," she quipped. "I'll only be down the road."

"Yeah, but still. It feels like a lot is changing all at once."

Jess looked up from the soapy dishes in front of her and eyed Rory. "Change is good, yes?"

Rory smiled to herself, her eyes glossed over as if she was recalling a memory. "Yes. Change is good."

Blake soared by them with full trash bags in hand. "It's over!"

Melanie followed, turning to the shelves behind them and sliding containers of candies and jimmies from the shelves to refill out front. "I can't believe it's already Labor Day. This summer season went by way too fast."

"It always does," Rory added. "But this time we're off to be studious college students. Or in Jess's case, a sexy baker with a hot new boyfriend."

She glared at her.

Melanie giggled. "Maybe that's what your bakery should be named, Jess! The Sexy Baker."

"It has a nice ring to it," she mused.

Rory and Melanie cackled. Jess smiled, finishing up the dishes and wiping her hands dry.

"Speaking of, how's the new roommate?" Rory teased.

Jess blushed, then pointed to the vacuum. "We need to clean. I don't want to be here all night."

"I take it things are going well," she jested back.

"Kevin told Calvin that every morning when he wakes up he's afraid it's all going to be a dream," Melanie explained, sealing the peanut butter cup container in her hand. "Then he sees her sleeping next to him and says he—and I quote—'falls in love all over again.'"

Her heart fluttered in her chest.

"My *god* he's so obsessed with you," Rory beamed.

"Yes, well, I have that effect on people."

Another cackle from the two of them.

Blake charged through the back door. "Guess who I found outside!"

Melanie smiled as Calvin walked in next, coming right up to her and whispering, "Hi, headband," as he cupped her face and kissed her greedily on the mouth, in front of everyone.

"Calvin, I presume," Rory deadpanned.

"No. I found all of them."

Rory perked up. "All of them?"

Blake smirked.

"*AHHH!*"

Rory ran out of the shop. They all followed, making their way around the brick building to the parking lot in front. Jess froze.

A canopy tent was set up in the center of the lot, covered in twinkling lights with lawn chairs scattered underneath. Multiple coolers were around a table tucked into the corner with pizza boxes piled high next to a small Bluetooth speaker. Honey's leash was tied up to the chair she sat on, her tail wagging enthusiastically as she took in everything around her, her tongue out and panting, her expression full of glee. And standing in a huddle, joking and laughing, were the familiar faces Jess had come to cherish deeply over the years.

Rory sprinted up to Tyler and shrieked as she jumped on him.

He caught her with a laugh and spun her around. "Hi, Ry."

"Ty, what are you doing here?! You have a game in three days!"

"I couldn't miss this," he explained, kissing his girlfriend on the cheek. "And I had to see my girl."

Rory's eyes twinkled, then she leaned down and licked his face. He balked out a laugh, mumbling a playful "You menace" before kissing her on the lips.

"*Jessica Valerie.*"

Everyone froze and glanced up at the man who stood on a cooler in the middle of the Scoops parking lot, his honey-blonde hair tucked behind one of his signature bandanas.

He held his arms out wide. "Today marks the end of an era."

Everyone cheered.

Jess crossed her arms. "Get down from there."

"No way. Not until I have thoroughly congratulated my girl for finishing her last shift at Scoops *ever—*"

More cheering.

"*And* for taking over Grampy's bakery in a few months—"

"I still wrap my head around that," Calvin chimed in.

"But she also did one very important thing this summer."

"Took off her clothes for you?" Jay joked.

The Scoopers howled as Jess flipped Jay off. He winked in response.

Kevin puffed up his chest. "Okay, *two* very important things."

He held out his hands to her. She grumbled as she stepped closer and placed her hands in his. He pulled her up on top of the cooler, then wrapped her in his arms. His smile was so infectious, she couldn't resist one of her own.

"You chose to be brave this summer, and did all the things you wanted to do. All before Labor Day."

"Even if I hadn't, you couldn't fire me now that I'm your *boss*."

He grinned and pressed his nose to hers. "Can I call you that later, *boss*?" he whispered for her ears only.

She rolled her eyes. "Always taking it too far."

Kevin hummed and curled a hand around her neck, then pulled her close, his lips caressing hers. "You're so beautiful, Jessica. I can't help it." Then he kissed her, and most definitely took it too far, slipping his tongue into her mouth and curling his free hand around her backside.

"Is this how it feels around me and Calvin?" she heard Melanie ask.

"*Yes*," everyone said in unison.

Jess and Kevin laughed as they turned to face the group. Calvin gave his girlfriend a bashful smile, curling his pinky finger with hers as he bent down and whispered something in her ear. She flushed.

"All right, y'all are making me sick," Jay teased, pulling his phone out of his back pocket. He tapped on the screen a couple times, then music blasted through the speaker.

They danced to the tunes as they placed greasy slices of pizza on paper plates and popped open cans of soda. There were tears and hugs and lots of laughter, because even if Jess knew these people would always have a place in her heart, it *was* the end of an era, and the start of something new. Something even more beautiful than the countless frosted ice cream cakes of her past, or the ice cream sundaes piled high with hot fudge and jimmies and bright red cherries.

Yes, they would always have Scoops. They would always have one another through thick and thin, because they'd been through so much. Together.

But this new life in front of her, full of endless possibility and hope? It felt like gold. The kind of gold from the rising sun of a new day. The sugary gold of a kanelbullar fresh out of the oven. The soft golden fur of a sleeping pup. Or the shining golden boy with dazzling hazel eyes that felt like home.

Epilogue

Four years later

Jess unlocked the door of the eggshell-blue house on Cherry Lane, the smell of freshly brewed coffee making her groan as she flicked off her shoes and went into the kitchen. "You better have saved some of that for me!"

Kevin smiled at her, peering up from his laptop. "My dear Jessica, how dare you think I wouldn't save you a cup of coffee. It's like you don't know me at all."

She smirked and leaned over to him, planting a soft kiss on his lips.

"Mmmm," he hummed. "You smell like fish."

"I *was* clamming for two hours."

"Kinky."

She rolled her eyes and made her way to the sealed carafe on the counter, then poured herself a cup, the coffee steaming hot. "Where's Honey?"

"Still sleeping in bed. I think we're going to have to start setting an alarm for her."

She took a sip of her coffee and sighed, the taste making

her feel all warm and tingly. She smiled, unable to contain her joy. It was a good morning. She's had *a lot* of good mornings lately.

She watched as Kevin's brow furrowed, concentrating on whatever new spreadsheet he was working on. "What are you looking at over there?"

"Figuring out how I can afford building a new storage space for the bikes," he said. "We're running out of room."

"Good thing you're selling them fast." She winked.

He sighed. "Yes, well, that won't be the case this winter. Plus, I don't want to take up more space than I have to in the café. It's always so slammed in there."

"Is the new patio situation helping at all?"

Kevin cocked a brow. "I don't know, *boss*. You tell me."

She grinned. "The café's daily revenue is up by thirty percent. Dad said they aren't turning away as many people now that they have more tables to work with. So I think yes, it's helping."

He chuckled, then glanced at the clock on the microwave above her head. "Speaking of alarms…"

Jess took one last sip of her coffee, then set the empty cup in the sink. "Yep, on it. I'll be ready in fifteen, it will be a quick shower."

He wiggled his brow. "Want me to join you?"

"Kev, emphasis on *quick*. Remember last time?"

His mouth twitched. "How could I forget?"

"We were thirty minutes late to Riley's dance recital. Dakota was *furious*."

"So, so worth it."

She took a step backward, pointing a finger in his direction. "Fifteen minutes. Don't distract me."

"Sure thing, boss."

Jess rolled her eyes, then bounded up the stairs. The

soft morning sun streamed in from the skylight windows along the hall as she made her way to the master bedroom. Sure enough, Honey was still asleep on the California King in her usual form—paws in the air, head lolled to the side, tongue out. Even after growing three sizes since they'd adopted her, her fur longer and darker, she still looked like that little pup when she slept. Like a reminder of their beautiful past, and their even better present.

As promised, her shower was speedy. She pulled on a pair of jeans and a T-shirt that said *Honey Sweet Bakery*, twisted her hair into a clip, and strapped on her favorite new pair of sandals. By the time she was coming down the stairs, purse and sunglasses in tow, Kevin was standing by the door holding the leash of a very enthusiastic and well-rested Honey, her tail wagging the second she saw Jess. She barked as well, the sound coming out loud and crisp.

Jess signed to her dog, motioning her to be quiet. Honey licked her hand and obeyed, then the three of them left the house and began their five-minute walk down to Main Street from their eggshell-blue house. Or as Kevin called it, their forever home.

He slipped a hand into the pocket of her jeans and squeezed. "I think these might be my favorite."

"You literally say that every time I buy a new pair."

Kevin grinned. "Yes, but *this* time I'm serious. I'm not sure how I can possibly go all day without a little squeeze," he said, his action supporting his words.

"Well then you better get your fill in now."

He looked down at her with that devious grin she'd come to recognize, the one he gave her when he had only one thing on his mind.

Kevin glanced around, making sure no one was looking as he snatched her hand and pulled her behind a tree. He dropped the leash; they never had to worry about Honey running away anymore. She was content to wait for them, always on the hunt for a flower bed to sniff or lie down in.

Jess leaned against the bark as Kevin slipped both hands in her back pockets, tilting her up as he pressed his body against hers and kissed her on the mouth. Even four years later, the sizzle was still there between them. She waited and waited during that first year with him in their tiny apartment, wondering when that moment would come and everything would finally shift; when the sizzle would slow, when the heated moments of passion became practiced ones of comfort. She waited for things to feel different after committing to therapy together, talking through her past wounds, developing tools that would ease her moments of panic, moments that were now few and far between. She waited for those changes, waited for things to fade.

But nothing ever changed; with Kevin, it was always good. She let go of her expectation and realized that she really had been wrong about relationships. A nine-year relationship with one person didn't make her an expert, especially when being with someone else could look so different. When being with someone like her golden boy set her world ablaze, where their love burned brightly and never snuffed out.

Kevin ran a hand up her thigh and traced his thumb across her jeans, right at the spot he knew well, the spot where she'd inked a climbing strand of ivy around her leg to match his own. It was a physical reminder that she, too, found her home.

He pulled back and nibbled on her bottom lip, then pressed his forehead to hers. "As much as I would love to lose track of time being utterly consumed by you, we need to get going."

She pouted. "Haverfest can wait. Zach texted me and said they already finished setting up."

"Yes, but there are things *we* have to do."

Jess cocked a brow. "I can't believe I'm saying this, but are you actually saying no to kissing me right now?"

Kevin groaned and squeezed his hands tight, then dropped her to the ground. "I can't believe I'm *doing* it, but yes. Trust me, denying myself my favorite thing is killing me on the inside."

She smirked. "Your *favorite* thing?"

He chuckled, patting her butt before twining his hand with hers. "Okay, my *second* favorite thing."

"Yeah, that's what I thought."'

They walked hand in hand down Main Street, following the double yellow line as they passed booth after booth preparing for the town's big annual celebration. She smiled, leaning her head against Kevin's shoulder as she gazed upon vendor tents, some faces she recognized, some she didn't. The town of Haverport had grown more popular over the years, people discovering how magical this little beach escape truly was. Jess knew part of it was likely Charlie's father and his successful restaurant that landed on the Michelin guide, the expansion of Cap's, and a few high-brow boutiques on properties he managed. Some townies complained about the changes, but Jess didn't mind; Honey Sweet Bakery was booming, and not because of Grampy's blueberry coffee cake that still had lines snaking out the door. It was because her kanelbullar was featured on multiple travel and food influencer accounts with hundreds of thousands of followers, originally in town to see the new developments, but finding her bakery to be the most exciting place to stop in at. She was selling bags of her signature cinnamon rolls at the same rate as the cakes these days—and handing covert bags outside the back door for townies. Three knocks for cake, four for kanelbullar. She hired a high schooler for the summer solely for that job.

Kevin slowed his walk, yards away from their booth next to the town green. Despite the commotion around them as artists and cooks set up for the crowds, the green was quieter. The white gazebo with views overlooking the ocean was completely empty, which usually wasn't the case during the summer months. Everyone loved to sit on the bench for a picture.

To her surprise, he guided her to the gazebo.

"Kev, what are you doing? You were in such a rush before to get to the booth."

"Wasn't exactly the booth I was going for," he mumbled. He stepped up onto the wooden planks, then dropped Honey's leash and signed for her to sit. She did, her tongue hanging open as she panted.

Kevin reached for her other hand and pulled Jess up with him, their bodies flush against one another.

"Jessica, I believe we never had the chance to finish your bucket list that summer."

Her brow furrowed. "What are you talking about? Yes, we did. I finished all ten."

"Yes, but you were so busy being brave, sweetheart, you forgot there was one more thing on there."

"I'm so confused."

He grinned, then reached into his back pocket for his wallet. He carefully pulled out a worn piece of paper, then unfolded it gently.

She chuckled at the familiar scrap of legal pad paper. "You still *have it?*"

He scoffed. "Of course I still have it, Jessica! Do you

think I would toss away the most important part of our history?"

"You're such a sap," she teased.

He grinned. "You picked your last thing on the list, but if you try to remember closely..."

She gasped and slapped her hand over her mouth. "You also added something."

"Sure did, sweetheart."

"Oh my god, I completely forgot."

He chuckled. "That's okay, we both said we would clock ours in at the time of our choosing. You chose the end of that summer. I choose now."

He handed her the paper. Jess lifted it and read through the list, smiling at the small doodles of dogs and beach waves and hearts that Kevin added throughout that summer. Check marks were ticked off for each number, until she reached the last one.

11. Say yes

She frowned. "Say yes to what?"

Jess looked up, realizing Kevin was gone. She dropped her arm and glanced around to find out where he went, then quickly realized he hadn't gone anywhere. He only changed his position, the piece of paper blocking him from where he now kneeled down in front of her.

Her mouth fell open.

Kevin beamed at her, then popped open the small maroon box in his hand, revealing the biggest diamond ring she had ever seen.

"Kevin...that ring is *huge*."

His grin was infectious. "It sure is."

"How did you even afford that?"

"Secret savings account. It's a good thing my hot girl-friend taught me how to budget. And I would very much like to make her my hot *wife*."

She kept staring at the ring—white gold band, yellow teardrop diamond.

"That thing looks like it has multiple carats."

"Good, because it does."

"*Kevin...*"

"Jessica Valerie, I love you so much it hurts. I've been wanting to get down on one knee since the day we made that list. Since the day I made the offer. You may think this ring is ridiculous, but so what? You deserve to be pampered and loved. I want to show you off because you sparkle even brighter than this ring, brighter than the ocean beside us, brighter than the sun above that beautiful head of blonde hair. I want the entire world to know that you're mine and I'm yours. You let me in and trusted me with your heart, and I intend on keeping it and protecting it for the rest of my life."

She grinned. "What's mine is yours and all that."

He laughed at the words he'd said to her four summers ago, when everything in her life changed. "Is that a yes?"

She kneeled next to him and brushed a hand through his hair, then linked her arms around his neck. "Well, I probably should finish this list, right?"

He pulled her close with that smile that still made her heart skip after all of these years, his eyes bright and full of adoration. His kiss was tender and slow, like they had all the time in the world. Because in their little world, they did. *Forever* was now on the table.

Cheers erupted out on the town green. Jess pried

herself from his clutches and noticed many familiar faces standing on the grass, clapping and hooting and hollering.

Dakota stood there with Jasper, Riley running around at her heels wearing the Piglet shirt Jess bought for her last Christmas. Her parents were also there, arms linked. Tears streamed down her father's cheeks, but Arielle was prepared, standing beside her parents with Kevin's dad in tow. She handed him a cloth napkin from her straw tote, the two exchanging watery smiles.

Calvin and Melanie had their arms around one another, the new shiny gold bands on their left hands sparkling under the summer sun, their faces full of hope and love after making their vows barefoot in the sand two months earlier.

Rory and Tyler stood beside them, Rory cheering obnoxiously loud for Jess as Tyler cackled, then tackled her from behind and peppered her cheek with kisses. The two looked just as posh as their SoHo apartment in New York, where they'd officially lived together for a year. Jess couldn't help but radiate with pride as she'd walked around Rory's place that spring, proud of the once messy high school girl and her transformation into a confident graphic designer at a big publishing house, finally living with her boyfriend after four years of excruciating long-distance. All of the Scoopers supported Tyler when he decided to leave football behind following his graduation from Rutgers. Or at least the side of football where he was *on* the field. Now he was working his way up to becoming a sports journalist, hoping to work off the field with a microphone, giving his insight on every play-by-play.

Jay was even there, his face covered with an expertly trimmed beard, his hand linked with Vanessa's, the two of them looking slightly rumpled from their plane ride all the way from San Diego.

Blake also looked a little disheveled, likely from his drive down from Boston where he was spending his summer interning at a marketing firm. He said it was nothing like working at Scoops, and commented on how his job at the ice cream shop may have been the best he'd ever had.

Jess agreed; they all did. Especially when you ended up with a beautiful family such as this.

"They're *all* here," Jess breathed.

Kevin kissed her cheek. "I knew I had the best chance of them all being home if I did it today. I had a feeling you wouldn't want this day without them."

A smile stretched across her lips. "Yeah. You're right."

"Are you going to put that giant rock on your finger or not?" Calvin barked.

"Hmm, I haven't decided yet," she teased.

"She's lying, she said yes," Kevin jested.

More cheering ensued. Jess shook her head as she held out her hand, letting her *fiancé* slip the massive teardrop diamond onto her finger.

Zach jogged up to the group. "Crap, did I miss it?"

Blake crossed his arms, looking irritated. Zach laughed, then threw his arms around his boyfriend and lifted him up before planting a kiss on his lips. Blake's face flushed like it always did when he was around him. Five years into dating and their attempt at doing long-distance didn't seem to slow down their affection. Even if a tiff ensued every now and then.

Jess knew they would make it, though. Because that's what you did with the person you loved. You kept trying. You kept showing up. You sacrificed...but you also communicated your needs. When you truly loved a person, you trusted them to take care of you as much as you took care of them.

Kevin slipped his hands around the curve of her waist, splaying them on her lower back. "Forever, my dear Jessica?

Her hands found his chest, and she beamed up at him. At the man who made her life feel like pure sunshine. "I like the sound of that offer."

Also by K.Sinko

THE SCOOPS SERIES

Safe Harbor

Always Choosing You

The Offer

STANDALONES

Sunday Supper

Call Of The Loon

NOVELETTES

Please Be Mine

Grampy's Blueberry Coffee Cake

Ingredients

For the Blueberry Cake

- 1/2 cup sugar
- 4 Tbsp butter softened (room temp)
- 1 egg
- 1 tsp vanilla
- 1 cup flour
- 1/2 tsp salt
- 1 tsp baking powder
- 1/4 tsp baking soda
- 1/2 cup sour cream
- 1 cup blueberries

For the Crumb Topping

- 4 Tbsp butter
- 1/4 cup sugar
- 1/4 cup brown sugar
- 1 tsp cinnamon
- 1/2 cup flour

Instructions

For the Crumb Topping
• Melt the butter in a medium-sized bowl.

• Add the sugar, brown sugar, cinnamon, and flour. Mix until combined, then set aside.

For the Blueberry Cake
• Preheat the oven to 350 degrees.

• Beat together the sugar and softened butter until fluffy —about 2 minutes.

• Add the egg and continue to beat for 1 minute.

• Add vanilla, beat for about 30 seconds.

• Mix together the dry ingredients for the cake (flour, salt, baking powder, baking soda) in a large bowl. Sprinkle in to the wet ingredients and beat until all the ingredients are combined—about 1 to 2 minutes.

• Using a rubber spatula, add the sour cream. "Fold" it in by stirring the sour cream in, moving your spatula from the bottom to the top until the sour cream is fully incorporated.

• Once incorporated, fold in the blueberries in the same way.

• Grease an 8×8" pan with some butter. Scrape the cake mixture into the pan and even it out.

• Sprinkle the crumb topping evenly on top.

• Bake for 30 minutes, or until a toothpick comes out clean when poking the center of the cake.

• Cut and serve in a brown paper bag after three knocks on the back door.

Acknowledgments

I've been waiting to write these acknowledgments until the last possible minute because once I write them, then this series is officially over...and I really don't want it to be over. Writing the Scoops Series has been the joy of my life, and watching you love these stories and rave about them online is a writer's true dream come true. Thanks for being on this journey with me.

Alas, I must write it, because I wouldn't be here without the following people who have been with me every step of the way.

To my beta reader team this time around, I am grateful for your kindness and your honest words. Thank you for loving Kevin as much as I do: Alexis Wierenga, Abby Hancock, Caitlin Goodey, and Marissa Kennedy.

Lexie, thank you for constantly being up for talking about romance novels, for finding frustrating plot holes and caring as deeply as I do about the Scoopers. I am so grateful for your friendship.

Abby, you have been my gal since day one when it comes to my books, my personal cheerleader. I am so glad we survived high school and came out the other side as stronger, confident women with the guts to follow our dreams. Thanks for continually telling me to never give up on mine.

My editor, Britt Tayler, who gave me the confidence to put these stories out there thanks to her keen eye and honest feedback. You make me look good on the page, and I am forever indebted to you for it. If I can find a way to mail you kanelbullar, focaccia, and blueberry coffee cake to the island, girl you know I will ASAP.

The stunning art behind the Scoops Series would not have been possible without the incredibly talented Jonny Ryley. His attention to detail with the coloring and the graphics does not go unnoticed. You are absolutely worthy of being nominated for that award. Thanks for being there with me since the day I said "I want to self publish my novel."

Caroline Palmier, thanks for the last minute proof read and for making my words shine.

I wouldn't have the confidence to be able to do what I do without the support of my family. Thank you for loving me for who I am, and for letting me talk endlessly about books. And for letting me ignore you sometimes so I can read in peace. True heroes.

And of course, the grumpy to my sunshine, my biggest supporter of them all. I don't even know how to convey in sentences how much you mean to me, how these books would never be possible without you. Thanks for always believing in me. I love you.

About the Author

K.Sinko is an indie published author with a deep love for love stories. She is the author of *Sunday Supper, Call Of The Loon, Please Be Mine,* and the Scoops Series—a trilogy of stand-alone romances featuring the of a fictional ice cream shop. Her debut novel *Safe Harbor* became an Amazon best seller for young adult contemporary romance and is the winner of two Indieverse Awards. Follow her on Instagram and sign up for her newsletter to get the latest book updates.

tinyurl.com/ksinkonewsletter

instagram.com/authorksinko